7/15

STEPHEN DANDO-COLLINS

CAESAR

the war dog

RANDOM HOUSE AUSTRALIA

A Random House book
Published by Random House Australia Pty Ltd
Level 3, 100 Pacific Highway, North Sydney NSW 2060
www.randomhouse.com.au

First published by Random House Australia in 2012

National Library of Australia
Cataloguing-in-Publication Entry

Author: Dando-Collins, Stephen, 1950–
Title: Caesar the war dog/Stephen Dando-Collins
ISBN: 978 1 74275 631 8 (pbk.)
Target audience: For primary school age
Subjects: Dogs – Juvenile fiction.
    Detector dogs – Afghanistan – Juvenile fiction.
    Combat survival – Juvenile fiction.
Dewey number: A823.3

Cover photographs: chocolate labrador © Brian Summers/Getty Images; Chinook
© iStockphoto.com/BreatheFitness; landscape © Asaf Eliason/Shutterstock.com;
camouflage pattern © italianphoto/Shutterstock.com
Cover design by Astred Hicks, designcherry
Typeset by Midland Typesetters, Australia
Printed in Australia by Griffin Press, an accredited ISO AS/NZS 14001:2004
Environmental Management System printer

Random House Australia uses papers that are natural, renewable and recyclable
products and made from wood grown in sustainable forests. The logging and
manufacturing processes are expected to conform to the environmental regulations of
the country of origin.

Dedicated to Sarbi the Australian Army explosive detection dog, Cairo the American Special Forces dog, Endal the British service dog, and all other dogs who have served humankind in peace and war. And in loving memory of my own labrador retriever, Zeberdy. With special thanks to Zoe, Catriona and Richard, and, as always, to my Louise, my commander-in-chief.

CHAPTER 1

The first time that Corporal Ben Fulton saw Caesar, he didn't think much of him. In fact, he walked by him twice without a second glance. When he finally came to a stop in front of Caesar, on his third inspection of the line of dogs, Ben had a perplexed look on his face. 'That has got to be ugliest labrador retriever I have ever seen,' he said.

Corporal Ben had come to Huntingdon Kennels to look for a new dog, one that he could train to become an Australian Army sniffer dog. Huntingdon Kennels raised dogs for use by the police, emergency services and military, and Ben had asked to see the kennels' labrador retrievers. In his experience, labradors made the best sniffer dogs. So, the kennels lined up a dozen young labradors for Ben to inspect. Some were sandy coloured, some were black, and some, like Caesar, were brown. They were all aged between eighteen months and three years, and they sat in a line like soldiers, facing Ben. All had been given obedience training by the kennels.

1

As a result, they sat still and quiet as Ben walked up and down the line accompanied by Jan, a young woman who helped run the kennels.

Ben was looking for a dog with something special. The animal he ended up choosing would spend the rest of his working days with Ben, and there would be times when Ben's life, and the lives of other soldiers around them, would depend on that dog. So, Ben had to be sure that he and the dog would get on well, and that the animal had what it took to be a war dog. Just as every man doesn't always make a good soldier, not every dog has the courage, strength and loyalty to be a good war dog. None of the dogs Ben had viewed that morning stood out. Except for Caesar – and he stood out for all the wrong reasons – with his snout puffed up like a balloon on one side, he was not a pretty sight.

'That's Caesar,' said Jan. 'He's always getting into mischief. He went and stuck his nose into a beehive and got stung on the nose three or four times. The swelling will go down in a day or two. It doesn't seem to have bothered him much.'

As the corporal studied him, the labrador returned his gaze, taking in this well-built soldier of average height with a round, open face and dark, short-cropped hair. Then Caesar lowered his head, almost as if he was embarrassed by his puffy nose.

Ben smiled broadly. 'Poor Caesar,' he said, kneeling

beside the sitting dog and rubbing him behind the ear, which dogs love. 'Those nasty bee stings would have hurt like hell. Didn't they, mate?'

Caesar, immediately taking a liking to him, responded by wagging his tail and trying to lick Ben's face.

The manager of the kennels now joined them. 'You're not thinking of taking Caesar, are you, Corporal?' he said. 'That would be the worst dog in the kennels. We were considering getting rid of him.'

'Why?' Ben asked, turning to look at him.

'Caesar's always sticking his nose where he shouldn't,' said the manager. 'And he's a digger, too. Some dogs love to dig holes, but labrador retrievers aren't usually that interested in digging. This labrador would dig all day if you let him, just to see what he could dig up. That's not good for a working dog. You want his full attention.'

Ben patted Caesar's shining chocolate-brown coat, then stood up. He looked down at Caesar, and Caesar looked back up at him with a wagging tail and gleaming eyes that seemed to say, *Take me!*

'You know what?' said Ben. 'I'll take him, I'll take Caesar. I like him.'

'Really? Why him, of all dogs?' the surprised manager responded.

'Curiosity,' said Ben. 'A dog that puts his nose into a beehive and digs to see what he can find has loads of curiosity. And in my job, that's just the sort of dog

I need. He's got to be curious enough to find out what's hidden in a package, or to locate explosives hidden in a culvert beside the road. A dog like that can save lives.'

The manager shook his head. 'Well, good luck with him, Corporal. But I don't think you'll find Caesar will be much use to the army.'

'What's his ancestry?' Ben asked.

'His father and mother are labradors,' said Jan. 'But his grandfather was a German shepherd.'

'A German shepherd?' said Ben, nodding approvingly. 'I thought I could see a hint of another breed in his long snout. German shepherds are even more intelligent than labradors. If this dog has the best qualities of the curious labrador and the smart German shepherd, we could make quite a team.'

'Please yourself,' said the manager, unconvinced. 'But don't blame me if he disappoints you and lets you down one day.'

Despite the manager's lack of confidence in this brown labrador, Corporal Ben had been working with military dogs for ten years, and he considered himself the best judge. Signing the necessary papers, Ben officially made Caesar a recruit of the Australian Army, and made him his new trainee war dog.

CHAPTER 2

In a green military Land Rover, Ben pulled up in the driveway of his neat modern brick house at 3 Kokoda Crescent, Holsworthy. Ben was stationed at the sprawling Australian Army barracks at Holsworthy, southwest of Sydney, and was allowed to live off the base with his family. Climbing down, Ben walked around to the back of the Land Rover and opened its rear door. Caesar sat in the back looking at him, with nose puffed up, tongue hanging out, and tail wagging expectantly.

'Okay, Caesar, come meet the Fulton family,' said Ben, taking hold of the dog's leash.

The labrador jumped down to the ground and waited, looking around at his surroundings and sniffing the suburban scents on the late afternoon air, as Ben closed the Land Rover door.

'Let's go, mate,' said Ben, before leading Caesar to the front door, the dog trotting along eagerly at his side. 'Where is everybody?' Ben called, as he led Caesar in through the door.

'I'm in here, Dad,' came the voice of Ben's son, Joshua Robert Fulton, or Josh for short. Josh, who had just turned nine, loved computer games and just about every sport there was, and had a vivid imagination. Other kids at Josh's school at Holsworthy had parents in the army, too. But Josh could only tell his schoolmates that his father was a dog handler. He wasn't allowed to say that his dad was a member of the Australian Army's Incident Response Regiment, the IRR, because it was a top-secret unit that dealt with terrorist threats. If anyone asked, Josh would just say that his dad worked with a sniffer dog, a dog which he often brought home. But Josh would neglect to include that his dad sometimes went away overseas on secret missions for months at a time. Ben couldn't tell his family exactly where he and his dog went, or exactly what they did while they were away, but he did tell Josh that the work they did on those secret missions was highly important. And Josh was really, really proud of his dad.

Josh was sitting at the dining table doing homework when his father walked in. Josh was the spitting image of Ben, with the same brown eyes and brown hair, the same round face with a dimpled chin.

'Got a surprise for you, Josh,' Ben announced.

'Really?' Looking around expectantly, Josh saw his dad with a brown dog on a leash.

'Caesar, sit!' Ben instructed in a firm voice.

Caesar immediately sat at Ben's side and looked at Josh, who looked right back at him. Josh frowned. 'What an ugly looking dog,' he declared, with disappointment in his voice, as he took in Caesar's puffed-up nose. 'Whose is he?'

'Ours, now,' said Ben, with a big grin. 'He's my new trainee war dog. His name is Caesar.'

'Ours?' said Josh with disdain. 'Why?'

'Caesar is the official replacement for Dodger. Say hello to him, mate.' Ben led Caesar across the room to Josh, and Caesar went to him with a wagging tail.

'I don't want a new dog,' Josh snapped, ignoring Caesar. 'I want Dodger.' Just two weeks before, his father's last war dog, Dodger, had passed away, and Josh, still hurting, was missing Dodger terribly.

Ben had been expecting his son to be overjoyed that they had a new dog so soon. 'Josh, mate,' he said, dropping to one knee in front of him, 'you'll grow to love Caesar as much as you loved Dodger.'

Josh looked at Caesar, who, standing before him, continued to wag his tail. But, to Josh, no dog could ever replace Dodger.

'Look, he likes you,' said his dad. 'Give him a pat, son. Just mind his nose – it's a bit sore. He managed to get it stung by bees.'

'Then he's stupid as well as ugly,' said Josh.

'But, son . . .'

'I've got homework to do.' Turning his back on Caesar, Josh returned his attention to the laptop on the table.

Ben, though surprised by his son's reaction, was prepared to give Josh some slack. After all, the family had been dealing with two tragedies this past year. Not only had they lost Dodger, but Josh's mother, Marie Fulton, had died eight months back after a battle with breast cancer. Ben's hope was that Caesar would help with his children's healing process. Maybe Josh's sister, he thought, would show more enthusiasm for the new dog. 'Where's Maddie?' Ben asked, coming to his feet.

'In the backyard, I think,' Josh answered, without looking up from his homework. 'And Nan's in the kitchen.'

Ben led Caesar toward the kitchen. As he did, fond memories of Josh and Maddie growing up with Dodger flashed through his mind. Dodger had also been a labrador, but a sandy-coloured one. After the children lost their mother, Josh in particular had become even closer to their four-legged playmate. That dog had seemed to know when Josh was sad, and whenever Ben brought him home, Dodger would go straight to Josh for a play with a tennis ball or a sandshoe, or for a wrestle. If Josh cried, Dodger had licked away his tears.

Two weeks ago, Ben had been faced with the task of breaking the devastating news to Josh and Maddie that their beloved dog Dodger had suffered a stroke. And how Ben had been forced to ask an army veterinary surgeon to put Dodger out of his misery with a lethal injection. Josh couldn't believe that dogs could have strokes, even though his dad had said it wasn't unusual for some labradors to have them, just like humans. To Josh, Dodger had seemed perfectly healthy the last time he had seen him. But Josh hadn't witnessed the effect of the stroke on Dodger, who had become partly paralysed and couldn't even walk. To Ben and the army, putting Dodger down was the kindest thing that could be done for him.

'How did you go today, Ben?' asked Ben's mother, Nan Fulton, as he entered the kitchen. She looked up from where she was peeling potatoes at the sink. A slim woman with short grey hair, she was fit and sporty, regularly playing tennis and golf in her spare time. After Marie's death, Nan, a widow herself, had moved in with Ben, Josh and Maddie. Ben called her their 'glue', for she had brought the Fulton family together in their time of grief, and had held them together.

'Mission accomplished, Mum,' Ben replied. 'We have a new dog. Meet Caesar.'

Wiping her hands, Nan bent and gave Caesar a pat. 'Hello, Caesar,' she said. 'Welcome to the Fulton household.' In response, Caesar licked her on the cheek, making her laugh.

'Josh wasn't particularly welcoming to Caesar,' said Ben.

'I overheard,' Nan responded, straightening again. 'Don't worry, he'll come around.'

'I know how much Josh is missing Dodger,' said Ben, nodding, 'but . . .'

'Just give him time to get over his grief for Dodger,' said Nan. 'It's a bit soon to expect him to fall in love with a new dog right away.'

'I know,' Ben agreed with a sigh. 'If we were an ordinary family, I would have left it a few months before I brought a new dog home. But we're not an ordinary family, and Caesar here is no ordinary dog. I have to get him trained up right away and then get back into the field. I've got a job to do, and the army waits for no one.'

'Maddie's out in the backyard,' said Nan. She put her hand affectionately on his arm. 'See what she thinks of Caesar.'

Ben slid open the glass back door and led Caesar out into the garden. Six-year-old Madeline Ann Fulton had fair hair and blue eyes, just like her late mother. Maddie loved animals and hoped that one day Father Christmas might bring her a horse of her very own. Like Josh, she had loved Dodger. Ben found her sitting on the back lawn, talking to a circle of dolls on the grass and waving a scolding finger at them. 'Maddie, what do you think of our new dog?' Ben called.

Looking up, Maddie spotted Caesar and let out a gasp. 'A new doggy?' she exclaimed. Jumping to her feet, she ran to Caesar and hugged him. 'He's lovely! Can we keep him?'

'You bet we can keep him,' said Ben. 'He's my new war dog. His name is Caesar.'

'Caesar,' Maddie repeated, continuing to hug the brown dog, whose tail wagged with delight.

'Caesar was the name of a famous general in Roman times,' said Ben. 'Pretty appropriate for an army dog, don't you think, Maddie?'

Maddie didn't care about Roman generals. But she did care about dogs. She didn't even seem to notice Caesar's puffy nose. 'Nice doggy,' she cooed. 'And you're all ours.'

Ben looked at Nan, who had followed him outside, and smiled. 'At least most of the Fulton family seems to like Caesar,' he said. 'All we have to do is win Josh over.'

'Like I said, Ben,' Nan replied, 'you can't push the dog onto Josh. You just focus on training Caesar, and let time take care of Josh.'

Ben nodded. His mother was usually not the most talkative of people, but over the years he'd found that when she did have something to say, it made a lot of sense.

Maddie was giggling as she continued to hug Caesar. The labrador, meanwhile, was twisting and turning as he tried to lick her face.

'So, Maddie, you like Caesar?' said Ben.

'I *love* Caesar, Daddy,' Maddie gushed. 'And I think

Mummy would have loved him, too, if she was still here. Don't you?'

Ben smiled wistfully. 'I think she would, sweetheart. I think she would.' To shake off the sudden wave of sadness that washed over him as he thought of the children's late mother, he bent to a pot plant beside the back door. Picking out an old, worn tennis ball that Dodger had always loved to play with, he handed it to Maddie. 'See if Caesar likes chasing balls,' he said.

As Maddie took the tennis ball, Caesar sat down, with his eyes fixed intently on the ball as if it was suddenly the most important thing in the world. Ben unclipped his leash.

'Fetch the ball, Caesar!' Maddie called, flinging the ball as far as she could.

When the ball bounced across the grass, Caesar watched its progress. But he didn't move, even though his front legs quivered in anticipation of the chase. Ben knew this was proof of excellent obedience training at the Huntingdon Kennels. As much as Caesar wanted that ball, he knew who was boss, and he was waiting for an instruction from his handler, Ben, before he moved.

Ben smiled approvingly then gave the command, 'Caesar, seek!'

In an instant, Caesar was up and bounding across the grass. Snaffling the ball in his mouth, he came loping back to drop it at Maddie's feet, before sitting and

waiting for another throw and chase. Time and again Maddie threw the ball, and time and again Caesar retrieved it. Ben, glancing back in through the dining room window, hoped that Josh might be showing some interest in what was going on in the backyard. To his disappointment, Josh's head remained down as he concentrated on his homework.

When Maddie's arm grew tired, Ben took over ball throwing duties. For a solid hour, Caesar chased and retrieved that ball, and Ben reckoned the brown labrador could probably have kept chasing it for another hour. Ben was pleased – Caesar's enjoyment of the task of chase and retrieval was a sign that he could make an almost tireless sniffer dog. For that was what explosives detection was all about – seeking and locating. Ben knew that sniffer dogs considered their work one big game. A dog that soon grew bored of a game of fetch would soon become bored with detecting explosives.

There were still months of training ahead, during which it might prove that Caesar was not cut out for war dog work, just as the manager of Huntingdon Kennels had said. Ben was determined to prove the manager wrong and to prove that Caesar had what it took to be a war dog. Ben knew that every dog, like every human, is different, and Caesar's future with the army would be all up to Caesar. Still, right now, that future was looking good.

CHAPTER 3

War dog training school began the next week. Caesar and Ben were among six dogs and six handlers assigned to the army sniffer dog school's training course for EDDs, or explosive detection dogs. The first part of the course would last two weeks, and would focus on dog and handler partnering skills. By the time the course began, Caesar's puffed-up nose had returned to normal, and he looked a much more handsome labrador than when Ben first saw him. The other dogs were a variety of breeds. But all were large, energetic animals that enjoyed working with humans, and were about the same age as Caesar.

Dogs mature very quickly, then age more slowly as they grow older. So, a two-year-old dog like Caesar was at his physical best, was alert and confident, and was learning all the time. The first week of his army basic training involved obedience. Even though Caesar had been well trained at the Huntingdon Kennels, the school's instructors wanted to see how well a dog bonded with its new master, and how well it obeyed that master's instructions.

That very first week, one of the dogs was expelled from the training course for disobedience. It occurred during an exercise where all six dogs were made to sit in a row, two metres apart from one another. To begin with, the handlers stood beside their dogs. Then, instructing their dog to 'sit', and then 'stay', Ben and the other handlers walked away without looking back and disappeared over the lip of a small rise. For thirty minutes, the dogs were left there, sitting in a row. But after twenty minutes, one dog, a blue heeler, became bored, and, getting up, went trotting away to sniff in the long grass, looking for something interesting to chase.

Ignoring the blue heeler, Caesar and the other remaining dogs stayed obediently where they were. Ten minutes later, their handlers reappeared and walked toward them. But even then, the dogs were expected to remain perfectly still. Ben and the other handlers returned to their positions beside their dogs and waited another minute until the chief instructor, Sergeant Angelo, loudly called, 'Fall out!'

Full of pride for Caesar and his good behaviour, Ben knelt beside him, gave him a vigorous pat and a cuddle, and praised him. 'Good boy, Caesar! Good boy!'

Caesar loved to please Ben, and loved praise. It didn't really matter what words Ben used to praise him. All dogs can sense from the tone of the human voice whether we're pleased with them or not. If Ben had said

'Good boy, Caesar', but in an angry tone, Caesar would have sensed that he was being scolded, and would have reacted accordingly. While Caesar knew straightaway whether Ben was pleased with him from his tone, he also came to associate the term 'good dog' with praise, and recognise that Ben thought he'd performed well. Praise is the best reward for any good dog, but during training Ben also gave Caesar a dog biscuit as a special reward for passing difficult tests like this one. As for the blue heeler, he was sent back to the kennels he came from. A good home would be found for him – but not with the army.

In the second week of training, Caesar and the four remaining dogs on the course were sent through obstacle courses: running along narrow tree trunks, through pipes and over walls on their handlers' command. All five dogs passed this test with flying colours.

Next, each handler stood a distance from their dog and fired a starting pistol into the air, with the dog expected to sit and not move when the gun went off. Caesar and the other dogs all passed this first stage of the important noise tests – a series of tests that would become more and more intense as the dogs were prepared for battle-field conditions. Dogs have much more sensitive hearing than humans and don't like loud noises. In fact, dogs can be panicked by a sudden, sharp noise, and many will instinctively run from it. But a well-disciplined dog will tolerate noise if it is with a master it trusts, a master who himself clearly isn't put off by the noise.

After the initial noise tests, the dogs walked with their handlers toward soldiers firing assault rifles into the air, to get them accustomed to the noise of automatic weapons going off. Then, on a firing range, the handlers themselves fired rifles and machineguns with their dogs tethered to their belts, sitting or lying beside them. Caesar took all these weapon noise tests in his stride. When Ben fired his gun, Caesar simply lay down beside him with his jaw on the ground, looking up at Ben as if wondering what on earth he was doing.

As their training moved to the next phase, the dogs were taken to a helicopter landing pad and made to sit with their handlers as helicopters landed and took off nearby. In combat situations, war dogs are generally fitted with special earmuffs to dampen the noise of weapons and machines, but first Caesar and the other dogs in his class had to pass the test without earmuffs. And they all did.

Caesar and the four other dogs came through all the noise tests, but a Belgian shepherd didn't reach the end of the course. As a sheepdog, its natural tendency was to round up things, herding them by circling them and nipping at their heels, forcing them to go in a particular direction. This Belgian shepherd – a large, fit dog – had once or twice nipped at the other dogs on the course during the two weeks, but on the last day, when it nipped the heels of an instructor, its fate was sealed. As a sniffer dog has to live and work with other dogs and with soldiers, Sergeant Angelo decided that this Belgian shepherd would be better at guard work, and sent him off to the air force dog school, which trains dogs to guard air bases.

Four dogs passed this two-week basic training part of the course at Holsworthy, and Caesar was one of them. In fact, the instructors told Ben that Caesar was one of the best dogs on the course, if not *the* best. With seventeen weeks of specialist sniffer training now ahead of them, Ben brought Caesar home for the weekend. Once again, Josh showed no interest in Caesar, and played computer games in his bedroom while Maddie played with the brown labrador in the garden.

The Fultons had a special visitor that weekend. His name was Charles Grover, but everyone called him Charlie, and he was Ben's best friend. Charlie and Ben had gone to school together and, years later, had joined the army together. While Ben had set his sights on becoming a dog handler, Charlie had always wanted to join the Special Air Service Regiment, or SAS, the elite special forces unit, whose motto is 'Who Dares Wins'. Both men had ultimately achieved their ambitions, with Charlie now a sergeant with the SAS. Charlie didn't have much family of his own, and he'd spent so much time with Ben and his family over the years that Josh and Maddie had come to think of him as an uncle.

Very tall, straight as a lamppost, and not as broad as Ben, Charlie had a slow, deliberate way of talking and of acting. Nothing flustered Charlie. To him, problems were always opportunities in disguise. A private man, Charlie didn't make friends as easily as Ben, which only made his firm friendship with Ben and the Fulton family all the more special to him. By contrast, Charlie and the friendly Caesar had become mates within minutes of Charlie's arrival, and Caesar soon had Charlie throwing tennis balls and an old sandshoe for him to fetch.

'Lunch is ready!' Nan called a little later, and Charlie joined the Fulton family inside for lunch, leaving Caesar in the backyard to amuse himself.

'Are you going away again soon, Charlie?' Josh asked as they ate. Josh knew that Charlie went away on special missions, just like his dad.

'Roger to that, Josh,' Charlie replied. As Josh knew, 'Roger to that' was army talk for 'yes'.

'Where are you going this time?'

'Can't tell you where, except that it's really hot there in summer and freezing cold in winter.'

'That narrows it down to about half the world,' said Josh, with a smile. 'I bet it's Afghanistan,' he added. 'A lot of the dads of army kids at my school are in Afghanistan, or have been there.'

Charlie shrugged apologetically. 'Can't tell you, mate, sorry. SAS movements are top secret.'

'Are you and my daddy sometimes soldiers in the same place, Charlie?' Maddie now asked.

'Sometimes we are, Maddie,' he returned.

'Good,' said Maddie, with a firm nod, and waving her knife airily about. 'That means you can look after Daddy while he's away.'

Charlie grinned. 'I'll do my best, Maddie,' he said. 'And he'll look after me.'

'Just like we've always looked after each other, ever since we were kids,' said Ben, and he and Charlie clinked their glasses together.

'Mates forever,' said Charlie.

After lunch, as Ben and Charlie helped Nan with the washing up, Nan glanced out the kitchen window and a look of horror came over her face. 'My roses!' she exclaimed. 'What has that dog *done*?'

Ben, looking out the window to see what his mother saw, groaned, 'Oh, no!' Putting down the plate he'd been drying, Ben opened the back door and stormed out into the yard. 'Caesar!' he growled unhappily.

Caesar was hard at work in a flowerbed, digging a hole with his paws, and having a great time. He wasn't looking for anything in particular, just following interesting scents in the earth. Around him were another half-dozen holes he'd already dug, uprooting a rosebush, and this latest hole was half a metre deep. Hearing his master's voice and his angry tone, Caesar stopped digging and looked around.

'Come away from there!' called Ben. 'Bad dog, Caesar. Bad dog!'

Caesar's ears immediately dropped. His head lowered. Both were signs of a dog that knew he was being scolded. Caesar trotted over to Ben, stopping in front of his master with his pink tongue hanging out the side of his mouth. He cocked his head to one side and looked up at Ben as if to say, *What's the problem, boss?*

'Bad dog!' said Ben, standing with his hands on his hips. 'You do not dig, Caesar. No digging!'

Looking past Ben, Caesar saw Maddie through the opening of the glass sliding door. Hoping to get a better reception from her, he bounded into the kitchen.

'Get outside with your dirty paws!' cried Nan. 'You naughty, naughty dog!'

Caesar, surprised and a little confused, quickly spun around and went trotting back out into the yard with his head down and tail low.

'Caesar, sit!' Ben commanded.

Caesar promptly sat. As Ben walked up to him and stood glaring down at him, Caesar looked guiltily away to the side, avoiding eye contact.

'You – do – not – dig – up – the – garden,' said Ben, stressing every word with a wag of the finger.

Caesar's head dropped a little lower.

'You know I like dogs, Ben,' said Nan, who had come outside with Charlie and Maddie to inspect the scene of Caesar's misdemeanour. 'But I *love* my roses.'

'Sorry about that,' said Ben, feeling responsible for the damage to the roses.

'I'm not sure this dog is going to meet your expectations, Ben,' said Nan unhappily. 'You can't have a sniffer dog digging holes when he's supposed to be sniffing out explosives. Dodger never dug up the garden.'

'No, he didn't,' agreed Charlie, who had known Dodger well.

'I know, I know,' said Ben. 'Huntingdon Kennels warned me Caesar was a digger. I'll just have to train it out of him.' He looked down at Caesar again, as the bemused labrador sat returning his gaze. Despite Caesar's digging habit, Ben still felt this brown dog had great potential. 'He's got everything else going for him – the temperament of a labrador and the superior intelligence of his German shepherd grandfather.'

'A German shepherd is smarter than a lab?' said Charlie with surprise.

'It's true,' Ben replied. 'Labradors are only rated the seventh most intelligent breed of dog. German shepherds are the third most intelligent.'

'Then why choose a labrador for your army work?'

said Nan. 'Why not get a German shepherd instead of Caesar?'

'German shepherds bark too much,' Ben replied, with a shake of the head. 'That's why they make such good guard dogs. They raise the alarm and scare the living daylights out of intruders, whereas labradors rarely bark – have any of you heard Caesar bark even once this weekend?'

'No, Daddy,' Maddie spoke up. 'Caesar hasn't barked once.'

Caesar was, meanwhile, watching them all talk, his head turning to each of them in turn when they spoke his name.

'You can't have a dog barking at every stranger it sees when it's supposed to be sniffing out explosives,' Ben continued. 'And while German shepherds can be intensely loyal, they're only loyal to one master. An explosive detection dog has to serve with groups of soldiers for long periods of time. In that sort of situation, German shepherds have been known to nip other soldiers in the group if they think their space, or their master's space, is being infringed. A lab like Caesar here will be mates with every man in a platoon.'

'Okay,' said Charlie. 'But if a labrador like Caesar here is only the seventh most intelligent, why not use a smarter breed, other than a German shepherd? Which dogs are the most intelligent of all?'

'Number one is the border collie, followed by the poodle.'

Nan laughed. 'A poodle? Second most intelligent? I can't exactly see a fussy little poodle going to war.'

'I wouldn't write them off just on appearances, Mum. Poodles were actually bred as hunting dogs by the kings of France,' Ben said, with a smile. 'But poodles and border collies don't have the stamina for our line of work. Besides, they can be too clever, too self-willed. On the other hand, a well-trained lab like Caesar here will obey his master through thick and thin.' Kneeling beside Caesar, Ben began to clean the dirt from his front paws.

Caesar, hoping that this was a sign he'd been forgiven, licked his master on the mouth, making Ben laugh and wipe his mouth with the back of his hand. He couldn't stay angry with Caesar. 'You are a silly boy,' Ben said, grinning and fondling Caesar's ears. 'But we'll have to get you out of that digging habit, my furry friend. You don't want to be rejected by the army like that dopey blue heeler the other day, do you?' Caesar nuzzled in against Ben's chest, seeking more reassurance that Ben had forgiven him, and Ben's heart ached. He had quickly grown fond of this cheeky brown mutt.

'Just keep him away from my roses!' Nan urged, as she headed back indoors.

'Can you train the digging out of him, Ben?' Charlie asked.

'I'll have to,' Ben firmly replied, 'if Caesar and I are to have a future together.'

The next afternoon, Charlie prepared to say goodbye to the Fultons after spending the weekend with them. He was wearing his army uniform now, complete with a sandy-coloured beret emblazoned with the dagger emblem of the SAS. He had spent an hour playing computer games with Josh that morning. Josh loved playing computer games with Charlie, who was a skilled player, and because Charlie let Josh win half the time. Josh's gleeful yells, groans and laughter could be heard all the way down in the living room, where Ben and Nan exchanged smiles – it was good to hear Josh enjoying himself for the first time since the family had lost Dodger.

As Josh and Charlie were finishing up, Maddie came wandering in. Caesar ambled in behind her, curiously sniffing all the new smells of Josh's room.

'Can I play?' Maddie asked.

'No, you're too young,' said Josh, with a frown. 'And get that stupid dog out of my room.'

'Come on, Caesar,' said Maddie, taking hold of Caesar's collar and tugging him from the room. 'Computer games are stupid, anyway!'

Charlie watched them leave, then turned to Josh with a questioning look. 'You don't like Caesar?'

'We *had* a good dog. We had Dodger.'

'But Dodger's gone, Josh.'

'Only because my dad killed him.'

'That's not fair, mate,' said Charlie. 'Your dad didn't want to put Dodger down – it was the last thing he wanted. Dodger and your dad were a team. But Dodger wasn't well, and your dad did the compassionate thing by putting Dodger out of his misery.'

Josh looked at Charlie with tears forming in his eyes. 'But I miss Dodger so much.'

Charlie put an arm around Josh. 'We all miss the old Dodger, mate – your dad most of all. But he has a job to do, just like I have, and that's why he's got Caesar now.'

'I would have looked after Dodger if Dad had brought him home instead of telling the vet to kill him.'

Charlie shook his head. 'After his stroke, Dodger had to be carried everywhere. You couldn't have been with him every minute of every day, Josh. You have to go to school. It would have been cruel to bring Dodger home in that condition, then leave him all alone.'

'I still don't think it was fair,' said Josh, snuffling up his tears.

'Some things in life aren't fair, mate. But your dad did the right thing, believe me. He put Dodger first. Sometimes, Josh, we have to put others before ourselves, and make sacrifices for the sake of others. To do that is the mark of a man of courage and compassion.'

Outside the door to Josh's bedroom, Ben had paused to listen, and smiled to himself as he heard Charlie's wise words. He opened the door gently and walked into the room. 'Time that Charlie hit the road,' he said, giving Josh a sympathetic smile. 'He has an overseas flight to catch tonight.'

So, Charlie bade farewell to the Fultons, with hugs all around, reserving his last goodbye for Caesar. Bending down and giving the cheerful labrador a pat, Charlie whispered, 'Now, you be a good dog for Ben, Caesar, and pass your training course. Then, maybe one day, we'll see each other on deployment somewhere.'

In response, Caesar licked him on the face.

CHAPTER 4

On Monday, Caesar and Ben were back on the EDD training course at the Holsworthy army base. Since Caesar had proven in the first two weeks of the course that he could obey Ben's orders like a good soldier, and that he could stand the noise of battle and machines, he and Ben now began the longer explosive detection part of the course.

Eight dogs took part: Caesar and the three others that had passed basic training the previous week, plus four experienced dogs who were being used to help train new human handlers. All eight dogs were taken out to the training area in the same truck each day, but after they reached the training area they were kept apart, with each team of dog and handler being trained at their own pace. Even though Caesar had performed well in basic training, if he proved to have poor detection skills, became bored with the job, or didn't continue to promptly follow Ben's directions, he would be ejected from the course.

The new dogs were going to be taught to use their incredible sense of smell, many times stronger than that of humans, to detect enemy explosives which might kill or injure soldiers in the field. While those explosives came in a variety of forms, they all had the same basic chemical ingredients. And it was those basic ingredients that military sniffer dogs were taught to detect.

Caesar's detection training began with a tennis ball. Ben stood with Caesar sitting by his side, and off his leash, while an instructor showed Caesar a tennis ball. The instructor then walked to a metal cage forty metres away and put the ball in it. Caesar had not taken his eye off the ball for a moment, but had continued all the while to sit obediently by Ben's side.

Then, pointing to the cage, Ben commanded, 'Caesar, seek on!'

In a flash, Caesar was up and bounding to the cage. Grabbing the tennis ball from inside, he came loping back and dropped the ball at Ben's feet, then sat in front of him, looking up, eagerly waiting for the 'game' to continue.

Squatting down beside Caesar, Ben patted him, ruffled his neck and praised him. 'Good boy, Caesar! Good boy!'

Before the training session had begun, the cage from where Caesar had retrieved the ball had been sprayed with traces of chemicals used in the manufacture of explosives. Humans can't smell those chemicals, but dogs can. As the ball game continued, with the instructor taking the tennis ball to the cage and Caesar bringing it back time and again to receive Ben's praise, Caesar began to associate the smell of those chemicals with the tennis ball and the order to seek on.

As the days progressed, the tennis ball disappeared, but when Ben ordered Caesar to seek on he would still dash to the cage in search of it. There, he would sit, looking at the cage, a little mystified, as if thinking, *So, where's the ball? I know it's here somewhere, I can smell it.* Caesar now associated the odour of explosives with the order to seek, and now knew that every time he located that odour he would receive Ben's praise. During the course, Caesar was exposed to different types of explosives, and even detonators. As the days stretched into weeks, the training moved on as Ben began to send Caesar into empty buildings to find the scent – into pipes and culverts, into an underground bunker, into trucks, cars, and an armoured personnel carrier. And, every time, Caesar would detect the odour in a container or package containing explosives that had been deliberately hidden for him to find.

Next, Caesar was taught to track the scent of explosives that were on the move. An instructor carrying explosives would lay a trail while Ben and Caesar waited. After thirty minutes, Ben would release Caesar and instruct him to seek on. As always, Caesar would bound away and follow the scent trail with his nose down to the ground. Every time, Caesar found the hiding instructor. Even when the waiting time was increased, Caesar could successfully follow an explosives trail that was hours old.

Another task involved training Caesar to inspect roads for hidden landmines or IEDs – improvised explosive devices, which are lethal homemade bombs. To perform this task, Ben trained Caesar to seek on up one side of a road until he was about forty metres ahead of Ben, then track back down the other side, always looking for the scent of explosives. During the training, genuine landmines and IEDs were planted in or beside roads. Caesar found every one. Each time, he would come to a sudden stop, turn in the direction of the explosives, then slowly ease his backside down into the sitting position and stare at the hiding place.

When dogs sense odours they have been trained to seek, all indicate their find in slightly different ways. Sniffer dog handlers call this the dog's 'signature'. Some dogs stare when they've located something. Some sit in front of it. Some stand frozen and seem to point with their nose. Others lift a front paw off the ground. Sometimes, when the scent is faint, making the dog uncertain, a handler has to be able to read a dog's changed behaviour – behaviour anyone else might not notice, or might dismiss as unimportant.

So, all through these weeks of detection training, Ben was undergoing a form of training of his own. He had noticed that Caesar would always stop and sit very slowly when he had found the source of the scent he was tracking, then stare at it with his tail rigid. If the scent was in a vehicle, Caesar would sit and stare at the vehicle. If it was carried by a human, he would sit and look up at the human without flinching a muscle. Ben also observed that when Caesar picked up a faint scent, his head would go down and he would keep it low to the ground as he sniffed urgently. When released from his leash, Caesar would quickly and methodically circle around and around, gradually increasing his search area until he picked up the scent.

In one exercise, Caesar was sent by Ben to inspect a group of unarmed Australian Army Engineers while they had lunch in the field. One of those soldiers had handled heavy explosives that morning especially for the training exercise. To a dog with a finely tuned nose, there would still be a faint scent of explosive chemicals on that soldier. Some dogs would miss it. Exceptionally gifted dogs would not.

At first, Caesar circled the group of soldiers, who were chatting and eating their lunch. As Ben observed from a distance, with chief instructor Angelo and a burly sergeant who was in charge of the Engineers, Caesar went around and around the group without seeming to pick up a scent.

'Which of your men was carrying the explosives, Sergeant?' Ben asked the engineer sergeant, as they watched Caesar continuing to circle the group.

'I expect your dog to tell us that, Corporal Fulton,' said the sergeant, with a chuckle. 'One of the other dogs picked up the scent when it was tested here yesterday. Looks like your dog's not up to it, though.'

Ben frowned. 'How long did it take yesterday's dog to find the scent?'

The engineer sergeant shrugged. 'Quite a while.'

'Was it at lunchtime, like today?' Ben pressed.

'No, it was after lunch. Midafternoon,' said Sergeant Angelo.

Ben nodded. 'The smell of cooking food might be masking the scent for Caesar,' he remarked.

'Sounds like a pretty good excuse for failure to me,' said the sergeant with a laugh. After a long pause, he looked at his watch. 'How long before your dog gives up?'

'Caesar never gives up,' Ben replied, with a proud smile on his face. 'He's proving to be the most persistent dog I've ever come across. He'd keep this up for hours, if I let him.'

'Well, we do have to go back to barracks before sunset, you know,' said the sergeant disparagingly, before turning to walk away.

'Wait a minute,' said Ben. 'I think Caesar's on to something now. Look.'

The sergeant stopped in his tracks and looked over at Caesar to see that the dog was still circling the Engineers. Shaking his head, he said, 'I don't see anything.'

'Look more closely,' Ben urged.

'What do you mean?' The sergeant scowled. 'He's still running around in circles! He's clueless, mate, admit it.'

'No, look more closely.' When the sergeant still couldn't spot any change in Caesar's behaviour, Ben had to spell it out for him. 'Look how Caesar stops in front of a particular man before he turns around and does another circle. It's always the same man he stops in front of. He's not certain, but he's troubled. I think Caesar has picked up a hint of a scent on the corporal with red hair.'

'Hell's bells, Fulton!' the sergeant exclaimed. 'You're either a freakishly good guesser, or you can read your dog like a book. The red-headed corporal was the one your dog was supposed to find – he was the one carrying explosives this morning.'

It was a double victory. Caesar had picked up a scent, faint though it was, and Ben had been able to read his dog well enough to realise when Caesar was on to something.

By the fifteenth week of training, while there was detection practice every day, new war dog skills were also being added. One day, Caesar was taught to relax when Ben picked him up and slung him around his shoulders like a very large furry scarf, then took a firm hold of his legs as they trailed down his chest, grasping two legs in each hand. This fireman's lift method would be used by Ben to evacuate Caesar if his dog was ever wounded in action or was otherwise unable to walk.

While Ben was holding Caesar like this, an instructor took a photograph of the pair. Caesar looked into the camera with a sad look, as if to say, *Why am I up here on Ben's shoulders? I just feel so silly.*

This fireman's lift practice also prepared Caesar for something that some humans, let alone dogs, find scary. At times, war dogs have to be winched in and out of hovering helicopters, or 'heelos', as soldiers call them. This was sometimes done with their handler, but other times circumstances required dogs to be lowered or raised on their own. For this, a long, thick winching wire hanging from the helicopter was attached to a heelo harness specially created for dogs. In these last few weeks of training, Ben put the harness on Caesar every day to get him used to wearing it. Caesar didn't even seem to notice he had it on.

Ben also had his own way of preparing Caesar for dangling beneath a helicopter. The weekend before he was due to take him to an army exercise area for Caesar's helicopter lift training, Ben took Caesar home as usual and tried out a device he'd rigged up in the backyard.

Josh was due to play school soccer on Saturday morning. As Ben drove him to the game, he said, 'Want to see how Caesar reacts to the heelo lift this afternoon, Josh? I'm going to try him in it from a tree in the yard. Remember how Dodger reacted when we tried him out with his heelo harness?'

'Nah,' Josh replied, looking out the window. 'I've got stuff to do this afternoon.'

Ben sighed with disappointment. But, remembering Nan Fulton's words after Ben first brought Caesar home, he didn't try pushing Caesar onto Josh. Though he did wonder how long it would take for Josh to finally like Caesar.

After Josh's team won their game and they returned home, the family had lunch, then Josh disappeared into his room.

'Josh's playing computer games again,' said Ben unhappily, leading Caesar out into the yard.

'Don't worry about him, Ben,' said Nan, as she and Maddie followed them out the back door to watch. 'He's okay.'

'I'm a soldier,' said Ben, taking Caesar to a large gum tree, tall, with a thick white trunk, by the back fence. 'I take orders. And I'm tempted to *order* Josh to get involved with Caesar. It's been months since I brought him home.'

'You can't order your son to love someone, Ben,' said Nan, shaking her head. 'Josh will warm to Caesar eventually. Just let him be.'

Maddie, as if she were in class at school, raised her hand. 'Daddy, *I* love Caesar,' she said.

'I know you do, sweetheart,' said Ben with a smile, as he knelt beside Caesar and attached a rope to the dog's heelo harness. 'And he loves you.'

Ben got up and heaved on the rope, which hung from a branch of the big gum tree, hauling Caesar several metres into the air until the brown labrador hung helplessly above their heads. As he slowly turned at the end of the rope, Caesar looked down at them from his harness with his tongue hanging out.

'He likes it!' Maddie cried with glee.

'I'm not so sure,' said Nan, with a worried frown. 'Look at poor old Caesar's tail.'

Sure enough, Caesar's tail was drooping. If he was enjoying this, his tail would be wagging. 'No dog enjoys this sort of thing,' said Ben, 'but Caesar's coping well. He's calm and accepting of his situation – that's good. He'll do fine when it's the real thing.'

Caesar did do fine in his heelo harness when it came to the real thing the following week. Caesar and the other dogs on the course and their handlers were driven to a live firing range outside Holsworthy. An army Black Hawk helicopter flew in, and hovered noisily above them as the men and dogs lined up. All the handlers were wearing ear-protectors, called Peltors, to reduce the noise, and goggles to protect their eyes from the clouds of dust raised by the helicopter's spinning rotors. Now, Ben and the other handlers fitted special dog goggles, called 'doggles', over their animals' eyes, along with canine ear-protectors, known as 'puppy Peltors'. Once Ben had fitted Caesar with his doggles and puppy Peltors, Caesar looked up at him as if to say, *What's this all about, boss?* Ben grinned and gave Caesar a pat. 'Caesar, mate, the doggles and Peltors suit you,' he yelled, above the noise of the hovering heelo.

Eight metal lines were then dropped down from the Black Hawk, which Ben and three other handlers hitched up to the heelo harnesses, first to their own then to those of their dogs. Dogs and handlers were lifted into the air as the heelo rose up and did several circuits of the area with the handlers and their dogs dangling beneath it, before returning and gently setting them back on the ground.

The morning was spent going through a variety of heelo lifts and drops, with all the dogs and handlers rappelling down together and then being winched back. One time, Caesar alone was winched all the way up into the Black Hawk's cabin, taken for a ride, then lowered back down, while Ben waited on the ground. All through this, Caesar was perfectly calm and accepting, indicating he had the right temperament for heelo work, as Ben had predicted.

Helicopter training ceased at lunchtime, with the handlers and instructors sitting down to an army ration lunch among the parked trucks and Land Rovers that had brought them out to the firing range. The dogs, on the other hand, were only given water, for they would have their only meal of the day at night. As the troops ate, the dogs were let off their leashes and allowed to roam free. The first thing that Caesar did was introduce himself to the other dogs by sniffing their behinds and letting them sniff his. This was a dog's way of getting to know other dogs – from their rear-end scent. Ben, sitting and eating from an MRE (Meals, Ready-to-Eat) pack, watched Caesar with the other dogs for a while, before becoming locked in conversation with chief instructor Sergeant Angelo.

After lunch, Ben went looking for Caesar. At first, he couldn't find him. Then, from beside one of the green Land Rovers, Ben saw earth flying through the air. Walking around the vehicle, Ben came upon Caesar digging a hole with a flurry of front paws. The hole was getting deeper with each second.

'Caesar, no!' Ben groaned. 'We've been through this before. No digging!'

Grabbing Caesar's collar, he tried to pull him away. But Caesar strained with all his might to return to his hole.

'Bad dog! Bad dog, Caesar!' Ben growled. 'Sit!'

Caesar looked around at him and let out a whine of surprise, then dutifully sat down.

Ben's scolding tone was heard by the chief instructor, who came walking around the Land Rover to see what was going on. 'Is there a problem, Fulton?' Sergeant Angelo asked. Then he spotted the hole. 'Oh. Did your dog do this?'

'Yes, Sergeant,' said Ben, guiltily. 'I thought he'd outgrown his digging habit. He hasn't done it in months.' Ben immediately became worried that this might count against Caesar, and might even result in his dog being kicked off the course – the tough chief instructor never gave a dog a second chance if it breached discipline. Both blue heeler and Belgian shepherd had been swiftly ejected for getting out of line during basic training.

Sergeant Angelo scowled as he looked at the hole. 'Your dog digs, does he? I'm not sure that's a good –'

Ben's heart sank, as he dreaded to hear the worst. 'It's just an immature habit of Caesar's,' he said, hurrying to defend Caesar. 'Don't worry, Sergeant, I'll train it out of him. It's not a big deal.'

But the chief instructor's attention had been caught by something in the hole. 'What's this?' he said, squatting to take a closer look.

Ben came and looked over Sergeant Angelo's shoulder, and saw a piece of curved grey metal in the earth where Caesar had been digging. 'Is that what I think it is?' he said.

Sergeant Angelo nodded grimly. 'It sure is, Fulton. An artillery shell. An unexploded round.' Coming to his feet, the sergeant yelled at the top of his voice, 'Clear the area! We have unexploded ordnance here!'

'Looks like Caesar knew what he was doing after all,' said Ben proudly, giving Caesar a pat. 'Good boy, Caesar! Good boy!'

As the men and dogs quickly evacuated the area, Sergeant Angelo was eyeing Caesar. He was not a man who often smiled, but a broad grin now creased his weather-beaten face. 'Your dog picked up the scent of the high explosive in the ground, Fulton. Well done to you both.'

Sergeant Angelo called in a bomb disposal squad, who were brought in by Black Hawk. While the handlers and their dogs waited a safe distance away, two bomb disposal soldiers in special padded suits and protective helmets carefully removed the large unexploded shell from the ground, then carried it away from the parked vehicles. With a boom, an orange flash and a cloud of black smoke, the shell was safely detonated a thousand metres away, in a controlled explosion.

As Ben led Caesar back to the vehicles once the all clear had been given, Sergeant Angelo came over to them. 'Fulton, you were saying that you would train the digging habit out of Caesar. I wouldn't do that if I were you. You never know when his interest in digging will come in handy on operations.'

Ben, smiling like a proud father, gave Caesar a pat. 'You hear that, Caesar?' he said. 'You can dig as much as you like – except when it involves Nan Fulton's roses.'

That night, as a special reward, Ben convinced a base cook to give him the best steak he had, for Caesar's dinner.

At the end of the seventeen-week course, Caesar and three remaining trainee dogs were all certified as trained explosive detection dogs, or EDDs, by chief instructor Sergeant Angelo. At a small ceremony, the four dogs and their handlers lined up and received special leather collars, into which metal tags were embedded. Caesar's metal tag read: *Australian Army EDD 556 Caesar*. This was now Caesar's official Australian Army service number – EDD 556.

As the other handlers marched away with their dogs, Sergeant Angelo took Ben and Caesar aside. 'Fulton,' he began. 'Your Caesar has done well – very well – and I think you're both cut out for Special Forces operations.'

'You do?' Ben responded with delight. This was a real

compliment but not a big surprise – he had always seen Caesar's war dog potential.

'In fact,' said Angelo, 'I'm assigning the two of you to immediate Special Forces insertion training. Good luck with it.'

The next day, Ben and Caesar were flown by helicopter to the Amberley Air Force base in Queensland. Their Special Forces training would commence the following week.

Over the weekend, Ben hired a car and, on the Sunday, drove to a secluded beach on the Queensland coast. All the while, Caesar sat on the back seat with his head out the open window, revelling in the rush of the slipstream against his face. At the beach, Ben stripped down to bathers, then let Caesar off the leash and raced him to see who would be first into the water. Of course, Caesar won the race – a man could never outrun a powerful labrador.

For hours, Ben and Caesar played in the water and on the sand. Labradors love the water. They even have webbed feet, like ducks, which makes them powerful swimmers, doggy-paddle style. Caesar swam on his own, at one point going way out beyond the breakers until he was just a dot, and Ben had to call him back.

Other times, Ben grabbed Caesar's new collar and let his dog pull him through the water. On the beach, Ben threw a stick for Caesar to fetch, both along the beach and in the water. By the time the sun was going down, Ben's arm ached, but Caesar was still keen to chase and fetch.

'Aren't you sick of seeking yet?' said Ben with a laugh, looking down at Caesar as the dog sat looking up at Ben with an expectant gleam in his eyes.

Of course Caesar wasn't tired of seeking. He had never had so much fun in all his life and he didn't want it to stop. He even barked impatiently at Ben, urging him to keep going with the game.

As Ben was towelling himself down and preparing to depart the beach, an elderly couple came walking by.

'Do you realise that dogs aren't allowed on this beach?' said the woman, looking disapprovingly at Caesar as he sat beside his master.

'Is that right?' said Ben, pulling on a t-shirt. 'I didn't know that.'

'People like you,' said the man angrily, 'should learn some discipline. Rules are made to be obeyed, young man!'

'And why aren't you doing something worthwhile with your time,' the woman added, 'instead of soiling a public beach with your animal?'

'Something worthwhile?' Ben responded, raising his

eyebrows, as the couple kept walking. Clearly, they weren't dog lovers. 'We'll see what we can do about that, lady.' He squatted and patted Caesar. 'Won't we, mate?'

'You do that,' the woman called back over her shoulder.

Little did the complaining couple know that Ben and Caesar were now among the most elite teams of Special Operations dogs and handlers in the world. But, because their work was top secret, Ben would have to let the woman have the last word.

That evening, as they made their way back to the airbase, Caesar fell asleep on the back seat of the rented car. Ben, briefly looking in the rear-view mirror as he drove, saw Caesar stretched out, his eyes closed. Caesar's nose was twitching, and one of his paws was quivering. He was dreaming, perhaps about chasing a ball or a stick – maybe even a cat or a rabbit. Returning his eyes to the road, Ben smiled to himself, knowing that Caesar was exhausted but happy.

CHAPTER 5

On the following Monday, Ben and Caesar began their three weeks of Special Forces insertion training, which prepared them for covert landings behind enemy lines on secret missions. First, they were trained to parachute from a Hercules transport aircraft. This big, four-engine plane has a ramp at the back which is lowered for the loading and unloading of cargo. For paratroops – soldiers who are parachuted into battle from aircraft – and for Special Forces, the Hercules' ramp is also lowered when the plane is flying over a target area, with the parachutists running off the ramp and launching themselves into the air. When a Special Forces dog and his handler jump together, the dog is strapped sideways on the front of the handler, at waist level, with both man and dog relying on the handler's parachute.

Caesar's tail was wagging as Ben, already wearing his parachute, led him into the hull of the vast Hercules aircraft for their training jump. A group of SAS men, or operators, as the SAS called its personnel, was going with them. The plane's engines roared deafeningly as a dozen men buckled into the webbing seats along the plane's cavernous interior. Caesar went around the SAS men, saying hello by looking up and wagging his tail at each soldier, and received plenty of pats in return.

As the Hercules taxied, Ben gave a gentle tug on Caesar's leash, and Caesar promptly returned to settle on the metal floor at his feet. Caesar lay contentedly there as they took off and flew toward the drop zone at 5000 feet. While the hydraulic tail ramp was slowly lowered, revealing clear blue sky behind the plane as far as the eye could see, Ben pulled his goggles into place and fitted Caesar's doggles. Then, with the help of an air force jumpmaster, who supervised the parachuting, Ben lifted Caesar up and attached the dog's heelo harness to his special jumping harness. This was like a giant sling, leaving Ben's hands free as Caesar hung in front of him.

All jumpers hitched up to an overhead wire that would automatically open their parachutes once they left the aircraft. They then shuffled into a line facing the open rear of the aircraft, like runners waiting at the starting line for a race to begin. Ben and Caesar stood behind them waiting to follow the SAS men out the open tail. Ben could feel that Caesar, not knowing what to expect, had tensed up, so he fondled his ears, bent close to him and said, reassuringly, above the roar of the engines, 'Everything's fine, mate. Just fine. Nothing to worry about.'

Caesar let out a little whimper, as if to say, *I hope you're right, boss. I'm not comfortable in this sling thing.*

A light flashed green, indicating it was time to jump. 'Go!' bellowed the jumpmaster, pointing toward the end of the ramp.

The SAS men ran along the ramp and launched themselves from the aircraft. With Caesar attached to him, Ben could barely run, so he waddled quickly to the end of the ramp, then pitched out into the sky after the others. Man and dog were flying together. Looking up, Ben could see the Hercules heading away and growing smaller with each second. Then the parachute line jerked and the parachute opened with a jolt, rapidly slowing their descent.

With Ben steering the parachute toward a large white cross marked on the ground, man and dog floated toward the target. Ahead of them, every SAS man had landed precisely on the cross. The ground came rushing to meet Ben and Caesar. Ben's feet touched the earth near the cross. Throwing himself to the right, Ben landed on his side to avoid landing on top of Caesar – which could injure them both. And then they were down, lying on the ground, with Caesar on top of Ben. Ben began to laugh, and Caesar leaned around and licked him on the cheek. 'Did you like that, Caesar, boy?' said Ben, as he set about unbuckling them both.

After Ben had released Caesar from the harness, and the two of them were standing free, side by side, an SAS trooper came by, gathering up his parachute. As the trooper passed, he noticed that Caesar was jumping up at Ben and nudging him with his nose.

'How did Private Woofer there like the jump?' the smiling SAS man asked.

'Look at the way he's acting now,' said Ben, ruffling Caesar's neck. 'He loved it and wants to go again!'

Ben was right. Just as Caesar loved the sensation of wind on his nose when he put it out a moving car's window, he had revelled in the sensation of slipstream on his nose when he and Ben jumped. As their Special Forces training continued, Ben and Caesar jumped again from a Hercules, this time from 20,000 feet, with both man and dog wearing special jumpsuits and oxygen masks. When the pair boarded the plane for the second flight, Caesar's tail was wagging even more vigorously than usual. Recognising the Hercules, he remembered what had happened the last time he'd been in one and couldn't wait to jump again.

This time, because they jumped from a much greater height, they freefell for some time and Ben had to pull the ripcord to open their parachute once they were nearer to the ground. A strong crosswind sprang up as they descended beneath the deployed chute, blowing them off course. With a splash, they landed in a murky brown river. The first thing that Ben did was unclip Caesar from the jumping harness. Only then did Ben worry about freeing himself from the dragging parachute. Caesar, swimming confidently, kept right beside his master as Ben unhitched himself. Ben then grabbed hold of Caesar's collar. 'To the riverbank, Caesar,' he instructed. 'Swim, mate. Swim!' Paddling strongly, Caesar towed them both to the bank. There, wet and muddy, Ben stripped them from their jumpsuits, before they jogged to the nearby landing zone.

The final insertion training phase involved Caesar operating at a distance from Ben. Only the best Special Forces dogs were used for this type of work. This was a night operation, involving Ben and Caesar being winched down into bushland from a hovering Black Hawk. This time, Ben was wearing full combat equipment including light, bullet-resistant Kevlar body armour and helmet, was carrying an assault rifle, had an automatic pistol holstered low on his right thigh, and had radio equipment and a laptop computer in his backpack. Caesar was kitted out, too, with a special black Kevlar dog vest fitted with radio and video equipment, plus the batteries to power them.

Ben's briefing from an SAS sergeant revealed that this exercise required handler and dog to hike overland for several kilometres after being dropped from a heelo, which was to disappear into the night after completing the insertion. At a designated point, Ben had to release Caesar and send him out on his own to locate insurgents – as local guerrilla fighters have come to be known. In this case, a platoon of Australian Army infantry recruits out on a night training exercise was playing the part of those insurgents. And those recruits had no idea that Ben and Caesar were being sent to locate them.

The recruits' orders had been to establish a night camp in the bush, make sure they could not be spotted, and be on the lookout for so-called 'enemy infiltrators'. Ben and Caesar were those enemy infiltrators. While the recruits would fail the exercise if their location was successfully identified by Ben and Caesar, Ben and Caesar would fail the exercise if they were spotted by the recruits first.

Finding a hiding place in the trees, and setting up his radio and computer, Ben then sent Caesar forward, with the infrared video camera attached to Caesar's vest set to broadcast pictures back to Ben's laptop. This enabled Ben to see what Caesar could see. There was also a radio speaker on Caesar's vest, through which Ben could speak to Caesar and give him instructions. For two hours, Ben had Caesar search the bushland until, at last, Ben saw movement on his computer screen.

'Caesar, halt!' Ben instructed with a hushed voice. 'Caesar, lie flat.'

Caesar lay on his stomach, and for several minutes Ben watched the pictures being transmitted back to him by Caesar's camera. Ben could see tents, camouflage nets, and shadowy human shapes. Taking out his operational map, he marked the location, then picked up his radio's microphone and called the SAS sergeant back at base.

'EDD team to Control. Twenty-plus insurgents sighted at the following grid reference,' Ben reported, before giving the reference number.

'Very good, EDD team, reference noted,' the sergeant replied. 'Well done, Corporal. Exercise complete. Those recruits are going to be surprised tomorrow when we can tell them exactly where they've been tonight. They thought they'd camouflaged their position so well. Collect your asset and return to the rendezvous point. Over.' In army talk, the 'asset' in this case referred to an EDD.

'Roger. EDD team out,' Ben returned, before using his radio to instruct his asset – Caesar – to return to him, which Caesar did, unerringly.

Back at base the next day, the SAS sergeant called Ben and Caesar to his office and congratulated them on a job well done. 'Caesar is one of the most efficient Special Operations dogs I've come across,' said the sergeant.

Both Ben and Caesar looked at the sergeant expectantly. 'What's next?' asked Ben.

'That's it,' said the sergeant. 'Your training is complete. I will now certify you two "insertion ready".' He started filling out a form which certified Caesar as fully trained. 'You and Caesar are ready for war.'

CHAPTER 6

Ben and Caesar returned to Holsworthy to await orders. Boring weeks passed, with Ben giving Caesar daily detection exercises to keep him fresh and interested in his work. Over a period of two days, they took part in an Incident Response Regiment joint operation with New South Wales Police to check a building where an important political conference was to take place, making sure that no terrorist bombs were planted there.

Then, one Thursday, deployment orders came for Ben and Caesar to replace EDD 523 and his handler in the Special Operations Task Group in Uruzgan Province, Afghanistan. Ben had three days to prepare Caesar and himself before taking off for the other side of the world the following Monday. The next day, Ben methodically prepared his and Caesar's equipment, then took Caesar home for the weekend. That night, Ben told Nan Fulton about his upcoming deployment. But he said nothing to Josh and Maddie for the moment, letting the weekend play out as it normally would. Then, after Sunday lunch, he took his children into the living room and sat them down on either side of him.

'I have something to tell you both,' said Ben, putting his arms around them. 'Caesar and I have received our orders. We have to go overseas.'

Maddie stiffened. 'When do you go, Daddy?' she asked.

'Tomorrow night,' Ben answered, steeling himself for what he expected to be an unhappy reaction.

Josh looked at his father with anxious eyes. 'How long for?'

'Only seven months,' Ben replied, trying to make it sound like a relatively short time.

'Seven months!' Maddie wailed, tears quickly forming in her eyes. She lay her head on her father's chest.

'Now, you've both been brave when I've been away on operations before,' said Ben, stroking Maddie's shiny golden hair. 'You'll both be fine while I'm away this time, too. Nan will be here to look after you, and you've got each other. I want you to be good to one another. Do you hear me?'

'Where are you going this time, Dad?' Josh asked. 'It's Afghanistan, isn't it?' There was fear in his voice now.

'Uh-huh,' Ben nodded.

'Where in Afghanistan?'

'Josh, you know I'm not allowed to tell you exactly where I'm going.' In a way, Ben would have liked his children to know precisely where he would be operating. At least that way they could look at a map and know where he was. Not knowing made their separation harder for them. But Ben had orders not to tell a soul where he would be based or operating, and he had to follow them.

'You won't get killed, will you?' said Maddie.

'Of course I won't get killed,' Ben assured her, gripping her little shoulder tightly.

'The father of one of the kids at school was killed in Afghanistan,' said Josh.

'I won't be killed,' repeated Ben, more firmly this time. 'All my training is about *protecting* lives – my own, and others. Trust me, the pair of you, nothing is going to happen to me. Besides, I'll have Caesar to look after me.'

'Oh, yeah, you will too,' said Maddie. Cheering up a little, she sat up straight again. 'Where's Afghanistan?'

Her father had been to Afghanistan before, but Maddie had been too young to take any interest back then. Ben brought out an atlas and showed them Afghanistan on the map.

'Why exactly are you going to Afghanistan?' Maddie then asked.

'To fight the Taliban,' said Josh. 'I've learnt all about it at school.'

'What's a Tabilan?' said Maddie.

'The Taliban are the cruel people who used to rule Afghanistan,' Ben explained, laying the atlas down and sitting back. 'They helped the bad guys like Al Qaeda kill innocent men, women and children. And they forced ordinary people to do things they didn't want to do. The Taliban even banned musical instruments and made it illegal for people to sing in Afghanistan.'

'People weren't allowed to *sing*?' said Josh, amazed. 'Not even "Happy Birthday"?'

'Not even "Happy Birthday",' his father affirmed. 'Crazy, isn't it? Now the Taliban are trying to overthrow the elected government of Afghanistan. Do you know, when the Taliban were in charge in Afghanistan, they wouldn't even let girls go to school.'

Maddie frowned. 'Why not? I'm a girl and I like school.'

'That's just how primitive and oppressive the Taliban are.'

'What's oppressive mean?' Maddie asked.

'That means they're mean bullies,' said Josh. 'Right, Dad?'

Ben nodded. 'When it comes down to it, yep.'

'Dad,' said Josh, 'will you make us a promise?'

'Name it, son,' Ben responded.

'Promise that you'll come back to us from Afghanistan? Promise that you won't leave us without both a mum *and* a dad.'

Caught off guard, Ben had to fight back a sudden surge of emotion. Every day, he tried to make it up to his children for the fact that they no longer had a mother. Every day, he fought with guilt at the thought that serving on army operations took him away from his children. But that was his job – what he was trained to do – and he was very good at it. He told himself that one day, before many more years had passed, he would be too old for war, and then he would be able to spend all the time in the world with his children. Until that day came, he would do the job he was trained to do, as best he could.

'Yes, Daddy, promise us!' Maddie urged.

Ben nodded slowly, and said, firmly, 'I promise that I *will* come back to you from Afghanistan.'

'Good,' said Josh.

'And Caesar, too, Daddy,' said Maddie. 'Promise us that he'll come back home with you.'

Ben smiled. 'I promise that Caesar will come back home with me, too,' he said.

'Good,' Maddie returned, satisfied. Slipping down from the sofa she turned to her father. 'Come on, then. Let's play ball with Caesar.'

Early Monday morning, dressed in his camouflage field uniform and ready to fly out that night, Ben said goodbye to his family before Nan dropped Josh and Maddie off at school. None of them said much. Nan gave Ben a long cuddle. Maddie gave him an even longer cuddle, but, being deliberately brave, she didn't cry. Josh, acting grown up, didn't cry either, and gave his father a handshake, then a cuddle.

Ben then brought Caesar in from the backyard. Caesar went directly to Josh, jumped up at him and licked him on the mouth.

'Caesar kissed you goodbye, Josh,' said Maddie with delight, as she reached out to Caesar and gave him a cuddle. Spluttering and laughing, Josh wiped his mouth with the back of his hand. 'How come Caesar came to me first?' he asked, surprised. 'Just like Dodger used to.'

'Caesar has no favourites in this family, Josh,' Ben responded. 'He loves us all equally.'

'Even though I don't like him?'

'You do like him,' said Maddie. 'You don't *hate* him.'

'No, I don't hate him,' Josh conceded, as Caesar went to Nan for his last goodbye.

'Of course you don't hate him,' said Nan. 'Caesar will be looking after your father in Afghanistan. How could you not care for a dog like that?'

'Well, I suppose I care,' Josh acknowledged. 'I don't want anything to happen to him, that's for sure.'

'And Caesar senses that you care,' said Ben.

Josh was impressed. 'Really?'

'Oh, yes,' said Ben, as Caesar came back to sit at his side. 'You'd be amazed what goes on inside this bloke's head. And in his heart.'

Two days later, Ben and Caesar were in far-off Kuwait in the Middle East. A Royal Australian Air Force Globe-master, a jet transport plane even larger than a Hercules, had brought them across the world from Australia. After ten days at a Kuwaiti airbase, several more flights brought them to Uruzgan Province, Afghanistan. Ben and Caesar were to be based in the southeast of the country at a town called Tarin Kowt, pronounced 'Tarin Kot', which sat in a valley surrounded by snow-capped mountains. There was a large military camp at Tarin Kowt, occupied by thousands of International Security Assistance Force (ISAF) troops from a number of countries including Australia and America, as well as local soldiers of the Afghan National Army (ANA) who had been trained by the Australians and other ISAF troops.

Behind high walls and barbed wire, the camp provided living quarters, dining facilities, garages and work-shops, a hospital, a long airstrip for military planes, and helicopter landing pads. There were also places where soldiers could relax during their time off. These were equipped with large-screen TVs, table tennis tables and computers, where men like Ben could play games, surf the internet and communicate with their families back home. There were two military kennel complexes where Australian and American war dogs lived while they were in the camp. The dogs even had military veterinary surgeons to look after them if they were sick or injured, with a large US Army war dog hospital in neighbouring Kandahar Province.

Ben and Caesar had been brought to Tarin Kowt to replace an Australian Army dog handler and his dog, after both had been injured by a roadside bomb. After flying into the base, Ben let Caesar have a good sniff around the Australian Army's kennels to get used to them. He also let Caesar introduce himself to two other Australian Army explosive detection dogs at the base – Zeke, a male kelpie, and Spider, a sandy-coloured female labrador. Both were about a year older than Caesar.

All three said hello to each other in the usual doggy way – sniffing each other's behinds – and were friends right away. As Ben watched the three dogs together, Zeke playfully tugged Caesar's ear. With a quick, low growl, Caesar let Zeke know he didn't like that sort of treatment, and Zeke promptly let go. Caesar was not letting any other dog mess with him!

Before long, Ben and Caesar would be assigned missions out in the countryside of Uruzgan Province. The landscape in that area varied from green and yellow valleys where famers grew a variety of crops, to rugged mountains and desert-like plateaus where nothing grew. The valley in which Tarin Kowt was located was dry and dusty. In the camp, it was all red earth and gravel underfoot, with no grass to be seen anywhere.

Ben had served here in Uruzgan Province before, with Dodger, so knew all about this place. Out there in the countryside, Taliban fighters came down out of the mountains to move about in small, heavily armed bands, attacking police, troops and government officials, and terrorising farmers. It was the job of the troops in the province to find those Taliban fighters and prevent them from making attacks. This was not easy as the Taliban dressed like local farmers, usually moved about at night, and never came out in the open to fight. Their regular tactic was to lie in wait to ambush police and military vehicles, then melt away into the countryside again.

Many of the Australian troops at the Tarin Kowt base were engineers, here as part of an international construction assistance program for Uruzgan Province. It would be the primary task of Ben and Caesar to help prevent those engineers being killed or wounded by the Taliban. But first, they had to protect the roads the engineers travelled on. The day after Ben and Caesar arrived at Tarin Kowt, they began training in the camp to detect the sort of bomb that the Taliban would have buried in roads throughout the province over the winter.

Explosive detection dogs like Caesar had become so good at detecting freshly made bombs, the Taliban had resorted to a new tactic – leaving IEDs buried for months, with the intention of detonating them later by remote control. Farmers and their animals passed over these buried bombs time and again, laying many different, confusing scents that masked the smell of explosives. To train recently arrived detection dogs to locate explosives hidden in this way, test explosives without detonators were buried near toilets and a waste dump on the Tarin Kowt base, as the soil was naturally impregnated with a variety of odours that could disguise the presence of explosives chemicals. When Caesar and several new American EDDs were given the job of finding them, Caesar not only located the buried explosives every time, he started digging for them.

One morning, an American engineer officer came to watch Caesar training. 'I've got me a mutt just like that back home,' he told Ben.

'Bet he can't do what Caesar does,' said Ben with a grin.

'You got that right,' the American replied with a chuckle, as he watched Caesar begin to use his paws to make a hole where he'd located explosives. 'Say, I heard that you Aussie soldiers were called "Diggers", but I didn't realise that went for your dogs as well. That dog of yours can come dig with my engineers any time he likes.'

At dawn every day, Ben would collect Caesar from the kennels and they would go for a long run together in the cool of the early morning, before the day heated up. Around and around the camp's exercise track, man and dog would go, side by side. They soon became a familiar sight in the camp and plenty of soldiers wanted to pat Caesar, who reminded them of their pet dogs back home. Loving the attention, Caesar would greet any friendly soldier with a wagging tail. He would even put a paw up on their leg, asking for a pat. Ben was happy to let Caesar mix with troops in the camp. In the weeks and months ahead, the pair would be spending a lot of time in the field with many of those men, and it was important that dog and Diggers got on well from the start.

Once a week, Afghan farmers would arrive by truck and donkey cart to set up a bazaar outside the military camp, and there the soldiers from the camp could buy local produce for themselves, and souvenirs for their families back home. Ben saw this as a good opportunity for Caesar to mix with Afghan locals and become accustomed to them. So the first time that a bazaar was set up outside the camp walls, he led Caesar out on a tight leash.

The first Afghan farmer that Caesar saw was quite a shock to him. The big brown dog had never seen anything like this before, and froze on the spot with his front legs planted in front of him to prevent Ben from leading him forward. Tilting his head quizzically to one side, Caesar stared at the man. The bearded farmer had a traditional Afghan turban on his head. Over a long, loose white shirt that fell over his trousers to his knees, he wore a sleeveless waistcoat. Ben didn't drag on the leash to force Caesar forward. He waited, knowing from his experience with Dodger that a military dog took a little time to familiarise itself with new surroundings and all the new scents that came with them.

The farmer, busy setting out melons on a makeshift table, ignored the corporal's dog. Afghans don't have the same affection for dogs that Australians and other Westerners do. While some Afghan farmers keep guard dogs, none have dogs as pets. As far as most Afghan men are concerned, a dog is just another mouth to feed. In a country where feeding your family every day is often a struggle, a dog is a luxury. So, as cute as a dog like Caesar was to Australians, none of the farmers here showed the slightest interest in Caesar. Unlike the soldiers, not one local would give him a friendly pat.

Caesar, meanwhile, was sizing up the Afghan farmer's scent. To dogs, every human and animal gives off a distinct odour. Just as we humans can identify each other by the sound of our individual voices, dogs identify each of us by our scent, which is based on what we eat. This Afghan farmer ate a very different diet to the Australian soldiers, and because of that, he gave off a whole new scent to Caesar.

Once he had taken in the man's scent, Caesar let Ben lead him through the bazaar. Ben smiled to himself as he watched his dog walk past the stalls and the chattering, laughing farmers, taking in and analysing their scents with a slightly puzzled look on his face.

This was another reason why Ben and Caesar had not been sent out on operations right away. Australian military commanders knew that their explosive detection dogs took time to familiarise themselves with the locals, and couldn't be rushed into service. Earlier experience had shown that when a dog was sent out into a strange environment without time for familiarisation, if faced with people or situations it was unfamiliar with, that dog could disobey its handler's orders. Worse, it could even become so unsettled that it would refuse to do its job, or run off.

The other Australian dogs, Zeke and Spider, were regularly going out of camp with their handlers on day-long patrols, but they had been working here for months and were accustomed to Uruzgan. For now, Caesar, the new dog, was confined to the daily grind of training in camp and mixing with locals at the weekly bazaars. But after more than two weeks of this, Ben was becoming frustrated, feeling sure that Caesar had gotten over his initial culture shock and was as good as, or better than, any other dog on the base when it came to detection work. But Ben was a soldier, so he waited for orders. To get rid of his frustration, he began to take Caesar for late afternoon runs as well as morning runs. It meant that both were at the peak of their fitness, and Caesar always enjoyed physical activities.

Late one afternoon, just as the sun was beginning to set behind the mountains, two dust-covered Australian SAS long-range patrol vehicles roared into base and pulled up close by the exercise track where Ben was taking Caesar for a run. Six SAS operators clambered down from the open, six-wheeled vehicles, then helped two blindfolded Afghan prisoners down. Both prisoners wore flat turbans. One had a bushy white beard. The other, a little younger, had a jet-black beard streaked with grey.

All six SAS men wore desert-patterned camouflage uniforms, sandy-coloured turbans and face coverings, and sunglasses. The fact they were Westerners was only revealed when they removed the face cloths. Australian soldiers in Afghanistan were expected to shave every day, but SAS men were different. Frequently going into enemy territory for long periods, wearing beards allowed them to more easily mix in with the bearded locals. Despite the beards, Ben now recognised one of those SAS men – the sergeant in charge – as soon as he removed his face covering.

'Charlie!' Ben called.

Charlie Grover turned, and on seeing Ben and Caesar, broke into a smile and ambled over to them. Caesar had recognised Charlie too, and was clearly pleased to see his master's best mate again. With fond remembrances of Charlie from his visit to the Fulton home at Holsworthy, Caesar wagged his tail so vigorously that his entire rear end was wiggling and waggling.

'G'day,' said Charlie. 'I heard that you two were here.' Charlie and Ben exchanged a firm handshake then a brotherly man hug, before Charlie squatted to give Caesar a hefty pat, receiving a lick on the face in return.

'You've been out on an op?' Ben asked.

Charlie nodded. 'Been out there for a week,' he said. 'Looking for a particular Taliban commander's father.'

'You got your man?'

Charlie, straightening, nodded again. 'Got the Taliban commander's father *and* his uncle. We're hoping they might tell us where we can find the Taliban commander – a bloke called Baradar.'

'Good luck with that,' said Ben.

'Have you and Caesar been out on ops yet?'

'Not yet,' Ben replied, sounding impatient for action. 'But we're ready to go.'

'Don't worry, mate,' said Charlie, flexing his aching shoulders after hours on the road. 'There's plenty of work out there for you. The Taliban are getting sneakier and sneakier. You two will soon be in the thick of it.'

Charlie was right. That night, Ben received orders – he and Caesar were to join an operation the next morning at a village thirty kilometres outside the camp. This would be their first mission in enemy territory.

CHAPTER 7

The sun was beginning to rise as a convoy of military and police vehicles travelled along a narrow yellow dirt road, leaving a trail of choking dust behind it. Most of Uruzgan Province's roads were unsealed. There were only a few bitumen roads, and many of those had been laid by foreign troops over the last few years.

In the convoy, Ben and Caesar were in the back of a bumping Bushmaster – a four-wheel drive, fully enclosed, armoured Australian Army troop-carrying vehicle. On top of the Bushmaster was a remote-controlled heavy machinegun. Inside rode a driver, a gunner and eight soldiers, sitting four down each side in full combat gear, plus, sitting contentedly between the legs of its master, one brown labrador EDD.

Caesar didn't mind being locked up inside the Bushmaster for hours at a time – it was air-conditioned, and wherever Ben went, Caesar was happy to go. He didn't like being separated from Ben for long, and Ben knew it. When Ben put Caesar in the metal dog box for the first stage of the flight to Afghanistan a few weeks back, Ben had deliberately acted as if they would be seeing each other in just a few minutes, not a day or so. Dogs have an uncanny ability of knowing when they are about to be separated from their masters, and Caesar had known. His tail had sagged and his ears had drooped as Ben patted a last goodbye before take-off. Such a strong bond had formed between dog and handler that Caesar would go anywhere, would put up with just about anything, as long as he was with Ben.

They were heading for a bridge over a small river east of Tarin Kowt. According to reports from locals, it had been damaged when a truck drove off the bridge and into the river. Ben and Caesar had been assigned to a party of engineers sent to clear and repair that bridge. A detachment of protecting infantry was also going along. So engineers and infantrymen were packed into the convoy of Bushmasters that wound along a dusty road through the valleys of southeast Afghanistan.

In the middle of the convoy there was a blue Toyota truck carrying Afghan policemen. As escort, an eight-wheeled ASLAV – an Australian light armoured vehicle – led the column, while another brought up the rear. A cross between an armoured car and an armoured personnel carrier, these formidable vehicles are fitted with swivelling turrets armed with a cannon and machineguns.

The valleys their route took them through were a patchwork of small family farms which grew crops and ran sheep, goats and chickens. These were very different to Australian farms. Each was centred around a kal, a large walled living compound that looked from the outside like a small prison. And every few kilometres along the dusty road there was a ramshackle village.

At each village the convoy slowly drove through, children shyly came out to watch them pass. But the parents of those children rarely took any interest. Some village men were working in the fields, others stood talking in the street, while all the women remained out of sight in their homes. Older houses in the villages were made from mud, more modern ones from concrete blocks. Few had electricity or running water. But on some distant yellow, lifeless hills there were mobile phone towers, powered by solar cells. Numerous families in these villages had mobile phones, and it was a profitable business for the few people whose homes had electric power provided by petrol-driven generators to recharge the batteries of other mobile phone users.

'I don't get it,' said a young Australian soldier sitting next to Ben. The soldier had never been to Afghanistan prior to arriving in the country a month before. 'Why doesn't the Taliban blow up the mobile phone towers? They blow up just about everything else.'

'Because the Taliban use mobile phones too,'

responded Ben, who had done several tours of Afghanistan and knew it as well as any foreign soldier could.

'To detonate remote bombs?' said the soldier.

Ben nodded solemnly. 'That, and to talk to their friends and agents.'

At a crossroads, near a fort on a barren hill, they passed an empty Australian Bushmaster being towed back to Tarin Kowt for repairs. One of the Bushmaster's front wheels had been blown off by a hidden IED, but the vehicle's V-shaped armoured hull had ensured that none of the soldiers inside had been badly injured by the blast. It was IEDs like that one that Ben and Caesar were here in Afghanistan to find – before those bombs took lives.

Australian Army engineers were already at work in one village the convoy passed through. They seemed to be dismantling what was left of a burnt-out building. As the convoy drove past, the engineers and their infantry escort gave their fellow Australians of the convoy a wave.

'What's going on there?' Ben asked the cavalry regiment driver of their Bushmaster.

'Last week, that burnt-out building was a new school,' the driver began in reply. 'Australian Army engineers built it for the village. It was the first proper school that village ever had. Four days ago, our blokes finished work on it. The very next night, as soon as we'd left the place, the Taliban turned up and burnt it to the ground. Before it even had a chance to open its doors!'

'That's just dumb!' declared the young soldier next to Ben. 'Why would the Taliban wreck a school? Schools don't hurt anyone. A new school would help Afghan kids, for God's sake!'

'It's because *we* built it,' the driver came back with a sigh. 'We're foreigners and we're not Muslims like the people here. Seems like the Taliban would rather Afghan kids didn't go to school than be grateful to us. A charity even provided books for the school. The books were all piled up, ready for the village kids to use. So what did the Taliban do? They used the books to start the fire.'

The soldier shook his head. 'I can't believe people could be so primitive in their thinking – could deprive their own kids like that.'

The driver shrugged. 'That's what we're up against in this country, mate. Primitive thinking. Self-destructive thinking. We build a school, the Taliban burn it down. We build the Afghan people a hospital, the Taliban will try to blow it up. We build them a road or a dam, they'll plant a bomb in it. We'll rebuild that school, and –'

'They'll try to burn it down again,' said Ben.

'Exactly,' the driver agreed. 'And we can't guard every building in Uruzgan. The local police are supposed to do that. But some police are in cahoots with the Taliban.'

'That's so frustrating,' said the soldier next to Ben.

The occupants of the Bushmaster all lapsed back into their thoughts. There were plenty of lulls between action for Australian soldiers to puzzle about the actions of their opponents. A lot of the time they simply couldn't work those opponents out at all – theirs was a totally different way of thinking to the Aussies.

After a long, careful journey, the convoy reached its destination. Once they'd passed through a village beside a stream, the vehicles spread out and came to a halt. As the rear doors of the Bushmasters opened, the heat of the day quickly replaced the air-conditioned cool of the vehicles. Wearing sunglasses to counter the glare of the bright sun, the troops piled out. Most quickly took up defensive positions with rifles and machineguns ready, watching the hillsides for signs of Taliban fighters.

Keeping a tight leash on Caesar, Ben dropped to one knee as he surveyed the situation. A hundred metres in front of them lay the bridge, made of stone. The old Russian truck that had gone over the side was still there, hanging at a crazy angle. Its nose sat in a rocky stream while one rear wheel remained on the bridge. In going over the side, the truck had broken through the bridge's parapet. Looking back the way they had come, Ben saw that the village they had just passed through was just as uninteresting and colourless as any they had seen that morning, with occasional patches of green grass and only a few trees.

An Australian infantry officer, a lieutenant, came up to Ben and Caesar. 'We've been watching the pictures from a drone all the way out here, Corporal,' he said. Somewhere, thousands of feet above them, an Australian Army drone aircraft was silently circling the area, transmitting pictures of the landscape around the bridge to the troops on the ground. 'Everything looks okay,' the lieutenant went on. 'There's no sign of Taliban activity. But we can't be too careful. Send your dog to the bridge to check it out for IEDs. This truck accident might have been set up as an ambush.'

'Right on it, sir,' Ben replied, pleased that he and Caesar were at last able to do the job they'd been sent to Afghanistan to do.

The pair began to walk toward the bridge. Forty metres from it, Ben instructed Caesar to sit, then dropped to one knee and unhooked his leash. Caesar's front legs were quivering with anticipation. He knew that he was about to go to work and couldn't wait. Then, Caesar heard the words from Ben that he'd been waiting for. 'Caesar, seek on!'

Caesar eagerly sprang forward and went trotting toward the bridge with his nose low to the ground. Behind him, Ben waited on bended knee, ready to use his rifle to protect his four-legged partner if need be. Caesar did as he'd been trained, moving quickly up the right side of the road. At a whistle from Ben, he turned and crossed to the other side. Checking the bridge, and then the crashed truck, Caesar then made his way back to sit at Ben's side.

Ben rewarded him with a hefty pat. 'Good boy, Caesar!' he said. 'Well done, mate!' The pair had just successfully completed their first explosives check in Afghanistan. Turning to the waiting lieutenant, Ben gave a hand signal and called, 'All clear!'

The lieutenant then sent forward two engineers with metal detectors to trace the same path as Caesar, and they also gave the all clear, as Ben knew they would. The engineers checked the bridge for damage. They reported that it was still sound and could support heavy loads. One of the armoured vehicles then moved forward, slowly crossing the bridge and edging past the crashed truck. The crew established a checkpoint beyond the bridge, with their turret pointing down the road to cover approaching vehicles. Ben and Caesar soon followed and joined the soldiers at the checkpoint. At the same time, a Bushmaster came up to attach a towrope to the Russian truck.

While the truck was being dragged back onto the road, it was the job of the troops at the checkpoint to stop and check all vehicles arriving on the scene. Several donkey-drawn carts came up, and Ben and Caesar checked out the carts and their drivers, who were made to wait. Then a battered old Toyota sedan drove up, and the driver and his passengers – a woman and three children – were told to get out.

'Caesar, seek on!' Ben instructed.

Ben quickly led Caesar around the family to see if he could pick up the scent of explosives on them. One Taliban tactic was to use suicide bombers with explosives strapped to their bodies beneath their clothes. These suicide bombers would set off the explosives when they were near troops or police, or in a crowd, blowing themselves up as well as everyone around them. A young man from Pakistan had done this in a Tarin Kowt market only a few weeks back, killing and injuring scores of innocent civilians.

Ben was pretty certain none of these family members from the car would have a bomb on them because suicide bombers almost always operated alone. Caesar, who hadn't indicated that he'd picked up the scent of anything suspicious on the family, seemed to back him up. Ben then let Caesar off the leash and pointed to their Toyota sedan. 'Check the car, Caesar. Check the car, there's a good boy. Seek on!'

Trotting with his nose down, Caesar did a quick circuit of the car without giving any sign of detecting explosives in the vehicle. Ben opened the driver's door. Without hesitation, Caesar put his front paws up on the driver's seat. He sniffed the air inside the car, this way then that, then hopped back down. Satisfied that the car was clean of explosives, Ben reattached Caesar's leash, planning to lead him back to their Bushmaster and let him rest in the shade of the vehicle.

'Are the car and occupants clean?' asked the sergeant in charge of the armoured vehicle. If he received the all clear from the EDD team, the sergeant would tell the Afghan family they could get back in their car.

Ben was about to reply when he felt Caesar pulling on the leash. Something was troubling him – something back in the direction of the Afghan family. Ben noticed that a breeze had just sprung up, blowing from the direction of the family to Caesar and himself. It was possible that Caesar had picked up a new scent on that breeze. Squatting beside his dog, Ben unclipped the leash again. 'Seek on, boy,' he said. 'Show me what's bothering you. Seek on!'

Ben watched as Caesar trotted back to the family. Around and around he went, circling the family, whose members watched him with anxious and uncertain looks on their faces. Caesar kept changing the direction of his circles, going one way and then the other.

'Is your dog onto something?' the sergeant called down from his turret.

'Something is bothering Caesar, that's for sure,' Ben replied. He then noticed that Caesar was stopping and turning in front of the man who had been driving the car, and Ben's memory went back to the day of the training exercise when Caesar had done the same thing in front of a red-headed corporal who had handled explosives. Based on that prior experience, Ben announced, 'The driver has been carrying explosives in the past twenty-four hours.'

'You're sure?' the sergeant asked.

'That's what Caesar is telling me,' Ben replied, nodding.

The Afghan police with the convoy were immediately called to the scene to question the driver of the car in his own language. It turned out that the driver was an off-duty policeman. But it was also revealed that he had been unloading ammunition at his police station the previous night, wearing the same civilian clothes that he was wearing today, which meant that those clothes still contained traces of explosives chemicals. Even though the car's driver turned out to be one of the good guys, Caesar had been right to be troubled by him, and Ben had been on the ball to spot Caesar's unease.

The lieutenant and the other Australian soldiers were impressed by the performance of the new EDD team. 'We reckon that dog of yours is a super-sniffer,' said one engineer to Ben. 'You two can work with us any time you like.'

For the remainder of the day, Ben and Caesar continued on duty at the checkpoint as the Russian truck was pulled back up onto the road and the engineers built a temporary barrier along the broken side of the bridge. Late in the afternoon, the troops climbed back into their vehicles, and the convoy rolled back into the Tarin Kowt base at twilight.

That night, after a shower, Ben used a computer in the recreation hall to talk to Josh, Maddie and Nan back at their home in Australia via Skype. He was able to do this once a week and it was a treat for him to see the faces of his children and his mother as he talked to them.

'How's the soccer going, Josh?' Ben asked, after he and Maddie had been talking for a while about Maddie's dance classes.

'Real good, Dad,' Josh replied. 'I scored a goal last Saturday and nearly got two more.'

'Well done, champ!' Ben responded with a grin. 'I reckon you'll be representing Australia at the World Cup one day.'

'I don't know about that,' Josh replied, 'but our coach says our team's on track to make the finals.'

'That's great, son.'

Josh smiled and leaned closer to the screen. 'Dad, if we make the grand final, will you come and watch me play?'

'The grand final? When's that?'

Josh dropped his eyes. 'September.'

Ben sighed. Moments such as these were one of the hardest parts about being away from home for such a long time. 'In September I'll still be over here in Afghanistan, Josh. You know that.'

'But if I make the finals, wouldn't the generals let you come home to watch me?' said Josh. 'It's really important.'

'Mate, they won't let me come home until my tour is over.' Ben felt terrible. He would love to see Josh play in his soccer final, but the army had other plans for him. 'Sorry, mate. I'm here to do a job for seven months. Don't worry, the months will fly by and I'll soon be home again.'

'But you'll miss my final,' said Josh, hanging his head.

'Look at me, son. I'll be home for Christmas. Okay?'

Josh wouldn't look at the screen. 'Christmas is *forever*,' he sighed. 'I'll be ten by then. You're even going to miss my birthday.'

'Sorry, mate,' Ben responded, feeling more and more guilty.

'You were here for Maddie's birthday,' said Josh, sounding increasingly peeved.

'Don't worry, Ben,' Nan Fulton piped up, putting her arm around Josh's shoulders. 'Josh will be fine. I'll go to his soccer final and I'll tell you all about how his team wins. Right, Josh?'

'I suppose so,' Josh agreed, glumly.

'Talking about winners,' Nan went on, 'look what I

won at golf last week, Ben.' She held up a shiny new golf trophy. 'You're looking at the new Holsworthy Lakes Senior Ladies' Champion.'

Ben smiled. 'What a family of champions we are! Well done, Mum.'

'Yes, we're all champions,' said little Maddie. 'Aren't we, Daddy!'

'We sure are, princess,' Ben replied. 'And look, I've got something to show you all.' Reaching over, he took hold of Caesar, who had been lying on a sofa beside him, and lifted him within view of the web camera. There was a floppy soldier's cap on Caesar's head, making him look almost human. From across the world, Maddie giggled with laughter.

'What a comical sight you are, Caesar!' said Nan.

Caesar's head cocked to one side as he looked at the computer screen. Recognising the voices of Nan and Maddie, he quickly became excited. His tail wagged so furiously that it thumped on the sofa and his hat fell off. He even barked in recognition. 'Caesar says hello,' said Ben.

'Tell him we miss him, Daddy,' said Maddie. 'We miss you, too.'

'Don't worry, time will fly,' said Ben, feeling emotional now, 'and we'll soon be home again – Caesar *and* me.'

'Keep safe, the pair of you,' said Nan.

'We will,' Ben assured her.

Ben sadly said his last farewells to his family, ended his session, then took Caesar back to the kennels, where Zeke and Spider were already asleep.

The next afternoon, Ben heard that an IED had that morning exploded on the same road that he and Caesar had used on the way to and from their mission at the bridge. The bomb had badly damaged an American Army vehicle and seriously wounded three American soldiers who were inside. The news sent a chill down Ben's spine. He realised that the Taliban who had set off that IED had probably been in the hills when he and Caesar had been at the bridge; that they may have been watching them as they did their work there.

The following day, Ben and Caesar went out on a regular patrol. Coming to a culvert as he inspected a section of road, Caesar slowly eased his rear end down to the ground and stared intensely at the culvert. 'Explosives here!' Ben warned the soldiers behind him. 'Caesar's found something.'

Caesar had made his first find of Taliban explosives.

CHAPTER 8

For a month, Ben and Caesar went out on day-long patrols checking roads, bridges, buildings and vehicles for bombs. Almost every other day, Caesar located explosives planted by the Taliban. His discoveries saved a lot of lives, but they also told the Australian and American commanders that the Taliban were becoming more and more active, and more and more daring, in the region of Tarin Kowt. It was decided that it was time that Special Forces operations were stepped up to counter the increasing Taliban presence.

Caesar's growing reputation as a super-sniffer, combined with the fact that he and Ben had passed insertion training back in Australia, resulted in the pair now being assigned to their first 'special ops' mission. It was to be carried out by just five SAS operators plus Ben and Caesar. And the man in charge was to be Ben's best friend, Sergeant Charlie Grover. In a meeting room inside the Special Operations Headquarters at the Tarin

Kowt base, Charlie led a briefing for the men taking part in the mission.

'Our codename for this job is Redback,' Charlie began. He pointed to a map projected onto a large screen. 'The target is this kal. We've received intelligence from locals that members of the Taliban under Commander Baradar are using this kal to store a large amount of weapons and ammunition. Our job is to find it. That's where Ben and EDD Caesar come in. Right, Ben?'

Ben nodded. 'If there's anything to be found there, Caesar will find it.'

'At 2330 hours tonight, we'll be landed by heelo here,' Charlie went on, tapping a hill shown on the map. 'We then hike to this other hill overlooking the kal, so we are in position to observe it come daylight. We watch the place all day and half the next night to see who comes and goes. At 0100 hours next morning, all being well, we enter the kal.' Charlie tapped some keys on a computer keyboard. An aerial photograph of a farm compound now appeared on the screen. 'One Section will go in via the western gate, here. Two Section will go through the southern gate, here. Ben, you and Caesar are with me and Bendigo Baz. We're One Section. Two Section will be led by Lucky Mertz. While Ben and Caesar search the compound from top to bottom, the rest of us will secure it and all occupants.'

'What happens if Caesar finds the Taliban weapons and ammo?' Corporal Lucky Mertz asked.

'We destroy it on-site, then pull out,' Charlie replied, 'taking the headman of the kal with us for questioning back here at Tarin Kowt.'

'How do we get back here?' asked another SAS man.

'We hike to an RP here.' He tapped the keyboard to bring up the map again, then pointed to a rendezvous point marked on it. 'The heelo will extract us at 0400 hours.'

'What's our plan B?' Ben asked. 'What happens if, for some reason, the heelo can't extract us?'

'That being the case, we might have to walk all the way back here to Tarin Kowt,' said Charlie with a wry smile.

'And what if we don't find what we're looking for at the kal, Charlie?' Lucky Mertz asked. 'What if the intel is wrong and there's nothing there? Information like that from locals has been wrong before.'

'Then, we say how sorry we are, give the owner of the kal some cash as our way of apologising for making a mistake, and get the hell out of there,' Charlie replied. 'Any more questions?' He paused. 'None? Then let's do it, you blokes.'

In darkness, they boarded an Australian Army Chinook helicopter at the busy Tarin Kowt airfield. Chinook helicopters, much larger than Black Hawks, are equipped with two sets of rotors, and, like Hercules aircraft, have a loading ramp in the rear that can be lowered and raised. Caesar, wearing his doggles and puppy Peltors, and trotting along on the end of a leather leash, happily went up the ramp with Ben and into the dark interior of the helicopter's cargo cabin.

Charlie and the four other SAS men had boarded ahead of them and were sitting along one side. All were wearing full combat gear including bulletproof Kevlar vests, gloves and infrared goggles, through which the night was lit up in an eerie shade of green. All carried forty-five kilo packs filled with food and water for three days, plus plenty of ammunition in case they got into a firefight with the Taliban and had to shoot their way out of trouble. Each man had a small personal radio attached to his camouflage tunic, just below the left shoulder. This enabled team members to communicate with each other during the operation. One trooper, a trained signaller, carried a much larger radio to keep the team in contact with base and support units. A trooper with medical training also carried medical supplies.

In addition to ammunition, a sleeping bag and rations, Ben was carrying extra litres of water and dog food for Caesar. In camp, Caesar lived on a diet of fresh meat and dried dog food, but out on missions like this, Ben could only take along the dried variety. Caesar didn't mind it, but he did really like a good steak, which was what Ben would give him back at base as a reward for a job well done.

First letting Caesar say hello to Charlie and the others, who all gave him a pat, Ben then eased down into a webbing seat and instructed Caesar to sit on the floor between his legs. With Caesar wedged between his knees, Ben could keep him from flying around if the helicopter bucked about in the air, which it often did, particularly if the pilot was avoiding enemy fire.

The Chinook's rear ramp came up. With a deafening noise from the engines and spinning rotors, the helicopter lifted off and was soon flying through the night at several thousand feet. Inside, Ben and the other members of the team sat in silence. In the glow of the dull red lights on the heelo's metal wall, some checked their equipment. Others closed their eyes and leaned their heads back against the wall. Caesar lay down on his belly and rested his head on one of Ben's boots. It was not long before the heelo began slowing and its ramp was lowered. All six men got to their feet and took hold of their weapons. Caesar, ready for action, also rose.

When the helicopter touched down at the designated landing zone, or what soldiers call an LZ, the six men and Caesar ran down the ramp and into a cloud of dust raised by the rotors. The men quickly fanned out and dropped flat, ready to answer fire from insurgents who might be in the vicinity. The Chinook, which had only been on the ground a few seconds, lifted off again. And with a wave from the helicopter's loadmaster, who stood at the open ramp, it rose up and swept away to the north. Soon, the heelo was gone, the dust had settled, and the chilly night was silent. Beside Ben, Caesar had lain down on command. Ben now removed Caesar's doggles and puppy Peltors, and stowed them in his pack.

Charlie briefly consulted his handheld military GPS, then pointed in the direction they had to go. Without a word, all six men and Caesar came to their feet. Lucky Mertz led out, the others falling in behind, stringing out with twenty metres between them. Ben and Caesar were second last in the line that warily made its way down from the barren hill where they had landed. For two hours, the team tramped across deserted countryside and over desolate hills. Finally, they reached a hilltop – their initial objective. From here, they could make out the kal they had been sent to raid in the valley below. It sat near a stream in the midst of dusty tracks and watered fields growing various crops. The kal was in darkness and not a sound was to be heard.

After establishing a watching position among large rocks on the hilltop, and covering themselves with camouflage netting that would hide any sign of them from prying eyes, the members of the team settled down to rest. Ben unrolled a sleeping bag from his pack and slipped into it, resting his head on the pack. When Caesar snuggled up against him and put his head on Ben's chest, Ben pulled him in close, to share body warmth. Soon, both dog and handler were fast asleep.

When dawn broke, the Australian soldiers were already wide awake and focused on the valley below. Through the day, as the sun beat down on them, they lay perfectly still and watched as men and boys came out from the kal and into the fields to work. Several light trucks came and went. In the compound itself, women could be seen working, and children playing. The compound was made up of high mud walls which enclosed a number of single-storey buildings and courtyards. Several related families usually lived and worked together in kals like this. At sunset, the soldiers watched as the men and boys left the fields and returned to the kal.

Nothing the SAS team had seen during the day suggested that any members of the Taliban were at the kal. This seemed to be a normal, peaceful farm. But, like the SAS, the Taliban moved about at night. So, with the darkness, the soldiers became extra vigilant, surveying all approaches to the kal to see if anyone came or went or acted suspiciously. The whole point of this waiting and watching was to make sure that the SAS team didn't walk into a viper's nest of Taliban insurgents when it moved down to the kal in a few hours' time.

The men on the hill now had their first meal of the day, and Ben gave Caesar a cupful of water and a ration of dried dog food that Caesar quickly wolfed down. The SAS men ate from MRE packs, and several gave Caesar their leftovers. With infrared binoculars, Charlie continued to watch the kal and its surroundings for signs of activity. Nothing moved in the valley.

By ten o'clock, the last oil-fired lamp in the compound had gone out. The hours ticked by. At midnight, the SAS men packed up their camouflage net, adjusted their night-vision goggles and prepared to go down to the kal. Just before one in the morning, Charlie gave the valley one more sweep with his binoculars, then nodded to himself. The coast seemed clear. With a hand signal, he gave the order to move out. Throughout the day, not a single word had passed between members of the team.

Up rose the advance man. As he made his way down the slope, the others set off, one at a time, with those remaining on the hilltop covering them. Then it was Ben and Caesar's turn, followed by the last man, whose job it was to guard their rear. Slowly, they came down off the hill, then split into two groups of three. Ben and Caesar went with Charlie and the short, stocky Bendigo Baz, who was carrying a machinegun that was almost as big as he was. Coming from different directions, the two groups stealthily approached two gates in the compound walls. When Ben, Caesar, Charlie and Baz reached a tall wooden gate in the southern wall, it wouldn't open. Charlie spoke softly into a small personal radio strapped to his shoulder. 'Lucky, this gate's locked.'

'This one is, too, Charlie,' came a radioed reply from Lucky Mertz, leading the second group of three.

'We'll blow them together,' said Charlie. 'On my lead.'

'Roger.'

Charlie then attached a small amount of plastic explosive, also known as PE, to the gate. Ben, knowing what was coming, led Caesar around the wall, then hunched down with him, putting a comforting arm around his neck. From around the corner came the sound of a dull explosion, like a paper bag being popped. Caesar didn't even flinch. From the other side of the kal another faint explosion followed, as Two Section blew open the western gate. Somewhere inside the kal, a guard dog began barking. Ben slipped his rifle from his shoulder. Ready to fire if he had to, he rose up, and with Caesar on a short leash, ran back around the corner. The blasted gate hung open on one hinge. Charlie and Baz had already charged through the opening. Ben and Caesar followed them into the compound.

Rapidly, the soldiers linked up and went from building to building, kicking open doors and searching for occupants. As outbuildings were cleared, Ben and Caesar went inside them, and Ben gave Caesar more leash so that he could check every room for explosives. Man and dog checked three outbuildings without finding any sign of explosives or weapons. When they emerged from the last one, Ben saw that lights were glowing inside one of the residential buildings, and he and Caesar made their way there.

They found that Charlie and the others had collected about twenty men, women and children in the one room. The children looked fearfully at Caesar. One girl of six or so cried out at the sight of him and clung onto her mother.

'Don't worry,' said Ben, thinking how much the little girl reminded him of his own Maddie back home. 'Caesar won't hurt you.'

Charlie, using the little he had learnt of the local Pashto language, was talking to the headman of the compound. The man, aged in his sixties, wore glasses and had a black beard flecked with grey. Charlie asked the headman if he had hidden any arms or ammunition for the Taliban at the kal, and the man shook his head. Charlie instructed Ben and Caesar to keep looking, and they did, going from room to room in every building of the compound. They even searched the outdoor lavatories. But, after thirty minutes, Ben reported back to Charlie that they had found nothing suspicious.

The headman smiled. 'This I tell you, soldier Australia,' he said in English. 'No weapons here. No bang-bang.'

Then his smile vanished and a scowl covered his face. 'You break into my kal. You come into my house wearing shoes!' In Afghanistan, it was very bad manners to wear shoes inside the house. Everyone was supposed to leave their shoes at the door. 'You frighten my children,' the headman went on. 'You break my gates. Not good. Not good, soldier Australia. You pay me money.' He held out his right hand.

Charlie sighed. Apologising for intruding on the family and pulling out a packet of local money, he handed over a wad of Afghani notes. The headman took the money and counted it. It amounted to about five hundred Australian dollars, which was more than most people earned in a month in Afghanistan.

'Not enough,' the headman said, waving the money in Charlie's face. In Afghanistan, men always haggled when it came to agreeing on a price for something. 'Not enough!'

'Mate, I don't have time to bargain with you,' Charlie responded, gently pushing the man's hand away. 'That's all you're getting. Let's go, you blokes.'

The SAS men began withdrawing from the room. Carrying oil lamps, the headman and several of his sons followed them outside, telling them in their own language that they had not been paid enough to make up for the intrusion by the Australians. Charlie and his men ignored them.

As Ben and Caesar were heading toward the broken southern gate, they passed a large wire chicken coop built against the outer wall. As they passed it, Caesar suddenly strained on his leash, pulling Ben toward the coop.

'What's up, Caesar?' Ben asked, stopping. 'You want to chase some chickens?'

It was a hunting dog's natural instinct to chase birds, including chickens. Dragging on the leash, Caesar led Ben over to the chicken enclosure.

'What's Caesar up to?' Charlie called. Noticing the dog's sudden interest in the chicken coop, he headed over to join Ben. 'Is he onto something? Or does he just fancy chasing chooks?'

'I'm not sure,' Ben replied.

'No, no!' the headman protested, sounding very worried all of a sudden. 'No let dog eat my chickens.' He and his sons hurried to the door of the chicken coop and stood in front of it, barring entry.

'Something in there's definitely taken Caesar's interest, Charlie,' said Ben, looking sideways at his friend.

'Is it chooks he's interested in or something else?' Charlie wondered aloud. 'Something more explosive, maybe?'

'I can't tell,' said Ben, as Caesar pressed up against the wire, his attention fixed on something beyond it.

'Only one way to find out,' said Charlie. He turned to

the headman. 'Open up,' he instructed, pointing to the gate of the chicken coop.

'No! No!' the headman protested. 'No kill my chickens. Great value. Great value.'

'Okay,' said Charlie. He took out all the Afghan money he had left and held it in front of the headman. 'How much for each chook the dog kills? That's if he does kill any when we let him in there.'

'No, no,' the headman responded, waving his hands. 'No want money. You no let dog in there.'

The fact the headman had suddenly lost his interest in money immediately made Charlie suspicious. 'Stand aside, mate!' he commanded.

When the headman and his sons would not move, Charlie ordered his men to drag them away from the gate, then go into the coop and clear it of chickens. Minutes later, the headman and his sons were standing unhappily to one side with SAS guns trained on them, and panicking chickens were running wild throughout the compound. The chicken coop had been successfully emptied. Caesar had watched with interest as the chickens were chased from the coop by SAS men, but his attention always returned to the place where the chickens had been kept. Ben finally let him off his leash and said, 'Caesar, seek on!'

Caesar immediately scooted into the coop and, with his nose down, went directly to a patch in the middle of the ground that was filthy with chicken droppings. He began to dig, his rapidly moving front paws spewing out the dry earth in a torrent, as if he was a digging machine. Ben and Charlie came to squat beside him and watch his progress.

'He's onto something,' said Ben, peering through the darkness into the growing hole in the dirt floor.

'Let's hope it's not just a bone,' said Charlie, wryly. Taking a black torch from his belt, he shone it into the hole. Now he and Ben could see objects that had been buried not far below the surface.

Ben pulled Caesar back and patted him vigorously. 'Good boy, Caesar! Good boy!'

Caesar, excited, wanted to keep digging. But Ben held him back as Charlie felt into the hole with a gloved hand. Using his commando knife, he enlarged the hole. Then, lighting it with his torch, he peered in and let out a low whistle.

'What have we got?' Ben asked, craning his head.

'Caesar hit the jackpot,' Charlie replied. 'It's PE, my friend.' Carefully, he removed a packet containing a yellow waxy substance like playdough. There was enough plastic explosive there to kill a hundred troops if the Taliban had the opportunity to use it. 'The headman has a lot of explaining to do,' Charlie added.

After digging a little more, Charlie also brought out detonators, a detonating cord and timing devices. And, later, several Russian-made anti-tank mines. These mines, so powerful they could disable a tank, would turn a Bushmaster into scrap metal in an instant.

'They thought they were clever, burying this stuff in the chook house,' Charlie remarked. 'They reckoned the smell would hide the explosives from any detection dog.'

'But they didn't reckon on super-sniffer here,' said Ben, giving Caesar a pat. 'Nice job, Caesar.'

Standing tall, Charlie walked out to where the headman and his sons were being held. 'I'll have that money back now, thanks, mate,' he said to the headman. 'And say goodbye to your family. You're coming with us for a little chat back at Tarin Kowt.'

'Taliban make me do it,' the headman now declared. 'They make me hide things here in my kal. They kill my children if I not help them.'

'Maybe they did make you do it, mate,' Charlie conceded, 'but you can tell that to the people back at base. You're coming with us.' He turned to his team members. 'Secure this bloke, then move out!'

The headman's glasses were removed, and he was blindfolded. His hands were secured behind his back with cable ties. Ben took charge of the headman's glasses. 'I'll look after them for you, mate,' he said, slipping them into one of his pockets. 'You'll get them back at Tarin Kowt.'

The headman's sons and other family members protested. The women wailed and tried to hold onto him to prevent him being taken away. Ignoring them, the SAS team carried on, hustling the headman from his kal. The explosives and mines found in the chicken coop were also brought out and piled in a field. Charlie took a photograph of the pile, as evidence of their haul, and for a split second, the camera's flash lit the dangerous collection and the men standing around it in the darkness.

Lucky Mertz then attached a small amount of their own plastic explosive to the pile. Once the team was five hundred metres away and had gone to ground, Lucky detonated the pile. It went up with a burst of orange flame and a loud boom that echoed off the surrounding hills.

Coming to their feet and tugging the headman with them, the team walked quickly back the way they had come, heading for the rendezvous point. They had to be there by four in the morning to be collected by helicopter. All being well, their hike would take them two hours, leaving them thirty minutes to spare. They walked in the same order as before, now with the headman stumbling along in the middle of the line. He did not speak, and neither did his captors.

For close to two hours they walked, until, passing through a fig orchard, they saw a hill looming ahead. Up the rocky hillside they climbed, to a flat plateau. It was three-thirty when they reached the RP. They settled among a collection of large boulders and, using the main radio, Charlie put in a call to 'Mother', the mission's codename for the Special Operations controller at Tarin Kowt. 'Mother, this is Redback. I am in position for extraction. Over.'

He received a brief and worrying reply from the controller. 'Er, Redback from Mother. Extraction delayed. Revert to Bravo. Mother out.'

'Extraction' was the military term for pickup by helicopter and 'Bravo' referred to the second letter of the alphabet, 'B'. The team was being told that their pickup by helicopter had been delayed and that they should revert to their plan B. This involved walking all the way back to Tarin Kowt, which could take days.

'Why would our extraction be delayed?' Lucky Mertz wondered out loud. 'They've got a lot more than one heelo at Tarin Kowt.'

Charlie shrugged. 'Who knows, Lucky, but the fact they haven't suggested a new extraction time means Mother has a problem at Tarin Kowt.'

There *was* a problem at Tarin Kowt. A big one. The Taliban had chosen this very night to launch an attack on Tarin Kowt airfield, using rockets and mortars. That attack made it too dangerous for helicopters and other aircraft to fly in or out for the time being.

As they were contemplating their situation, Trooper Baz, who was on watch with night-vision binoculars, called a warning. 'We've got company! I can see movement down the hill behind us.'

Charlie quickly focused his binoculars in the direction Baz had indicated. He could make out a number of men climbing the slope, moving from the cover of one set of rocks to another. 'We've been followed!'

'Do you think the headman's sons followed us?' Ben asked.

'It's possible,' Charlie responded, 'but whoever they are, they're armed.'

'Do we stay and fight, or move out?' Ben asked.

Before Charlie could answer, a rocket-propelled grenade – an RPG – came flying up from below and burst close by. The shockwave from the blast knocked Charlie off his feet and sent him sprawling into the open. Bullets fired from AK-47 automatic rifles, carried by the men climbing the hill, now began to spray around the Australian soldiers, chipping the boulders and humming by their heads. Four of the SAS men began to return fire, but Charlie was not moving.

Ben wasn't firing. His eyes were on Charlie's still form. Letting go of Caesar's leash, he was tensing his muscles to leap into the open and grab his best friend when Caesar himself jumped up and dashed out to Charlie. Caesar, much lower to the ground than Ben, grabbed hold of Charlie's backpack with his teeth. Slowly, Caesar began dragging the sergeant toward Ben, who, on his hands and knees, scrambled to join his dog and get Charlie back behind the boulders.

'Well done, Caesar!' Ben yelled, above the noise of weapons going off all around them. 'Good dog! Brave dog!'

Ben took hold of Charlie's Kevlar vest, and between Caesar and himself they were able to drag Charlie behind cover. Fortunately, Charlie had not been seriously injured. He had only been knocked out by the blast, and was now coming round.

Looking up at Ben, Charlie said, groggily, 'Someone pulled me into cover – was that you, Ben?'

Ben burst into a grin. 'Yep, but with a lot of help from Caesar. That wasn't something he learnt at training school, I can tell you.'

Slowly sitting up, Charlie reached over and patted Caesar. 'Thanks, Caesar, mate,' he said. 'We'll have to get you a medal, for bravery above and beyond the call of duty.'

In response, Caesar let out a little whine, as if to say, *I hope you're all right, Charlie*, and licked Charlie's face.

All around them, the four other SAS men were laying down a fierce response to the attack from below, firing machineguns, grenade-launchers and rocket-launchers down the hill. As a result, the bottom of the hill was being lit up by explosions, and hostile fire quickly slackened.

With his head beginning to clear, Charlie looked around the small group and called, 'Where's our prisoner? Where's the headman?'

'Fear not, Charlie boy,' Bendigo Baz cheerfully called back. 'The headman isn't going anywhere.'

Peering through the darkness, Charlie and Ben were able to make out the sight of Baz sitting on top of the very unhappy headman, who, still blindfolded, was lying on his stomach. Using the headman as a seat, Baz was all the while firing his machinegun at their Afghan attackers down the hill. As Charlie rejoined the battle, firing his carbine at flitting shapes and muzzle flashes, Ben attached Caesar's leash to his belt, then he too opened fire with his rifle. As Ben fired, Caesar lay down beside his master, with his head resting on his paws, and waited for the noise to stop. After several minutes of intense shooting, Charlie called on the others to cease fire. No longer was there any return fire coming from below.

'If any of those blokes down there are still breathing, they'll either be calling in help from their Taliban mates or moving around to cut us off,' said Charlie.

'Or both,' said Ben.

'One way or another,' Charlie responded, 'we can't

stay here. Any of you blokes been hit?' When the others all replied that they were unhurt, Charlie said, 'Okay, let's move out!'

Pulling the terrified headman to his feet, they set off again, marching quickly over a flat plateau toward the north and then slipping and sliding down a rocky slope to reach another valley dotted with farms. They kept walking until the sky to their right began to streak with the yellow rays of the rising sun. Charlie then led the way up onto a rocky ridge. From there, they had a good view of their surroundings. The men and Caesar lay down among the rocks and covered themselves with the camouflage net. It would be too dangerous to travel in daylight – they would be spotted by Taliban, or by friends or spies of the Taliban among the farmers and villagers of the district.

All day they lay there, watching vehicles travel distant roads, hoping that no bad guys would come looking for them. The whole point of a Special Forces operation like this one was to slip in, do a job and slip out again without attracting attention. They were not supposed to get into a firefight. The team was heavily armed – more heavily armed than ordinary infantrymen – to enable them to fight their way out of trouble if they found themselves in a tight corner. But that was supposed to be a last resort. This morning's short, sharp encounter had shown just how lethal they could be, despite their lack of numbers. But it had also alerted the Taliban that a small Special

Forces operation was going down in their midst. And the Taliban would now be out looking for them – in big numbers.

Through the day, Caesar lay by Ben's side, panting in the hot sun. After a while, Ben unravelled his camouflage-patterned sleeping bag and put it over them both to create a little shade. But the air was thick with heat. Occasionally, Ben would give Caesar a little water from a plastic cup, and Caesar would gratefully lick it empty. For a large, energetic dog like Caesar, it was difficult to remain in the one place for so long, and several times throughout the day he became restless and got to his feet. Each time, Ben pulled Caesar back down beside him, ruffled his neck, tickled his ears and spoke quietly, soothingly to him, telling him that they would be on the move again soon enough, but that, for now, they had to stay where they were.

On another occasion, Ben felt something drop onto his stomach. Looking down, he saw a round stone the size of a golf ball lying on his tunic. Caesar sat looking at him expectantly. Ben smiled to himself as he realised that Caesar had dropped the stone there, wanting Ben to throw the stone so he could fetch it. 'No, mate,' he said softly, 'we can't play yet.' Pulling Caesar close, he tickled his ear. 'Later.'

Several times, the headman, a Muslim, asked permission to pray to meet the requirement of his religion to kneel, face east and pray five times a day. But Charlie, wary of an attempt by his prisoner to escape or attract Taliban attention, wouldn't permit it.

After sunset, the men and Caesar ate their day's cold rations, and Caesar, again, scored a few leftovers. The soldiers offered the headman an MRE pack, but, refusing to eat their Western food, he would only take water. Again, he asked permission to pray, and now that it was dark, Charlie agreed and freed the headman's hands. As he knelt and prayed, still blindfolded, two of the SAS men guarded him with their rifles at the ready. When he had finished his prayers, his hands were bound once more behind his back and he was again made to lie in the midst of his captors.

By midevening, the last light in the distance went out. The valley below was going to sleep. Charlie checked his GPS, then got back on the radio.

'Redback now at X-Ray Victor 9,' he reported to Tarin Kowt. 'All intact and with one guest. Request extraction. Over.' He didn't mind walking all the way back to Tarin Kowt through enemy territory, but there was an unwritten SAS rule: only an idiot looks for an unnecessary fight. A lift from a heelo would eliminate the risk of another dangerous engagement with the Taliban on their way back to base.

'Wait, Redback,' came a brief reply. 'Mother out.' Twenty minutes passed. Then, the radio crackled in

Charlie's waiting ear. 'Redback, this is Mother. Extraction at 0100 hours is now possible, at X-Ray Romeo 8. Advise. Over.'

'Wait, Mother.' Charlie checked his GPS, assessing the time it would take for them to walk the distance from where they were to the new grid-reference point. 'Roger, Mother,' he then advised. 'Redback can do. Over.'

'Roger, Redback. X-Ray Romeo 8 at 0100 hours. Do you copy? Over.'

'Copy that. X-Ray Romeo 8. The spider will be on the toilet seat at 0100 hours. Redback out. Over.' He switched the radio off.

'How far do we have to walk this time?' Bendigo Baz asked, as Charlie packed the radio away.

'A few clicks,' Charlie replied. 'Just a stroll for a fit bloke like you, Baz. Okay, let's pack up and make tracks, people, before the moon rises and lights us up on the skyline.'

They were soon back on their feet and on the march again. Caesar's tail was wagging excitedly. He hadn't enjoyed being cooped up under the camouflage net all day and was glad to be on the move. Keeping to high ground, the team made good time and reached the new RP a little after midnight. First, they found a piece of clear, level ground that would serve as an LZ for a helicopter. Then Charlie turned on an electronic homing device that would allow a friendly helicopter to pinpoint their location. Again, the men and Caesar settled down to wait.

Just before one in the morning, Ben noticed Caesar's ears prick up and felt him tense a little. Caesar had heard something – something the humans around him could not hear. Not only did the labrador have a far better sense of smell than humans, his hearing was more acute, too. And Caesar's ears had picked up a high-pitched sound emitted by a powerful helicopter's engines. Not long after, Ben and the others heard the deeper *whoosh-whoosh* sounds of an approaching helicopter's spinning rotors, coming from the direction of Tarin Kowt.

On hearing this, Charlie and Lucky took flares from their backpacks and lit them, marking the LZ to guide the helicopter's pilot. At the same time, Ben fitted Caesar with his doggles and puppy Peltors, then slid his own goggles over his eyes. Out of the darkness came a Chinook, descending with its flat underside at an angle, tail first. The downwash from the rotors kicked up a small dust storm, which swirled around the landing zone. The helicopter's rear wheels touched the ground first, followed by its front wheels.

'Let's go!' Charlie yelled above the noise of the helicopter, while tugging at the headman's arm.

But the headman refused to budge. 'No!' he cried. 'I no go! They torture me at Tarin Kowt.' He threw himself to the ground.

'Mate,' said Charlie, slowly, deliberately, 'my orders were to bring you in if we found Taliban explosives at your kal, and that's exactly what I'm going to do. Baz, give me a hand with this bloke.'

Charlie took the headman under one arm and Baz took him under the other. Between them, they half carried and half dragged him up the ramp and into the hull of the waiting Chinook. Ben and Caesar followed close behind. Lucky Mertz and the two other SAS men in the group, who had been covering the landing of the Chinook, now rose up from where they were lying and came running up the ramp.

The Chinook's loadmaster, standing at the mouth of the ramp, spoke briefly to the pilot via his headset microphone, telling him that all passengers were aboard. The tail of the Chinook immediately rose up, followed by its nose. As the big helicopter swiftly gained height, Ben half fell into the webbed seating and strapped himself in, then pulled Caesar in between his legs, giving him a solid pat and ruffle of the neck. Bending low to the labrador's ear, and lifting one side of his puppy Peltors, Ben told him, 'The mission's almost done, Caesar – you did a great job. Good boy!' And Caesar's tail wagged with delight.

The Chinook returned them to Tarin Kowt without incident. As the headman, minus the blindfold but with his hands still tied behind his back, was being handed over to waiting US Army Intelligence officers, Ben returned the man's glasses, slipping them in place for him. The headman looked away while Ben was doing this for, in Afghanistan, it is considered rude to look someone in the eye for any length of time.

'Taliban – they are forcing me to help them, soldier Australia,' he said glumly, bowing his head. 'I am having no choice.'

'So you said before,' Ben replied, wearily. 'But if the Taliban had a chance to use what my dog found in your compound, they could have killed a lot of my comrades. Maybe even my dog and me. Whether you wanted to or not, you would have helped the Taliban kill people. Probably including innocent civilians.'

The headman didn't reply. If he was telling the truth, Ben could feel some sympathy for him. It was widely known that the Taliban threatened to kill local people if they failed to help them, and often carried out those threats. But a lot of locals in Uruzgan Province helped the Taliban voluntarily. After all, it was in Uruzgan that the chief of the Taliban, Mullah Omar, had been born. It was possible this headman was lying. Maybe he secretly supported the Taliban, had willingly buried those explosives, and would gladly see Ben and his mates blown to smithereens.

As the headman was led away, Charlie came over and patted Ben on the back. 'We got a good result out of this mission, mate – and all because of you and Caesar. It was great working with the pair of you. Let's hope we can do it again sometime.'

'We hope so too, Charlie,' Ben replied.

Caesar, nuzzling up against Charlie's leg with a wagging tail, seemed to agree.

CHAPTER 9

The day after returning to Tarin Kowt, Ben gave Caesar a bath. All dogs hate being bathed, even labradors like Caesar who will swim and romp in open water with the greatest of glee. A bath of soap and water is, to them, a mild form of torture. But Caesar was in dire need of one – his brown coat was greasy, and smelled of dirt and dust and chicken droppings.

Caesar stood on a cement pad in the base kennels, covered in soap suds, his tail drooping. Looking up at Ben, he had a sad, sad look in his eyes, as if to say, *Was this really necessary, boss?*

'Caesar, you can't make me feel guilty for giving you a bath,' said Ben, with a chuckle. 'It's for your own good, mate. And you'll be getting steak for dinner tonight as a reward for a job well done.'

After Ben hosed him down, Caesar shook himself to dry his coat, but to dry him off completely, Ben still had to kneel beside him and towel him down. Caesar liked that. He liked the closeness. As Ben towelled,

Caesar turned and licked him on the face, making Ben laugh.

'Seems like you two are having fun, Corporal,' said a voice behind Ben.

Turning in the direction of the voice, Ben came face to face with two officers. One was a general – Major General Michael Jones, commander of the Australian forces at Tarin Kowt. The other was a captain, the general's assistant. Ben immediately sprang to his feet, came rigidly to attention and saluted. And Caesar, without being told to, sat down, soldier-like, beside his master.

'Stand easy, Corporal,' said Major General Jones, returning his salute. 'I wanted to congratulate you on an outstanding job on the Redback operation. Outstanding.'

'All the credit goes to Caesar, sir,' Ben replied. 'If he hadn't led us to the chicken coop, we would have missed the Taliban hoard.'

'He's one heck of a fine EDD, by all accounts,' the general acknowledged. 'But like a soldier, an explosive dog is only as good as his training. Full marks to you for giving him that training, Fulton.'

'Thank you, sir. But,' Ben said, shaking his head, 'with respect, there are some things you can't train a dog to do – things some dogs do purely by instinct. My last dog was terrific, but Caesar has instincts that make him just about the best EDD I've ever come across.'

The general nodded. 'Well, we'll be making full use of his special talents. Make sure you look after him. We need him, and you, here in Uruzgan.'

'I sure will look after him, sir. And he'll look after me,' replied Ben, smiling fondly at Caesar.

'I imagine he will,' said the general, smiling. 'Carry on, Corporal.'

Charlie and Ben soon got their wish to work together again. After several weeks of routine explosives patrol work on roads and in villages, Ben and Caesar received orders to join a major Special Forces mission. When Ben reported to the Special Operations Headquarters for the mission briefing, he found Charlie there along with Lucky Mertz, Bendigo Baz and eight other Australian SAS men.

The briefing was led by an American Special Forces colonel, a man with a thick bull neck and a shaved head. He told the Australians they were being airlifted into an FOB, a forward operating base, named Python. This FOB was a hundred kilometres to the north of Tarin Kowt, deep inside what the Australian and American troops called 'bandit country'. A dozen American Special Forces soldiers were already located at FOB Python, along with soldiers of the Afghan National Army.

It was late August, and the winter weather would soon arrive in Uruzgan Province. Before long, snow and ice would make travel by vehicle impossible, and the Taliban would melt away into the mountains to await the next spring, when they would return to launch new attacks. While the weather was still favourable, the Australians were to join the troops at FOB Python for a week, carrying out missions in the area to seek and capture as many Taliban insurgents as possible before winter. In particular, they were to try to seize the Taliban's most senior man in the region, Commander Baradar, who was reportedly operating in the valley. The American strategists behind the seven-day joint operation had given it the codename Operation Comanche.

'Okay, Aussies,' the colonel finished up. 'Make me proud of Operation Comanche. Go kick some Taliban butt!'

Ben immediately went to prepare his and Caesar's gear and, shortly after sundown, they were on a Chinook that flew them north to FOB Python along with Charlie and the other SAS men assigned to the mission. When they landed at the base, which sat on a rise on the valley floor, they were greeted by American Green Berets, members of an elite Special Forces unit, who would be their partners for the next week. These bearded, heavily tattooed Green Berets looked more like pirates than soldiers. They showed the Australians to their quarters – an old shipping container. In these cramped quarters, Caesar would sleep on his own mattress beside Ben.

That night, the Americans gave the Australians a hot meal, followed by chocolate-chip ice-cream, of which they seemed to have an endless supply. Their cook even had a steak to spare, for Caesar, and a bone. Downing a soft drink and chatting with the friendly Yanks as Caesar lay at his feet gnawing at the bone, Ben found the Americans had been feeling isolated at this distant outpost and were pleased to have Aussie company. He also discovered that there was a US Army EDD at the base – a Belgian shepherd named Butch. His handler was Sergeant Mannie Madrid from Arizona. Mannie and Butch came and introduced themselves, and Ben and Caesar hit it off with them right away. Caesar was pleased to have some doggy company, and Ben watched with a smile as the two dogs romped like schoolboys.

After Mannie and Butch turned in for the night, Ben and Caesar were briefly joined by Charlie for a chat. Charlie had been talking with the commander of the US Special Forces team on base, learning more about their planned week-long mission.

'All set for tomorrow?' Ben asked.

'All set,' Charlie returned, as he fondled Caesar's ears. Caesar, for his part, rested his head on Charlie's knee and lapped up the attention. 'Are you in touch with Josh and Maddie back home?' Charlie asked.

Ben nodded. 'We Skype every week like clockwork. I told them you were doing ops with Caesar and me. They were really pleased.'

Charlie took a swig of his drink, then asked, 'How are the kids handling your being away?'

'Pretty well. I mean, I know they'd rather have me at home than away. And I do miss them . . . but I've got a job to do.' He let out a long sigh.

'I don't know if I'll ever end up having kids of my own, but if I do, I wouldn't mind a couple just like Josh and Maddie. Those two are the best, mate. You are a great dad to them.'

'As a special treat,' said Ben, 'I thought I might take them to Disneyland in California when this tour ends and Caesar and I get back home.'

'To Disneyland?' Charlie smiled. 'Mate! Wow! Would you take Nan Fulton too?'

'Absolutely. Nan goes wherever we go. A pity we can't take Caesar with us.'

'Now that, mate, I would like to see!'

Not long after, they went to bed. The men and Caesar had to be up at dawn.

For six days, as August gave way to September, the Australians, Americans and Afghan soldiers based at

FOB Python moved methodically from one end of the valley to the other, carrying out sweeps in search of the Taliban. They found deserted Taliban hill camps, and kal occupants who, when questioned, told them that the Taliban were active in the area. That was made obvious when both Caesar and Butch discovered IEDs in and around the roads they travelled. But the Taliban themselves seemed to be deliberately keeping out of their way.

'It's a worry,' Charlie said to Ben on their sixth night at FOB Python. 'The Taliban are usually spoiling for a fight. I wonder what they're up to.'

'Maybe they're waiting for us to leave the valley,' Ben suggested.

'Maybe.' But Charlie was unconvinced, and he went to bed with a feeling of foreboding about the next day.

The following morning, the captain in charge of the Afghan troops at FOB Python was told by a local that Commander Baradar himself was using a particular kal about five kilometres from the base. The combined Special Forces group had checked that kal earlier in the week, but the informant said that Baradar had since slipped back into it. As the Australians were supposed to be airlifted back to Tarin Kowt that evening, Charlie radioed headquarters for permission to stay on for one more day to take part in a raid on the compound in question. With the hope of securing Commander Baradar, Charlie's superiors gave their approval, and the Australians prepared to join their comrades at FOB Python in a raid on the kal that very night.

At twelve-thirty that night, thirty-six men – twelve Australians, twelve Americans and twelve Afghans – and two dogs set off to raid the kal and, hopefully, bag Commander Baradar. They travelled in five Humvees, the standard American four-wheel drive military vehicle. Ben and Caesar were in a Humvee along with Charlie, several other Australians including Bendigo Baz and Lucky Mertz, plus a smiley, round-faced Afghan Army interpreter named Kareem and an American driver and gunner.

In bright moonlight the little convoy trundled away from the base, making its way north. Half a kilometre out from the target kal, the vehicles stopped and the Australians, most of the Americans and some of the Afghan soldiers clambered out. Ten men remained with the vehicles. The American sergeant in charge of the raid, Sergeant 'Duke' Hazard, sent one of his men out in front to lead the way, then stood watching the other men pass him in single file as they trooped after the pathfinder. When Charlie drew abreast of him, the bearded Hazard, who wore a black baseball cap and chewed gum perpetually, fell in beside him and walked part of the way at his side.

'My guys and the ANA will take the northern gate,' said Hazard. 'I want you and your Diggers to take the southern gate.'

Charlie nodded in acknowledgement. 'Gotcha.'

'I'm feeling good about this op,' said Hazard.

'Uh-huh,' Charlie returned. He felt just the opposite. After going to bed the previous night with a bad feeling about the day ahead, he was still uneasy. To him, something about this mission didn't feel right – something he couldn't quite define – and he wasn't going to pretend otherwise. With nothing concrete to support his unease, Charlie had to simply get on with the job.

'This your first tour of Afghanistan?'

'No,' answered Charlie, concentrating on the way ahead.

'Don't talk much, do you, Aussie?' said Hazard.

'Only when I have to,' Charlie responded.

Hazard shut up after that and rejoined his men.

Not far behind Charlie, Ben and Caesar were in the middle of the little force of twenty-six men making their way on foot and in single file toward the target kal. The American dog Butch and his handler were toward the rear. On a two-metre leash held in Ben's left hand, Caesar trotted by Ben's side, alert and ready for work. With Ben and other familiar Australian soldiers all around him, Caesar was feeling part of the team.

The mud walls of the target kal loomed up ahead, looking spooky in the green light of Ben's night-vision goggles. This kal was much the same as countless others that Ben and Caesar had visited in Uruzgan. Roughly square, it had high mud walls around the perimeter, and contained the usual collection of small buildings and dirt courtyards. Back at FOB Python, Ben had seen an aerial photograph of it taken from a drone, so knew its layout.

As Hazard had instructed, the assault team split into two sections, with the Australians moving to one closed gate, and the Americans and Afghans to another. Using plastic explosive, both gates were blown open at the same time. The troops swept in through the gateways, weapons at the ready. The Australians, with Ben and Caesar to the fore, checked half of the compound. The Americans, with Mannie and Butch leading the way, checked the other half. The kal was deserted. Not a single soul was found. Nor was there any sign of weapons, ammunition or explosives. In the building that clearly served as the main living quarters, Charlie, Lucky, Ben and Caesar linked up with Duke Hazard and several of his men. Oil lamps had been lit by the Americans, and they shone a golden glow around the humbly furnished room. There weren't even chairs for sitting. Like most traditional Afghan homes, there were simply cushions on a rug on the floor, where everyone sat to dine and talk.

In the improved light provided by the lamps, Ben slid his night-vision goggles up onto his forehead. After instructing Caesar to sit, Ben turned to his companions. 'So, where's Commander Baradar?'

'It was all a freaking wild goose chase!' declared an angry Sergeant Hazard. 'The intel was bogus!'

'Either that,' said Charlie, 'or Baradar got wind of us and skipped out of here before we arrived.'

'Or, we've been lured into a trap,' said Ben, offering a third, more worrying alternative.

The others nodded. Most agreed that Ben's suggestion was most likely the case. But Sergeant Hazard didn't agree. 'If it was a trap, this place would have been booby-trapped to hell,' he said. 'The informant lied for money. The locals do it all the time.' He shouldered his rifle. 'Okay, you guys, move out. I want to be back at Python before sun-up.'

The others began to withdraw from the room. But Ben still suspected a trap. Why, he wondered, was the kal deserted? It was full of personal belongings. People *lived* here. But where were they? Had the Taliban told the occupants to clear out before the foreign Special Forces troops arrived? As Ben stood there thinking these thoughts, the Americans began dousing the oil lamps.

Looking down, Ben noticed that Caesar had come to his feet and was looking at the white wall at the far end of the room. It wasn't Caesar's usual detection signature, but it seemed that something had attracted the dog's attention.

Sergeant Hazard was about to extinguish the last lamp, but Ben called to him. 'Can you leave that lamp burning for a minute longer, Sergeant?'

'Why?' Hazard irritably responded.

'I think my dog's on to something,' Ben replied. Squatting beside Caesar, Ben unfastened his leash. 'Caesar, seek on!'

As Ben and Sergeant Hazard watched, Caesar moved forward and stood just centimetres from the wall at the end of the room, staring at it. Joining his dog, Ben said, 'What have you found, Caesar, mate?'

Caesar looked up at him for a moment, then returned his attention to the wall. He stared at it unwaveringly.

'Explosives?' Sergeant Hazard wondered aloud.

'I'm not sure,' Ben responded. Removing a glove, he ran one hand over the wall's bumpy surface. Then he took a black torch from his belt and shone it on the wall. 'The wall's colour is slightly different here,' he said, 'as if it's been patched.' Slipping his knife from its sheath on his belt, he stabbed the wall. Mud crumbled away as he dug a hole five or six centimetres deep. Bending down so it was eye-level, he shone his torch into the hole.

'See anything?' asked Hazard, who had brought the lamp closer. Intrigued, he was now paying close attention.

Behind them, Charlie and several other soldiers had returned. 'Has super-sniffer hit the jackpot again?' asked Charlie.

'Looks like he might have done,' said Ben, peering into the hole. Carefully reaching in, he took hold of an object and withdrew it.

'Is that a mobile phone?' said Charlie.

'Yep,' Ben replied, handing a grubby phone to Hazard before reaching back into the hole and bringing out seven more. Finally, he retrieved a clear plastic packet containing detonators. It had been the detonators' faint aroma, even though they were hidden behind a mud wall centimetres thick, that had attracted Caesar's attention.

'Interesting,' said Sergeant Hazard. 'Could be this place has been used by the Taliban after all.'

'And if there are detonators,' said Ben, 'chances are they've been making IEDs here.'

'And the mobile phones?' said Hazard. 'You think the Taliban have been using them to communicate with each other?'

'To communicate with their contacts and spies in the towns, I reckon,' said Ben.

'The bears would love to get their hands on those phones,' said Charlie. 'Bears' was military slang for the military intelligence personnel, who had the equipment that would enable them to work out the phone numbers of incoming and outgoing calls on the phones. Once they had those numbers, the intelligence officers would be able to track down their owners, the Taliban contacts and spies.

Ben squatted and gave Caesar a hearty pat. 'Good boy, Caesar! Good boy! You've done it again, mate.' Caesar's tail wagged away, showing his pleasure at Ben's obvious approval.

'You got yourself one hell of a smart dog there, Digger,' said Hazard to Ben.

'Don't let Caesar hear you say that, he'll get a big head,' Charlie joked.

'You know what?' said Ben, as he put the phones and detonators in a small canvas bag that he'd taken from his backpack. 'I think the Taliban have probably planted their IEDs on the road back to FOB Python. They lured us out here on a wild goose chase, and plan to attack us on our way back to base when our guard is down.'

'Then ... *kaboom*!' said Charlie, raising his eyebrows. 'Ambush.'

'I'm not a gambling man,' said Ben, 'but I'd bet a hundred bucks they're out there now, waiting to ambush us on the road back.'

Sergeant Hazard was rubbing his bearded chin. 'Trust those tricky Taliban to think up something as devious as that,' he growled. 'Okay, we keep off the roads going back. We'll go overland.'

'What if they've thought of that, too?' said Charlie.

'Yeah, what if they've mined the countryside?' Ben added.

'They can't mine every square inch of this valley!' Sergeant Hazard countered. 'We'll have to take our chances.'

The raiding party quickly withdrew from the compound and returned to the waiting Humvees. On Sergeant Hazard's orders, once all the troops and dogs were aboard, the five vehicles pulled off the road. Bumping over rough, open and often rocky terrain, they began to slowly head back toward the safety of FOB Python on the hill five kilometres away.

In the back of Ben and Caesar's shuddering Humvee, Kareem the interpreter had headphones on. He was listening to the Humvee's military radio, slowly scanning the radio frequencies that the Taliban were known to use. Suddenly, Kareem stiffened and listened intently. Turning to Charlie with a worried look on his face, he said, 'Sergeant Charlie, I can hear them – I can hear the Taliban. They are talking in plain Pashto.'

'What are they saying, Kareem?' Charlie asked.

'I can hear a Taliban commander,' Kareem replied. 'He is saying, "The infidels are coming! The infidels are coming! Be ready! Be ready!"'

Ben knew that 'infidels' was what the Taliban called those who did not observe their Muslim faith. 'The question is,' he said, 'are they talking about us, or about some other luckless infidels a valley or two away?'

'We'll soon find out,' said Charlie. 'We could have an interesting night ahead of us, boys. Lock and load.'

Charlie slipped the carbine from his shoulder, checking it and the ammunition magazines on his belt. As all the men in the vehicle followed his lead, preparing their weapons and equipment for action, and sliding their night-vision goggles down over their eyes, Charlie used the vehicle's radio to warn Hazard, who was riding in the Humvee behind them, telling him what Kareem had heard. Hazard replied that his interpreter had picked up similar radio chatter from the Taliban. 'Could be they're just trying to scare us, knowing we're listening,' Hazard said. 'Could be there's no ambush.'

From experience, Charlie knew that an increase in Taliban radio chatter always preceded an ambush. 'And *could be* my old man is Santa Claus,' he replied, unable to hide his sarcasm. He was now convinced that an ambush was imminent.

'Okay, okay,' Hazard came back over the air, sounding exasperated. 'We'll divert along the creek bed ahead. Should make better time using that, and we can get the hell outta here. Meantime, tell your people to keep their eyes peeled for the bad guys.'

Caesar was sitting between Ben's legs as usual, looking up at him with his tongue hanging out the side of his mouth. If there was a battle ahead, Ben needed both his hands free to use his weapons. But he didn't want to be separated from Caesar, so he fastened the end of Caesar's leash to a clip that was on his belt for just this purpose. With the pair of them connected by the two-metre length of leather, and with both hands now free, he slipped his rifle from his shoulder and prepared for action.

Leaning down to Caesar, Ben spoke into his nearest ear. 'Stay close, Caesar. Whatever happens, we'll get through this together.'

Caesar licked him on the cheek.

Ben grinned and ruffled Caesar's neck. 'Yes, I love you too.'

Charlie was looking at him. 'If things get hairy, Ben,' he said, 'you worry about keeping Caesar safe. It's not as if he can defend himself against the Taliban. And he's a valuable asset. Let the rest of us do the shooting.'

'I might not have much choice in the matter, Charlie. We might need every gun we have.' Ben knew that the Taliban usually only staged ambushes when they outnumbered the opposition. And if they were waiting for this little convoy out there in the night, as he had predicted, then they had planned this ambush with care. The Taliban commander would have called in as many men and as much weaponry as he could. Soon, Ben suspected, he and every one of his comrades could be depending on each other to get out of this mess alive.

Just as Ben could feel his own muscles tense and his heart pounding in his chest, he felt Caesar, sitting between his knees, also tense up. More than just picking up Ben's increased alertness, Caesar, like Ben, could sense danger – and that danger was real and growing closer by the second.

CHAPTER 10

Whoomp! Dust and smoke billowed up in a cloud. An IED had exploded beneath the front right side of the leading Humvee. The vehicle, its front right wheel blown off, was thrown up onto its side. Its ANA occupants, some wounded, tumbled out and scrambled to hide behind the upturned wreck.

The convoy had been following a dry creek bed back toward FOB Python – just as the Taliban had expected it to. At a bend in the creek, the insurgents were waiting for them, and had planted the bomb in the riverbed. The creek bank directly ahead and a low ridge to the right of the line of Humvees sparkled with flashes from the muzzles of AK-47s and machineguns fired by Taliban insurgents lying in wait.

'Contact! Contact! Two o'clock!' yelled the American gunner in Ben and Caesar's Humvee, the third vehicle in line. Taliban bullets splattered against the Humvee's lightly armoured sides. Moments later, the gunner was letting rip with his 50-calibre machinegun, and its *tat-tat-tat* joined the harsh concert of battle sounds that now filled the previously still night. Ben and Caesar's Humvee slithered to a halt.

'Why are we stopping?' Charlie called.

'The way's blocked!' their driver yelled back. Ahead, the second Humvee was trying to reverse away from the overturned lead vehicle.

'We're sitting ducks!' Lucky Mertz shouted. 'Back up!'

'I'm trying! I'm trying!' the driver cried, his voice high-pitched with alarm. In his panic, the driver reversed their vehicle into the Humvee behind – Sergeant Hazard's vehicle. With a metallic crunch, the two Humvees collided and briefly became locked together.

'This is like dodgem cars at the Royal Melbourne Show!' Bendigo Baz exclaimed. 'And I don't like dodgem cars!'

'Most of the fire's coming in from the right,' said Charlie, calmly assessing the situation. 'Everyone dismount, take up firing positions and engage. Go left! Go left! Now!'

Throwing open the left side doors, they sprang from the Humvee. Ben went out the rear door with Caesar just as, with a roar of its engine, the Humvee directly behind them managed to free itself and reverse away. Then it too stopped, as its occupants tumbled out and landed on rounded but hard river stones. As they hit the riverbed, an RPG hit the front of the Humvee that Ben and Caesar had just left.

Aimed at the American machine-gunner, who had remained behind and was continuing to direct fire at the enemy with his big weapon, the RPG blast took away part of the right side of the vehicle. The machine-gunner, instantly wounded, sagged back down into the blackened wreckage. The Humvee's driver reached back into the cabin and dragged his injured countryman from the vehicle, then started to apply first aid.

Meanwhile, Ben was crouching, with Caesar on his belly at his master's side. Caesar's tail and ears were drooping – both signs that he was clearly unsettled by the incoming fire.

Charlie was close by. 'Too much fire's coming our way,' he yelled to Ben, as bullets whizzed by, just overhead. He pointed to Sergeant Hazard's stationary Humvee behind them. 'Use that as cover, and keep your heads down.'

'How many hostiles are we up against?' Ben called.

'A lot!' Charlie returned. 'Now get into cover, and stay low! That's an order.' He tapped Bendigo Baz on the shoulder. 'Baz, give Ben and Caesar cover.'

'Your wish is my command, oh master,' Baz replied, and up he popped with his machinegun, to let off a long, fanned burst at the enemy.

Ben, hunching low, led Caesar back to the next Humvee. Enemy bullets chopped up gravel nearby as they ran. Sergeant Hazard and a mixture of Australian and American soldiers were using the fourth Humvee as cover – bobbing up to fire to the right, then bobbing back down again. Ben could see that the Humvee at the tail end of the convoy was blocking their way back out of the creek bed. It too was stopped. And it was on fire, with orange flames licking the metal and rising up into the night sky. It had been hit by two RPGs.

Ben recognised the tactics used by their attackers as those of a classic convoy ambush – destroy the first vehicle and the last, trapping the remaining vehicles in between. It occurred to Ben that the Taliban commander responsible for their predicament knew exactly what he was doing, and had probably done this many times before.

Over at Humvee number three, Charlie found Kareem the interpreter huddled beside the vehicle. 'Kareem, are you okay?' Charlie asked.

'Yes, Sergeant Charlie, I am okay,' Kareem replied. But terror was painted across his face. 'I am thinking of my wife and dear children. The last thing I heard the Taliban commander say on the radio was "Kill them all! Kill them all!". Please tell me, Sergeant Charlie, are we all going to die here?'

'Not if I can help it, mate,' Charlie replied, slipping a grenade into the grenade-launcher attached to his carbine. Rising up, Charlie took in the line of enemy muzzle flashes, some as close as 100 metres away. Aiming at a machinegun position, he fired, then dropped back down onto one knee behind the Humvee. That the grenade detonated right on target was evident by a fresh, black hole in the glittering necklace of muzzle flashes.

Ben, sitting with his back to the side of Sergeant Hazard's Humvee, pulled Caesar in close and aimed his rifle at the far bank of the stream, ready to fire on any Taliban fighters who might appear there, coming at them from behind. Beside him, Sergeant Hazard was still chewing furiously on gum as he fired a carbine into the night.

Before long, Charlie came in a running crouch to join them. 'We can't stay here, Hazard,' he said, speaking loudly to be heard above the din of gunfire and explosions all around them. 'Hostiles are ahead of us and on our right flank. And they've got mortars. Won't take them long to completely surround us.'

'How many do you figure we're up against?' Hazard asked.

'A hundred, maybe more,' Charlie replied. 'The longer we stay here, the more hostiles are likely to arrive – and the sooner they'll surround us. I say we break out via the open side of the stream while we still can.'

'And leave a couple of Humvees behind?' said Hazard, unhappily.

'You can come back for the wrecked Humvees in daylight,' Charlie insisted.

'Hell no, I'm not running from a fight!' replied Hazard. 'I'm calling in an air strike. We'll bomb the crap out of those freaking hostiles!' Grabbing the radio, Hazard called headquarters in Tarin Kowt. When he finished the call, he threw down the handset in disgust and looked at Charlie. 'There's not a single F-16 on standby in all of Afghanistan tonight! Can you believe it? They have to call in an air strike from *Kuwait*!'

Charlie was shaking his head. 'We can't wait that long. We'll all be history by the time that arrives.' As he spoke, an enemy mortar bomb exploded nearby.

'What a screw-up!' Hazard snarled.

Then, suddenly, bullets kicked up river stones just five metres behind them. Those bullets had been fired from the rear of the convoy. This made Caesar jump up. Facing the direction of the unseen Taliban gunman, the brown labrador began barking defiantly into the night. Caesar rarely barked, but when he did, he meant it.

'You tell 'em, Caesar,' said Ben with a proud grin, gripping him firmly by the collar and pulling him closer.

'They're behind us now,' said Charlie. 'We have to move!' He glared at the American sergeant, ready to order his own men to get the hell out of this death trap if Hazard didn't act soon.

'Yeah, yeah!' Hazard conceded. 'Is your vehicle operational?'

'We'll give it a go,' said Charlie, before he dashed back to the third Humvee.

Like Australian-made Bushmasters, American Humvees were built to be tough and to withstand punishment, so when the driver of the third Humvee climbed back behind the wheel, its engine started on his first attempt. Charlie ordered the wounded to be loaded into the damaged cabin and onto the small flat tray on the back, then instructed all able men to walk and run alongside the Humvee as it struggled up the creek bank, using it as mobile cover, and firing as they went.

Following Charlie's lead, the men at the second and fourth Humvees did the same, and those sheltering behind the first and last wrecked vehicles scrambled to join them. Ben and Caesar ran alongside Sergeant Hazard's vehicle as it turned left and went up the side of the creek's bank, its furiously spinning wheels spewing out stones behind it. With roaring engines, and with Taliban fire pouring their way, all three Humvees climbed up the stony side of the creek, flopped over the bank and reached flat ground. More men were wounded in the process, and they were bundled into the vehicles as the Humvees continued to roll at walking pace.

Ben and Caesar kept near the crouching Sergeant Hazard, alongside his Humvee. So far, in the first twenty minutes of battle, none of them had been hurt. But the battle was far from over. As the three Humvees rolled along, with their machineguns blazing away and with the able men who kept pace beside them also firing, the Taliban followed them in pursuit. Keeping behind natural cover, the Taliban fighters would run to new positions ahead, then resume firing. It was a moving battle and every few metres brought more wounds to the Special Forces group.

Half an hour into the battle, a US Air Force F-16 arrived from Kuwait. Without warning, the jet roared in low overhead, mistakenly dropping a bomb on a distant kal, not on the Taliban. And what seemed like a hundred Taliban weapons pointed skyward, spitting fire at it as the jet soared away. Coming back for another run, the F-16 dropped a second bomb. This time the target was a ridge from which heavy Taliban fire had been coming. Flame and smoke mushroomed into the air where the second bomb landed. And the jet was swallowed by the blackness of the night as it headed back to Kuwait, leaving the men on the ground on their own again. Taliban fire had not even faltered during the air attack. Tough, brave and determined, the insurgents had no intention of letting these Special Forces infidels escape them.

Two hours after the first contact with the enemy, the nonstop battle had brought the three Humvees to within a kilometre of FOB Python. So many men had been taken out of the fight by wounds by this time that Ben had disobeyed Charlie's orders and was using his rifle against their attackers. When he checked his ammunition, he found that he'd fired all his magazines except for one. Then he saw Bendigo Baz, who had been walking and firing beside the Humvee in front, go down with a head wound. The Humvee continued on, leaving Baz lying out in the open.

'Come on, Caesar!' said Ben, and he dashed forward to help Baz, with Caesar scuttling along beside him. Grabbing Baz beneath each arm, Ben hauled him to the middle vehicle. Caesar, tugged along by the leash attached to Ben's belt, came too. Charlie appeared at the left rear of the Humvee and helped Ben lift the unconscious Baz up onto the vehicle's rear tray. Ben saw that Lucky Mertz was among the wounded lying on the tray. Lucky's camouflage trousers were red with his blood. Yet, despite the wounds to his legs, Lucky had swapped his sniper rifle for someone else's carbine and was still letting off bursts at the enemy, at the same time abusing them at the top of his voice. Then Ben recognised the face of Kareem the Afghan interpreter also among the wounded on the tray. Kareem's eyes were glazed, as if he didn't know where he was or who he was.

Without a word, Charlie moved off, now armed with a shoulder-fired rocket-launcher. Ben, meanwhile, was just taking up a new firing position at the rear of the Humvee when, five metres away, an RPG detonated. Shrapnel, or 'frag', flew through the air, hitting the lower rear parts of the Humvee. One piece of frag hit Ben in the back of his left leg. Another neatly sliced through Caesar's leash, severing it from Ben's belt. All of a sudden Caesar was running free, finding himself in the open between the middle and last vehicles.

'Come, Caesar!' Ben yelled, grasping his left leg with one hand and beckoning Caesar with the other. 'Caesar, back here to me, boy!'

Caesar looked around at his master as Ben continued to move further away, forced to keep pace with the moving Humvee.

'Caesar, come!' Ben called, urgently.

Caesar had just started to move back to Ben when a mortar bomb lobbed down in the open between the middle and last Humvees. Frag from the explosion scythed through the air and hit the dog's front left leg, bringing a pained yelp from Caesar. With a cloud of dust and smoke rising in front of him and blocking his view of Ben, Caesar turned and limped away, seeking shelter he could see at the last Humvee. When the dust cleared, Ben was relieved to spot Caesar limping along beside the rearmost vehicle. His furry mate was keeping close to the Australian SAS men there, knowing from their familiar scent that they were friends.

Fifty moonlit metres now separated each of the Humvees. Taliban bullets and mortar bombs were kicking up the earth between each, and Ben knew that if he tried to cross those exposed fifty metres to reach Caesar, he wouldn't make it. He thought of Josh and Maddie. For their sakes, he could not risk his life trying to go across that killing zone. He could see Caesar, and Caesar could see Ben, both locked in each other's sight. Ben could only hope that Caesar would stay with the last Humvee and, with it, reach safety. Ben resumed firing. He had just forty-two rounds remaining, so he selected his targets carefully. Every now and then he looked back to check that Caesar was okay. 'Keep coming, Caesar!' he yelled. 'Keep coming!'

With the terrain becoming less difficult to cross, and with FOB Python getting closer, the leading Humvee began to speed up. The second Humvee did the same, forcing Ben, Charlie and the others beside it to break into a trot to keep up. Ben, ignoring the wound to his left leg and regularly looking back to check where Caesar was, struggled to stay with the vehicle. The third Humvee also sped up, but not as much as the first two. The gap between middle and last vehicle was increasing. Ben could still see Caesar, who was coming as fast as his injured leg would allow, managing to stick with the last Humvee and the men alongside it. 'Good boy, Caesar!' Ben yelled. 'Keep coming, mate! Come on!'

With the gap increasing between them, and with Caesar obviously struggling to keep up, Ben was considering making a dash to the rear vehicle to get him after all when an RPG rocketed in and hit the ground right under the Humvee beside him. The explosion rocked the already battered vehicle up on to its left wheels, tipping three of the wounded men who were lying on the tray off onto the ground. When the vehicle's right wheels hit the ground again, the driver kept going, and the damaged Humvee pulled away, leaving the men lying in the open. Ben hadn't been hurt by the blast, but he was now fearful for the trio left behind. One of them was the Humvee's American gunner. Another was Kareem. And the third was Bendigo Baz.

Ben bashed on the Humvee's left rear window. 'Stop! Stop!' he bellowed to the driver. 'You're leaving people behind!' But the driver, unable to hear him above the din of the battle, drove on.

'Ben, I'll give cover while you grab Baz,' said Charlie, appearing beside his best friend. Exposing himself to enemy fire, Charlie then ran out into the open and launched anti-tank rockets from his shoulder-launcher. Ben, meanwhile, dashed out, and for the second time during the battle, took hold of an unconscious Baz. Looking around, Ben saw that the middle Humvee had come to a stop after all and was waiting for them. Grateful for that, he dragged Baz to it and, with Lucky's help, got him back onto the tray. An American had meanwhile followed his example and retrieved the American gunner. Only Kareem remained in the open.

As Charlie continued to fire rockets, and attract Taliban fire from all directions, Ben started back for Kareem. He had only gone half the distance when a mortar bomb landed in front of him, blowing him off his feet. He landed on his back and lay there, stunned, as a sea of red washed over his eyes. And then he blacked out.

CHAPTER 11

With a splitting headache, Ben regained consciousness. His brain swimming, he tried to work out what was happening. He was on the back of a Humvee, lying with Kareem beside him and partly on top of Baz, who was still unconscious. Lucky and other injured soldiers lay all around him. The Humvee was speeding toward the gate of FOB Python as machineguns on the post's wall joined the battle, covering their retreat.

'Lucky, how'd I get here?' Ben asked, shaking his groggy head.

'Charlie got hold of you and loaded you on here with the rest of us,' said Lucky. 'He went back for Kareem, too, and brought him in. Then the silly bastard went out and started laying down more covering fire for us. It was then they got him.'

Ben froze. 'They got Charlie?'

Lucky paused, then said, 'An RPG cut his legs from under him.'

'Is Charlie still out there?' Ben tried to sit up and look back the way they had come.

'I think the last Humvee picked him up . . . I hope it did, anyway.'

'And what about Caesar?' Ben asked. 'Did anyone see what happened to Caesar?'

'Sorry, mate,' Lucky replied. 'I lost sight of him a while back.'

They were soon inside the comparative safety of the FOB. All three Humvees made it back, loaded with casualties. As Lucky had hoped, Charlie had been collected by the last Humvee, Sergeant Hazard's vehicle. But Charlie was unable to walk. He couldn't even feel his legs.

Charlie, Ben, Lucky and Baz were among the nine Australians who had been wounded. Only three of the SAS men came out of the three-hour battle unhurt. Most of the Americans had also been wounded. Mannie Madrid, Butch's handler, had been seriously injured, although Butch himself had returned to Python without any injuries. But Caesar had not been brought in, and there was no sign of him.

'Please, has anyone seen Caesar?' Ben pleaded with the American medic who swabbed Ben's bloodied face and bandaged his head. Only Ben's eyes remained uncovered – protected by his goggles during the battle, they had been unaffected by the mortar bomb's blast.

'Who's Caesar?' the busy young medic asked as he worked on Ben.

'My EDD – my dog.'

'Dude, do I look like a veterinary surgeon to you?' the medic said, grumpily. 'Humans are my only concern. Dogs can take care of themselves.'

'Please, Caesar was with the third Humvee the last time I saw him,' said Ben. 'Can you ask around? Can you ask the people who were with the last Humvee? They must have seen what happened to him.'

'I'll see what I can do,' said the medic, as he cut away Ben's camouflage trousers to tend to his leg wound. 'When I find the time – *if* I find the time.' He worked away, soon commenting, matter-of-factly, 'Nothing major to worry about with the leg.'

'Great,' said Ben, grimacing a little at the medic's touch. Now that the adrenaline rush of battle had worn off, the leg wound and his face were both starting to really hurt. But if the medic said his leg was okay, he was happy to believe him. 'So, I'll walk again?'

'Oh, sure. Your face will be a mess, though.'

'Thanks for breaking that to me gently,' Ben returned, bemused by the medic's lack of bedside manner.

The medic momentarily raised his eyes. 'Honesty, I find, saves a whole lot of time and trouble.' The medic bandaged the leg before inserting an intravenous drip into one of Ben's arms to feed a painkilling drug into his

146

bloodstream. Then, peeling off his surgical gloves, the medic said, 'You're good to go, Aussie.'

As the medic went to leave, Ben reached up and grasped his arm. 'My dog,' he pleaded. 'Please. Will you ask around about him?'

'I told you before, I'll see what I can do,' the medic impatiently replied, before moving on to his next patient across the room.

Moments later, several Afghan soldiers appeared, and, taking hold of Ben's stretcher, placed him to one side with other wounded soldiers from the battle. All were waiting for a medivac Chinook to arrive and take them to the military hospital at Tarin Kowt. Ben found several wounded men around him who had been with the last Humvee. One Australian said he was sure that Sergeant Hazard must have been the last to see Caesar. Hazard, it turned out, had been the only man with the rearmost vehicle to come out without a scratch. Ben, fighting the wooziness brought on by the painkillers, begged everyone who passed to send Sergeant Hazard to him. Determined to know what had happened to Caesar, he fought to stay awake, wafting in and out of consciousness.

'You wanted to see me, soldier?'

It was Sergeant Hazard's voice. Ben forced his eyes open to see Hazard standing over him. Still chewing gum, and with his hands on his hips, the sergeant looked down at Ben.

'My dog, Caesar,' said Ben weakly. 'Did you see what happened to him?'

'Your dog was left behind, buddy,' the sergeant told Ben, matter-of-factly. 'Sorry about that. We had to get the hell outta there, so we put the pedal to the metal. Your canine just couldn't keep up.'

Ben was appalled by Hazard's devil-may-care attitude to Caesar. 'Couldn't you have stopped for him? You could have put him in the Humvee. He was injured – I could see he was limping.'

'Soldier, I don't run a taxicab service for mutts.'

'Send some men back out to look for him. *Please.*'

'Back out there?' Hazard scoffed. 'Friend, the bandits are in control out there now, and they know it. I figure we just came up against at least two hundred Taliban fighters. No one is going out this camp's gate. The only way in or out of Python in the foreseeable future is by heelo.'

'But Caesar is one of ours,' protested Ben. 'We can't leave him out there.'

'He'll come in of his own accord, you wait and see. If that dog is as smart as I think he is, he'll be scratching on the base's front door in time for supper.' And with that, Hazard walked away, and Ben dejectedly closed his eyes again. All he could see in his mind's eye was his last memory of Caesar, limping along beside the rearmost Humvee. Within minutes, Ben lapsed into sleep.

Before long, the sun rose on a new day, and a Chinook was making a noisy arrival at FOB Python, escorted by a pair of Apache helicopter gunships. The wounded were carried aboard the big heelo once it touched down, and the other Australian and American Special Forces men at the base joined them. All were being withdrawn to Tarin Kowt.

When the Chinook lifted off a little later and turned south with its Apache escorts, Ben awoke. Lying on a stretcher on the helicopter floor, dazed, drugged and weak from loss of blood, he reached out instinctively to feel Caesar at his side. But, of course, Caesar wasn't there. Ben, more worried about Caesar than he was about his wounds, prayed that Sergeant Hazard was right – that Caesar would come into FOB Python of his own accord. Nothing was more important to him right now than knowing Caesar was safe.

All the shooting and explosions had ended a long time earlier. All day, as the sun travelled across the sky, Caesar had lain in a ditch near a road. After being unable to keep up with the last Humvee and being left behind, Caesar had found a hole in the ground where he took shelter. Picking up the scent of Afghans and hearing the voices of Taliban fighters shouting with glee after sending the Special Forces troops fleeing back to FOB Python, Caesar had lain low until he could no longer hear or smell them.

Then, cautiously, he had come out of hiding. After looking around unsuccessfully for signs of Ben and the other Australians, Caesar had limped east to a road, and there beside it he had rested, and waited. Remembering that he and Ben had come to this place by road the previous night, Caesar decided that Ben and the other soldiers might come along this road again. When he heard vehicles, he would emerge from hiding – that was his plan, anyway. But not a single vehicle came along the road as he lay there. Late in the day, Caesar decided to try to find Ben. Pain shot through his bloodied left leg every time he put his paw on the ground, so, keeping his front left paw off the ground, Caesar limped along the road in the direction that he believed would lead him back to Ben.

In twilight, Caesar limped up to the gate of FOB Python. A breeze had been blowing his way and, a long way out from the hilltop base, he had picked up the aroma of cooking food. That, combined with scents he associated with the base, and with Ben, had acted like a beacon to Caesar. In a metal tower rising above the camp wall beside the main gate, two soldiers of the Afghan National Army on guard duty spotted Caesar approaching. Sergeant Hazard had been right about the missing dog finding his own way back to base in time for supper, but no one had told the two Afghan sentries that an Australian military dog was missing and to be on the lookout for it. As Caesar limped up, the sentries thought he was nothing but a stray kal dog.

First, they yelled at Caesar to go away. In response, Caesar barked at them, as if to say, *You silly humans, I'm on your side! Let me in!* One sentry, angered by this barking dog, turned his machinegun Caesar's way and fired a short burst of bullets into the air. When Caesar stood his ground, the sentry fired off another, longer burst now in Caesar's general direction. This time, Caesar shied away. Getting the message that he was not wanted here, he withdrew into the growing darkness.

CHAPTER 12

Eight wounded Australian soldiers lay in the same ward of the Tarin Kowt military hospital. Ben Fulton was one of those eight. In beds either side of him were Bendigo Baz and Lucky Mertz. Both had been shaved by nurses, and Ben hardly recognised them. Baz's head wound was not as serious as had been first thought, and he was likely to be the first of the SAS men to be released from hospital. Lucky, on the other hand, had leg, arm and shoulder wounds, and would take a while to recover fully. As for Ben, the grumpy medic at FOB Python had been right – his leg wound would soon heal, and, while his face had been chewed up, it was not a life-threatening situation.

A party of Australian and American officers now entered the ward and came to the eight Aussies. Leading the group was Australian commander Major General Jones.

'How are you blokes going?' General Jones asked. 'Are you getting everything you need?'

'General, this place is like a six-star resort,' Baz joked. 'I'll have to book in here again sometime.'

General Jones smiled. 'I'm glad you're in good spirits, Trooper, but I wouldn't want to see any of you men back here in hospital any time soon.'

'Where's Charlie Grover, sir?' Lucky asked. 'Why isn't he here with the rest of us?'

The general's smiled faded away. 'Sergeant Grover's condition is pretty serious, men,' he replied. 'His legs were chopped to pieces. The doctors stabilised him, then flew him out to Germany last night.' The Australians all knew that the US military maintained a vast military hospital in Frankfurt, Germany, with all the latest equipment and the best doctors. Any American or coalition troops seriously wounded in Afghanistan were sent there.

'Will Charlie pull through, sir?' Baz asked, sounding worried.

'I'm sure the docs will do everything they can for Sergeant Grover,' General Jones replied. 'I also wanted to tell you all that your families back home in Australia have been notified of your wounds.'

Ben's thoughts immediately went to Josh and Maddie, and how they would take the news that their father had been wounded. But knowing they were mentally strong, and that he would be going home to them, his main concern was for his lost labrador. 'Any news of Caesar, sir?' he asked.

The general looked at Ben's heavily bandaged face, and frowned. 'Caesar?'

'We had to leave him behind out there,' said Ben, his voice quavering.

A look of dismay came over General Jones. 'One of our men was left *behind*? Why wasn't I told?' Angry now, he turned to his subordinates. 'Is a Trooper Caesar missing in action?'

'Not *Trooper* Caesar, sir,' said Baz. 'Caesar, Ben's super-sniffer.'

The general turned to him, looking puzzled. 'I don't understand.'

'Caesar's my EDD, sir,' said Ben.

'EDD? Ah!' A look of realisation lit up General Jones's face. 'Is that you, Corporal Fulton? I didn't recognise you under all that bandaging. You say that your dog was left behind?'

'Yes, sir,' said Ben. 'Caesar was with the last Humvee, but he'd been hit by frag and couldn't keep up.'

'Leaving an EDD behind is almost as bad as leaving one of our men behind,' the general said to his subordinates.

'Caesar might come into Python under his own steam, sir,' said Lucky. 'We hope so, anyway.'

'Caesar is our mate, sir,' said Baz, and all the other wounded SAS men in the ward agreed.

'Poor old Ben is miserable without him,' said Lucky. 'We have to get Caesar back, General! That dog is one of us.' Again, the other SAS men agreed.

'Leave it with me, men,' said Jones. 'We will do everything in our power to locate Caesar. You have my word.'

True to his word, Major General Jones returned to his office and drafted an order for all Australian personnel to be on the lookout for Caesar, wherever they were in Uruzgan Province. He then paid a visit to the American general in overall command at Tarin Kowt, and told him about Caesar. The American general, agreeing with General Jones that no soldier or dog serving in Uruzgan Province could or would be forgotten, issued an order to all troops in the province. That order required them to make it a priority to seek, recover and return Australian Army EDD 556 Caesar to Australian forces at Tarin Kowt.

Like many dogs, Caesar had a strong in-built homing instinct. Sensing that he had to go south to find Ben, after being frightened away from FOB Python, he began to slowly head in a southerly direction.

During his first full night on his own, Caesar came to a fast-flowing stream of clear, fresh water, and he lapped up his fill. He was hungry, but the water would keep him going for now. He slept under a bridge that night, then next morning limped across the bridge and continued south. His experience with the Afghan soldiers outside the gate of FOB Python made him wary of locals, so that whenever Caesar caught a whiff of the scent he associated with them, or heard vehicles approaching, he would leave the road and hide nearby. He spent his second night under the shelter of overhanging rocks. There he curled up in a brown ball and, hungry and exhausted, he slept a fitful sleep.

The next day, still limping and growing weak for lack of food, Caesar continued his slow journey southwards. Late in the afternoon, he picked up the scent of meat being cooked. Desperately hungry now, he followed it with his nose, leading him to a kal. Pausing outside, he sniffed the air. The scents he was picking up were all of Afghans, but overriding those was the aroma of stewing meat. His stomach now drove him forward. The kal gates stood open, so Caesar limped in through one of them. Away to his left, he heard children laughing. One of those children was a girl and her laugh reminded Caesar of Maddie. He limped in the direction of the laughter.

Two children were playing with an old car tyre, rolling it around a dusty compound. The girl whose laugh had caught Caesar's attention was eleven-year-old Meena. Wearing a shirt and trousers, Meena was playing with her ten-year-old brother Hajera, the youngest of eight children in their family. When Meena was little, because it was easier for her to say Haji than Hajera, she had called her younger brother Haji, and the other children of the family had followed her example. The very same year that Hajera was born, the children's father had undertaken the Hajj, the Muslim pilgrimage to Mecca, where the prophet Mohammad was born. And men who complete the Hajj often add the term Haji to their name to celebrate their act of faith. Because of this coincidence, the family had considered Hajera's nickname lucky. So, while the boy's official name would always be Hajera, within the family he was called Haji.

Now, Haji looked around and saw Caesar standing there watching them. Having established eye contact with the boy, Caesar sat down, still keeping his injured paw in the air, and looked expectantly at brother and sister. Perhaps, Caesar hoped, they would give him food.

'A dog,' said Haji, thinking aloud. 'Where did it come from?'

'This dog is hurt, Haji,' said his sister Meena. Letting go of the rubber tyre, Meena advanced toward Caesar, then squatted down in front of him and surveyed him. 'Where did you come from, dog?'

'Be careful, Meena,' said Haji, taking more care to approach the strange brown dog. 'Remember what Father says – wild dogs can bite and kill you.'

'This is not a wild dog, Haji. Look, he has a collar. This is a dog that is owned by some person. And look here.' She took hold of the severed end of Caesar's leash. 'This dog has run away from his owner. Or perhaps he was stolen.'

Finding more courage now, Haji also squatted in front of Caesar and studied him. Caesar, meanwhile, sat there panting, his pink tongue hanging out, in turn observing this boy in a long white shirt, white pants and small round white cap.

'Do you think, Meena,' Haji asked, 'that this dog's owner is a very important person? The President of all Afghanistan, perhaps?'

'The President of all Afghanistan lives far away in the city of Kabul, Haji. I do not think that his dog would run all the way here to our kal from Kabul. Do you?'

'Hmmm.' Haji thought for a moment. 'A governor's dog, perhaps? Or a general's dog?'

'A general's dog?' said Meena. 'It is possible, Haji. It is a very fine dog. If it is a general's dog, I would not be surprised if that general would pay a reward for his return. Father would be pleased.'

'And if it is not a general's dog, perhaps Father will allow us to keep it, Meena.' Haji was excited by the prospect.

Meena frowned. 'What do you mean, "keep it"?'

'As a guard dog, perhaps,' Haji suggested.

'Ah.' Meena nodded. 'It is true we no longer have a guard dog since our last one died. But Father would gain great honour if he were to return a general's dog to him.'

'This could well be our family's lucky day, Meena. And this could be a lucky dog.'

'This lucky dog looks thirsty, Haji. We should give it water to drink.' The two children filled a plastic container with water from the kal's deep well, then set it in front of Caesar, who drank it dry.

'This lucky dog was indeed thirsty, Meena,' said Haji, inspecting the empty container.

'Haji,' Meena said, looking around the compound, 'we should tie up this lucky dog so we can show him to our father when he returns home.'

Finding a length of rope, the pair attached one end to Caesar's collar and the other to a post. Caesar didn't resist and let them tie him up. The children had been kind to him, and he could smell that tantalising aroma of meat cooking coming from close by. For food, Caesar was prepared to put up with almost anything. Before long, a truck brought some of Haji and Meena's older brothers, sisters and cousins home to the kal from the village school. They, too, all squatted around Caesar and gazed at him. And Caesar gazed back.

'How do you know this is a general's dog?' said Haji and Meena's sceptical fourteen-year-old brother Nasir. Nasir was growing a wispy beard, and considered himself a man. He was jealous of Haji, who seemed to him to be the favourite son of their mother and father, and could do no wrong in their eyes.

'I did not say that he was a general's dog,' Haji replied. 'I only said that it *could* be a general's dog.'

'Why would a general's dog come to our kal?' said Nasir, standing straight again. 'This dog is a wild dog. Father will only shoot it, and then beat you and Meena for bringing it into our kal.'

'We did not bring it in,' Haji retorted. 'It came of its own desire. I think it is a lucky dog, and that it was meant to come into our kal.'

'And how could it be a wild dog, Nasir?' said Meena. 'See how it wears a collar.'

'Then it is a wild dog with a collar,' Nasir came back, with a shrug.

'How can a wild dog wear a collar?' Haji countered.

'Because . . . because it was in prison,' Nasir said, starting to walk away. 'A prison for wild dogs.'

'You are making that up,' said Haji. 'There is no such thing as a prison for wild dogs.'

'There is too,' Nasir called back over his shoulder. 'I learnt about it at school.'

'No, this is a lucky dog,' Haji said stubbornly.

Meena intervened. 'Father will know what to do with him,' she said with confidence.

That evening, their father, uncles, older brothers and cousins came in from the fields. Told of the new arrival, the children's father, who was headman of the compound, came to view the strange brown dog. Tall, slim and bony, like most adult men of Afghanistan, he wore a dark beard on his face and a turban on his head. His name was Mohammad Haidari. With a scowl, he studied the brown dog. Caesar, meanwhile, a little restless, kept moving positions from being seated to lying down, then back again. This man was an adult Afghan man, and Caesar had never been completely at ease with adult Afghan men.

'This is not an Afghan general's dog,' the children's father pronounced.

'It is not?' said Meena, disappointed.

'Look here, child,' said her father, bending and grasping Caesar's collar with its metal identification tag. 'This is written in a foreign language. This is an outsider's dog. And the only outsiders in our country with dogs are foreign soldiers. This is a foreign soldier dog.'

'A soldier dog?' said Haji, greatly impressed. 'Then, could we perhaps keep it as a guard dog, Father? We need a new guard dog. And what better guard dog could there be than a soldier dog?'

'A guard dog? This dog?' Haji's father laughed. 'Boy, look at it. Has it barked once? I am a stranger to it, yet it has not barked at me. That is the job of a guard dog – to bark at strangers and warn the household. Watch me now.' He held out his right hand to Caesar.

'Be careful, Father, the dog may bite you,' Nasir warned.

The children's father shook his head. 'This dog will not bite me, Nasir.' He continued to hold his hand under Caesar's nose.

Warily, Caesar sniffed the farmer's hand. Then, he licked it, as if to say, *Be my friend, mister*.

'You see,' said the children's father, withdrawing his hand with distaste and wiping it on his shirt. 'This dog would only lick intruders to death.' Nasir and some of the other older children laughed at this. 'Such a dog would be useless as a guard dog,' their father added.

Nasir was smirking. 'I told you so,' he said to Haji and Meena. 'You heard our father – this dog would be useless as a guard dog.' Nasir turned to their father. 'You should shoot the dog, Father, and beat Haji and Meena.'

With that, the children's father cuffed Nasir's ear with the back of his hand. 'Where is your respect, boy?' he growled. 'You do not tell your father what to do!'

Nasir let out a pained cry.

'Father,' said Haji, 'could we perhaps train this soldier dog to be a guard dog?'

His father shook his head. 'No, my little Haji. Such a dog cannot be trained to bark and bite. I have seen its like before. Such a dog will only wag its tail and eat our food. Get rid of it, Haji. Get rid of it, do you hear?'

'How should I get rid of it, Father?' Haji asked, clearly disappointed.

'How did you come by it, boy?'

'It just wandered into our kal, Father.'

'Then make it wander out again, boy,' said his father.

'Father, could you not sell the soldier dog back to the foreign soldiers?' said Nasir, trying to regain his father's favour.

But his father was a man who tried to steer a middle course in the war that gripped his country. And giving the dog back to the foreign soldiers might be seen in a bad light by the Taliban. 'No, Nasir!' he snapped. 'Haji, do as I tell you. Get rid of the dog! And, all of you, prepare for dinner.'

As their father strode off, the other children laughed at Haji and Meena, then hurried away to get ready for dinner as they had been instructed.

Haji looked at Meena, then at Caesar. 'Father did not say *when* I should make the soldier dog wander out again, Meena,' he said, with a cheeky grin.

Meena's eyes widened. 'You do not mean to keep the dog, Haji?'

Haji nodded. 'I will keep him for a little while. Perhaps we can train him to be a guard dog, and then Father will change his mind about him. You must help me hide the soldier dog, Meena.'

Ben was lying in another hospital bed, this time back in Sydney, Australia. He gazed dreamily out the window to the distant ferries and sailboats on Sydney Harbour, thinking and worrying about Caesar. Sensing that he was not alone, he looked around. Nan Fulton stood in the doorway with Josh and Maddie at her side. Nan had dressed the pair in their best clothes, and was holding a big bowl of fruit – a gift for Ben.

Both Josh and Maddie had shocked looks on their faces. Nan had tried to prepare them for the sight of their father with a heavily bandaged face, but the reality of that sight still rocked them. Between the bandages, Ben's eyes peered out through one slit, while his lips, cut and swollen, protruded through another. Nan brought the children to Ben's bedside.

Ben tried to smile, but that only hurt. 'Hey, don't you two look great!' he exclaimed.

'Daddy, can we kiss you?' Maddie asked.

'There's nothing to kiss,' Josh said, glumly. 'He's

all covered with bandages. He looks like an Egyptian mummy.'

'You can hold my hand, Maddie,' said Ben, raising a hand that had been protected by his combat gloves during the battle. Maddie took his hand, then stood holding it, and wouldn't let go.

Fighting back tears, Nan set the bowl of fruit down on the bedside table. 'I brought you some fruit, Ben.'

'Thanks, Mum.'

'Does it hurt, Dad?' said Josh, gazing at his father's bandages and puffed lips.

'Not a bit,' Ben lied.

'When are you coming home?' Maddie asked.

'Not for a while yet, sweetheart,' Ben replied.

'But you will get better?' said Josh anxiously.

'I sure will, mate,' Ben replied. 'These bandages will come off before long, and I'll stop looking like an Egyptian mummy.' He shifted, gingerly, to look at Josh. 'The doctors tell me my face will be a bit messy for a while, but they're going to tidy that up, and in the end I'll look like new.'

'It was the Taliban that did this to you, wasn't it, Dad?' said Josh. 'It was on TV, how you and a lot of other Australian soldiers were in a big fight with them.'

'It *was* a big fight,' Ben agreed with a sigh. 'You know that Charlie was badly hurt in that same fight?'

'Our Charlie?' said Josh, worriedly.

'But Charlie's not going to die, is he?' said Maddie with concern.

'No, princess, Charlie's not going to die. But, from what I've heard, he won't be able to walk. He's in hospital over in Germany and could be there for a long time.'

'He can't walk? Oh.' Maddie found the idea of big strong Charlie not being able to walk hard to come to terms with. 'Not at all? Ever?'

'I'm not sure,' Ben replied.

'And Caesar?' said Nan. 'What about him, Ben?'

'Yes, where's Caesar?' said Maddie. 'Will he be coming home with you, when you come?'

Ben paused. He had been dreading this moment. 'I'm afraid that Caesar is lost, Maddie, somewhere in Afghanistan.'

Maddie was amazed. 'Lost? Why?'

'Yeah, how come?' Josh echoed, with concern.

'Wasn't Caesar supposed to be looking after you?' said Maddie.

'He *did* look after me. Caesar helped save my life and a lot of other soldiers' lives while we were over there. He even helped save Charlie's life one time.'

'How?' Josh asked.

'He grabbed hold of Charlie's vest with his teeth, and dragged him into cover, after Charlie had been knocked out by an RPG blast.'

'Whoa!' Josh responded, impressed. 'So, how come Caesar's lost now?'

'We were separated during the battle,' Ben explained. 'I kept an eye on him for as long as I could. In the end, in all the chaos of the battle, he got left behind. I wanted the others to go back out looking for him, but they couldn't.'

'What will poor Caesar do all alone over there?' Maddie asked. She looked like she was about to cry.

'I think he'll try to find his way back to Australian soldiers,' Ben returned. 'I hope he will.' He gave Maddie's hand a reassuring squeeze. 'He's clever, and brave. If any dog can find his way back, Caesar will.'

'Poor Caesar,' said Maddie sadly. 'He must be very frightened.'

'The general told me that every soldier in the province has orders to be on the lookout for him,' Ben assured them all. 'Caesar will turn up. I know he will.'

'Yes, of course he will,' Nan agreed, also trying to put on a brave face.

'But we can play our part, too,' said Ben, as an idea formed in his mind. 'Josh, can you do me a favour? I want you to look for any information that might lead us to Caesar.'

Josh frowned. 'How do you mean, Dad? Where would I look?'

'Online. There are government websites, news sites

and podcasts. And then there's the radio and TV. They might mention that a brown labrador has been sighted, here or there in Afghanistan. Somewhere, sometime, someone might make mention of a sighting of Caesar. While I'm stuck here in hospital, you can help search for news of Caesar from home, every day.'

The responsibility suddenly seemed daunting to Josh. He looked worried. 'But, what if I miss something?'

'Don't worry, son, the more you look, the more likely it is you'll come across something.'

'Your dad's right, Josh,' said Nan. She realised that not only did Ben genuinely want to find Caesar, he had another motive. A year back, Josh hadn't been able to do anything to save Dodger, but now he could help save Caesar. It would be good for Josh, and Ben had recognised that it would give his son a cause to focus on while his father was in hospital. 'Josh, we owe it to Caesar to do everything we can to track him down,' Nan went on. 'Caesar didn't ask to be taken over there to Afghanistan, or to be left behind. We have to help him.'

'Yes, we have to help Caesar!' Maddie adamantly agreed.

'And, Josh, you're the master of the internet in our house,' Ben added. 'If anyone can find any mention of Caesar, you can. Will you do it every day, without fail, and report back to me?'

'It'll help your dad recover all the quicker, Josh,'

said Nan, 'knowing that you're on the job, looking for Caesar.'

'Well . . .' Still Josh hesitated, uncertain of himself.

'Think of it as detective work,' his father suggested.

'Detective work?'

'Yeah, detective work,' said Ben. 'Who knows what you'll turn up?'

'Do it for your dad, Josh,' Nan urged, 'as well as for Caesar. Go on.'

'If it's for Dad, as well as for Caesar, I suppose I could give it a try,' Josh agreed.

'Good on you, mate,' said Ben, producing a painful smile.

'I'll help look, too, Daddy,' said Maddie. 'Josh and me, we'll both be doggy detectives.'

Back in Afghanistan, Caesar was being hidden by Haji and Meena in a storage shed in their kal. Every night after dinner, Haji would sneak out to the shed and feed a little meat to Caesar – meat that he secretly kept from the evening meal. Sometimes it was goat meat, sometimes it was mutton. Occasionally it was chicken. And Caesar would gratefully wolf down all the food that his new young friend brought him. Except for the time Haji brought him a ball of spiced rice – Caesar only sniffed that, then left it alone. Meena often came with Haji, and she also brought a clean cloth with which she and her little brother bandaged Caesar's bloodied leg.

During the day, whenever he had a spare moment, Haji would sneak into the shed to see Caesar and talk to him. 'Soldier dog, you will make a fine guard dog,' Haji said to him one day, sitting in front of him. 'But you must learn to bark. Like this . . .' Haji pretended to growl, and then bark, like a dog.

With his head tilted to one side, Caesar looked at Haji as if to say, *What are you doing, my new friend? You aren't a dog.*

Not long after Haji left the shed, he bumped straight into his older brother Nasir.

'What were you doing in that shed, Haji?' Nasir demanded.

'Er, Father told me to tidy it,' Haji replied. It was no lie – his father had told him to tidy that shed . . . months before.

'Did I hear a dog growl and bark?' Nasir then demanded.

'Oh, that was me,' Haji replied, grinning cheekily. 'We do not have a guard dog any longer, so I thought I could make the noises of a guard dog to scare away intruders. Like this . . .' He growled and barked, as he had done in front of Caesar.

Nasir shook his head and rolled his eyes. 'What a

stupid little brother you are, Hajera Haidari. You cannot be a guard dog. Or would you have our father chain you up outside all night to frighten away intruders?' He laughed. 'Now that I think about it, that would be a very good use for a stupid, annoying little brother.' Laughing to himself, Nasir walked away. 'I will suggest it to Father.'

'I am not the stupid annoying brother in our family,' said Haji, half to himself.

For two weeks, Haji and Meena succeeded in keeping Caesar hidden from their father and from everyone else in their kal. But then, one night, Haji's secret was discovered. Because he was the youngest boy in the family, it was Haji's job to serve his father and all the older males at dinner every night, while Meena, the youngest girl, had to serve their mother and the other females. The men of the family ate in one room, and the women in another, as was the custom in Afghanistan. Dinner was a series of courses, usually various meats plus rice and vegetables. Haji would carry in plates loaded with one course or another from the kitchen and offer them to the diners one at a time. He would start with his father, the headman, then move to his uncles, then his brothers and cousins. If a male guest was visiting the kal, that guest would always be the first to be offered food. The diners, sitting cross-legged on cushions on the floor, would select food from the large plate and eat with their fingers. In the case of rice, they would roll it up into a ball to eat.

As the waiter, Haji was able to steal a little extra meat from the plate as he was serving, slipping it into a pocket of his trousers. Later, he would take the meat to Caesar. This meat would soil his pocket, but when his sisters washed his trousers once a week, along with all the other clothes from the kal, none of them paid attention to this. But one night at dinner, Haji's jealous brother Nasir happened to look up just as Haji, standing behind their father and uncles as they ate, slipped a piece of meat from the serving plate and into his pocket. Nasir frowned to himself at this odd sight, but said nothing. When the meal was over, Nasir watched Haji leave the room, then, suspicious of his youngest brother, followed him out into the night.

Droning noisily in a shed away to Nasir's right was a petrol-driven generator, which supplied a limited amount of electric power to their kal every night for cooking and light, and for radio or television broadcasts on special occasions. When everyone in the kal went to bed, it was one of Nasir's daily chores to turn off the generator. Hanging back in a doorway, Nasir watched as Haji crossed the courtyard illuminated by the bright moonlight and disappeared around a corner.

Hurrying to the corner, Nasir then peeked around it to see Haji walking toward a shed against the far wall. When Haji reached the door to the shed, he paused and looked back the way he had come, making sure he was not being watched. Seeing Haji stop, Nasir quickly withdrew back around the corner so Haji did not spot him. When Nasir looked back around again, Haji had disappeared inside the shed. Nasir quickly crossed the courtyard to the shed. And, putting an ear to the closed door, he heard Haji talking to someone inside.

In the shed, Haji lit a candle then knelt in front of the sitting Caesar. 'Here I am again, my friend,' he said. Taking a piece of meat from his pocket, which bulged with the night's food collection, Haji held it high in the air. Caesar's eyes were locked intently on the meat in Haji's fingers, his front legs quivering with anticipation. But, as hungry as he was, he did not move. The well-trained labrador was waiting for his cue.

'What must you do, soldier dog?' said Haji. 'What does a good guard dog do? Woof, soldier dog. Woof!'

Caesar barked, but once only.

Haji, knowing that the sound of the dog's bark would not be heard at this time of night because it would be drowned out by the noise of the generator, smiled broadly. 'Good, soldier dog,' he said. 'Again. Woof!'

Again, Caesar barked.

'Again. Woof!'

Caesar barked a third time.

'Very good, soldier dog.' Haji held the piece of meat out to Caesar, who gently, politely took it from the boy's hand and downed it. Behind Haji, the door suddenly burst open. With a gasp, Haji, still on his knees, swung around to see his brother Nasir standing in the open doorway.

'So, Haji, I have caught you!' Nasir declared, with a victorious grin on his face. He looked at Caesar. 'You disobeyed our father and kept this dog. You are in trouble now, little brother. Wait until I tell Father!'

'No, Nasir!' Haji protested in sudden fear. 'Do not tell him. Please!'

But it was too late. Nasir was already running back to the living quarters to inform their father of his discovery. Feeling as if the sky was about to fall in on him, Haji looked back at Caesar, who barked, as if to say, *Quick, give me the rest of the meat while you can.* Seemingly picking up the dog's message, Haji emptied his pocket and lay several more pieces of meat in front of Caesar, who quickly devoured them. Haji knew that it was pointless trying to run or hide. Getting to his feet, he moved over beside Caesar and sat down cross-legged beside him, then put an arm around the dog.

'Together, soldier dog,' Haji said with a sigh, 'we shall await my father and my punishment.'

Caesar responded by licking him on the cheek.

And so the pair waited. It was not long before Nasir returned, bringing with him their father, uncles, brothers and cousins. Haji's father had a fierce look on his face.

'See, Father?' said Nasir, almost dancing with glee as he pointed to Haji and Caesar.

'Hajera, my son, what have you done?' The boys' father stood in the open doorway glaring at the pair who sat together in the flickering candlelight. Both boy and dog looked guilty. The tone in the Afghan man's voice was enough to tell Caesar that the man was displeased, so Caesar lowered his head and did not look at him.

Haji decided to try to charm his father. Forcing a smile, he said, 'You did not tell me *when* I should make this soldier dog wander away, Father.'

'Do not be cheeky with me, boy!' his father growled. 'You disobeyed me!'

'But, Father, I thought that if I could train the soldier dog to be a guard dog, he would be of much use to you.'

'Is that so?' Haji's father returned. 'And have you trained this dog to be a guard dog? I think not.'

'I think not either, Father,' said Nasir, delighting in the moment.

'Be quiet, Nasir, I was not speaking to you,' he commanded, cuffing Nasir around the ear.

'Ow!' Nasir grabbed his stinging ear. 'But, Father –'

'Be quiet, Nasir.' Returning his attention to Haji, his

father said, 'Well, Haji? Have you trained this dog to be a guard dog?'

'Oh, yes, Father,' Haji replied.

'Then show me.'

'Yes, Father.' Jumping to his feet, Haji turned to Caesar. Hoping that this was going to work, and save him from a beating by his father, Haji lifted his right hand high as he always did when he had a piece of meat for Caesar. Caesar's eyes followed the boy's hand. Then, clicking his fingers, Haji said, 'Bark, soldier dog, bark! Woof! Woof!'

And, as Haji had hoped, Caesar barked. It was only a solitary bark, but it was a bark.

'You see, Father,' Haji said, smiling with relief. 'Now the soldier dog barks like a real guard dog. I have trained him to do it, you see?'

His father tried to hide a smile. 'One bark does not make a guard dog, my son. And would you stand on guard with him to tell him when to bark?'

'He can do more than bark, Father,' Haji insisted. 'He can chase intruders. See how he runs? Come, soldier dog.' Quickly untying the rope, Haji led Caesar past the men and out into the courtyard. There, he squatted and unfastened the now grubby cloth that Meena and he had tied around Caesar's injured leg. Fortunately for Caesar, the injury had not been serious and no bones had been broken. The deep cuts caused by flying mortar bomb fragments had healed during the past two weeks. But never again would fur grow on that part of the leg where he had been cut, and where an ugly weal would remain. While his paw was still a little tender, the pain had gone, and Caesar could once more walk and run freely.

Haji led Caesar on a run around the courtyard at the end of the rope. Caesar trotted along with a wagging tail. He was enjoying stretching his legs for the first time in weeks. Then Haji came to a halt and, while pointing a finger at Caesar, said, 'Sit, soldier dog.'

Caesar couldn't understand Pashto, the language that Haji and his family spoke. He could understand at least two hundred words in English, and had always immediately known what Ben meant when he said words like 'seek on', 'come', 'heel', 'stop', 'lie flat', 'sit', and so on. He also knew English words such as 'shoes' and 'newspaper', and would fetch both on command. He knew 'food', 'car' and 'swim', and would become excited when he heard them. He knew 'bath', and would try to hide when he heard that word. But he also connected various motions by Ben – and others such as little Maddie back in Holsworthy – with their commands. To Caesar, Haji's pointing finger meant he was to sit, so Caesar sat.

'You see, Father,' said Haji, proudly, 'the soldier dog obeys my commands.'

'Very impressive, Hajera,' said his father, 'but I fear that this dog is still not a guard dog that will bark and bite and scare away intruders. You must get rid of him. Today! Do you hear me?' His eyes narrowed. 'And this time, my son, you must not disobey me.'

At this point, one of Haji's uncles took his father's arm. 'Mohammad, a word,' he said, before steering Haji's father aside. Haji watched, full of hope, as the two elders of the family spoke in whispers for quite some time. Perhaps, Haji thought, his uncle was speaking up for him.

Then, Haji's father returned and said, thoughtfully, 'I am reminded by your uncle that we are to host an important visitor for dinner tomorrow evening. This important visitor may be interested in your soldier dog. The dog will remain, until tomorrow evening.'

CHAPTER 14

Every day, Josh and Maddie had phoned their father at the hospital, and every weekend Nan took them to visit him. After the first-time shock of seeing their father swathed in bandages, they had almost forgotten the bandages were even there. On their latest visit, Josh was especially excited. He had brought the Fulton family's laptop with him. He set up the computer on the roll-away table that usually went over Ben's bed at mealtimes.

'Here, Dad, look what I found,' said Josh, pointing to the computer screen. 'Like you said, I did lots of detective work. To begin with, I thought it'd be impossible – Google 'Caesar', and you get zillions of mentions of Julius Caesar, the ancient Roman general. But look here. See what I found on this website? There's a story about *our* Caesar. He's been seen in Afghanistan!'

Following Josh's pointing finger, Ben saw an article by an Australian newspaper reporter named Amanda Ritchie. Headlined 'Australian War Dog Missing in Action', this was the first mention by the Australian media of the fact that Caesar had been with the Special Forces during Operation Comanche, and of how he had been left behind during the battle outside FOB Python. Ben read the article, his heart beating a little faster toward the end of it when he saw the words: 'The Australian Army has recently received a report that their missing dog Caesar turned up at the gate of the forward operating base the night after the battle. The Afghan guards did not know that Caesar was missing and, thinking the dog a local stray, they shooed him away.'

Ben was smiling by the time he finished reading. 'Good job, son! This means that Caesar definitely survived the battle. He's out there in Uruzgan Province somewhere and he's alive.'

'Does that mean Caesar will be coming home?' Maddie asked.

'We hope so,' said Nan, placing a hand on the little girl's shoulder.

'He will,' said Ben definitely. 'Caesar will find his way back to Australian troops. I'd bet my last dollar on it. Meanwhile, Josh Fulton, super detective, keep up the good work, please. There are sure to be more mentions of Caesar on the net in future.'

Josh was smiling from ear to ear. 'You can count on me, Dad.'

180

A little fearful, Haji lingered in the doorway as the barefoot men sat down to eat. The family's special guest had arrived, and he was the first to sit in the circle of cushions on the floor of the dining room. Haji's father also took a seat, then turned to Haji and clicked his fingers. 'Food and water, boy. Bring the water for Commander Baradar and his men at once.'

The family's guest of honour was the famous Commander Baradar, the very same Taliban commander who Ben Fulton, Caesar and the Special Forces troops had hoped to capture during the failed Operation Comanche. The commander had come with two of his fighters, and now all three bearded, turbaned visitors joined the men of the Haidari family for dinner. A solid man with deep-set eyes, Baradar had ugly scars on the back of both his hands. These scars were a graphic reminder of burns he had received years ago during a US Air Force attack on the mountain cave where he had been hiding. After they sat down, he and his men placed their AK-47s on the floor in front of them, close enough to grab if they needed their weapons in a hurry.

Haji quickly brought bottled water and filled the cups of Commander Baradar and his men, and of the others present. This bottled water, purchased in the local village especially for the visitors, was more drinkable than the kal's well water. As Haji worked, he listened intently to the conversation that passed between the men.

'Thank you, Mohammad Haidari, for allowing my men and myself to eat with you,' said the Taliban commander.

'You honour my household with your presence, Commander Baradar,' said Haji's father, with a bow of the head.

Anxious not to miss any of the conversation, Haji hurried from the room to bring in the first plate of food from the kitchen. When he returned, the men were talking about farming and the weather. It was the Afghan way to take time to reach the actual subject of a meeting. It was only after many courses that Commander Baradar spoke of what was really on his mind.

'Mohammad Haidari, you know that devil soldiers of Australia took my father and uncle to prison in Tarin Kowt?' he said.

Haji's father nodded. 'I also heard that your uncle was before long released, Commander Baradar.'

The commander nodded. 'That is true. But my father is still being held. My father has done nothing to deserve being locked away, other than be the father of a son who fights the infidels. How many of your sons fight the infidels, Mohammad Haidari?'

'My sons are all very busy,' Haji's father replied. 'They either do their schoolwork, or help their father and uncles in the fields. We have many mouths to feed in this kal.'

'You could not spare even one son to join me and my men fighting the infidels?'

Haji's father shrugged. 'My first duty is to my family.'

'You know, Mohammad Haidari, the infidel generals say that in time they will beat the warriors of the Taliban because they have the superior weapons. But time is something we have much of. Time is our weapon. This is our land, and we have been fighting infidel invaders for a thousand years. And we have always won, in time. We have won because men, like yourself, have supported us. God willing, we shall win again. But the time has come for you to play your part in this war, Mohammad Haidari. You will give me a son to fight with my men, or you will allow us to use your kal to store weapons and ammunition, and allow us to hide here when we have need to hide. Perhaps you will do all three of these things.'

Haji's father had been expecting an ultimatum of this kind from the Taliban. For years, he had been polite to them, to the Afghan Government, and to the foreign soldiers who supported the government. He had never told one what he told the other, and he had been trusted by all sides. This war was not his war. He was from a different Afghan tribe to that of the Taliban leaders. He thought that the government in Kabul was corrupt, but he also thought that the Taliban were cruel and were trying to hold back his country. He particularly wanted his daughters to receive an education, and that was something the Taliban didn't agree with.

But, eventually, Haji's father knew, the day would come when he would have to choose sides. Whichever side he chose, it would be at the price of offending the other. If he chose the Taliban, he was sure that government soldiers would one day discover arms and ammunition if the Taliban stored them at his kal. Then he would be arrested and taken away, or, worse, an American jet could drop a bomb on his kal and kill his family. On the other hand, if he chose the Afghan Government, he knew that the Taliban would come to his kal, shoot him, and take his sons away to fight, and die, for their cause.

'I will need time to think,' said Haji's father with a sigh.

'Time?' Baradar smiled, revealing a mouth missing several teeth that had been lost in battle. 'Of course, my friend, you shall have time to consider. As I said, time is something we have plenty of in Afghanistan. One of my men shall return in a week for your answer.'

Then one of Haji's uncles said, 'Mohammad, tell Commander Baradar about the dog.'

'Ah, the dog,' said Haji's father, nodding. 'Commander, I have a gift for you.'

'A gift?' said Baradar with surprise. 'Is it not the custom for the guest to provide the gift?' Baradar had left the traditional gift of fruit at the door when he had arrived.

'This gift may be of some use to you,' said Haji's father. 'And perhaps it may show that my family can be of aid to you in ways other than those you suggest. Sometimes, it is useful to have a man such as myself as a *malek*, a go-between. In walking the road that separates you and the infidels, perhaps I can be of more use to you . . . over time.'

'Is that so?' Baradar returned, unconvinced.

Haji's father turned, and, clicking his fingers, called, 'Haji, bring the soldier dog for Commander Baradar to see. At once!'

Haji's heart sank. 'Yes, Father,' he glumly replied. Haji hurried out to the shed that had become Caesar's temporary home. Caesar was curled up, asleep, when Haji opened the shed door. 'Come, soldier dog,' said Haji, as Caesar opened his eyes and lifted his head. Tugging on the rope attached to the labrador's collar, Haji led Caesar out into the night. Then he paused, and, squatting down in front of Caesar, he whispered, waving his finger at him, 'Soldier dog, you must be a *bad* dog for Commander Baradar. He must not like you, do you understand? If he does not like you, he will not take you away, and then you will be able to stay here at our kal with me.'

Caesar cocked his head questioningly to one side, as if to say, *What's that, new friend? What are you saying?*

'Come, soldier dog,' said Haji. Rising to his feet, he led Caesar across the courtyard. Haji's father, Commander Baradar and his men, and all the men and boys of the kal came to stand outside the door to the building. Here, with several of Haji's brothers holding lanterns to light the scene, Haji presented Caesar to the commander.

'This dog, Commander Baradar,' said Haji's father, as they all studied the brown labrador sitting by Haji's side, 'came into my possession only recently. If you look at its collar, you will see that it bears the identification of a soldier dog of the foreigners.'

Baradar walked to Caesar and, bending, looked at the tag on the dog's collar. 'Indeed, an animal of the Americans or Australians,' he deduced. 'Two such dogs were seen with the infidel force that my men and I thoroughly defeated outside the base they call Python, some weeks ago. Could this be one of those animals, I wonder?'

'It is a very naughty dog, Commander Baradar,' Haji spoke up. 'It would not be of any use to you.'

Haji's father glared at him. 'Boy, you know that you only speak when you are spoken to! Not another word from you!'

'Yes, Father,' said Haji, dejectedly sinking his head onto his chest.

'I would be honoured, Commander Baradar, if you were to accept this dog as a gift,' said Haji's father. 'And to accept my services as a malek.'

'Indeed?' said Baradar, thoughtfully rubbing his whiskered chin.

Haji's father was clearly offering the Taliban leader a deal. If Commander Baradar accepted the dog, he would also have to accept the offer from Haji's father to act from time to time as a go-between, an envoy between the Taliban commander and the government and military. If Baradar did that, he would have to give up his demands that one of Haji's older brothers join the Taliban, and that the Haidari kal be provided as a hiding place for the Taliban's weapons, ammunition and fighters. On the other hand, Baradar knew that if he accepted the dog, it would add to his prestige among Taliban fighters to have a captured infidel soldier dog as his prisoner. That would be almost as good as having an infidel soldier as his prisoner.

'Of course,' said Haji's father as the Taliban leader hesitated, 'if you are not interested, I could offer this soldier dog to the government, to be returned to the soldiers who owned it.'

'No,' said Baradar firmly. 'It will not be necessary to do that. As you say, it is sometimes valuable to have a malek one can rely on. I will take the animal off your hands, Mohammad Haidari.'

'Then it is agreed?' Haji's father responded.

'It is agreed,' Baradar replied. Turning to one of his men, he said, 'Abdul Razah, you will take charge of the infidel soldier dog.' Abdul, an obese man with a double chin and a broken nose, came forward and snatched the rope from Haji's hands.

'You will be kind to him?' said Haji, softly, to the Taliban fighter, realising that Caesar was being taken from him. 'He is not really a naughty dog.'

'Dogs are a burden, boy,' said Abdul gruffly. He looked down at Caesar. 'Dogs are only good for eating.'

Caesar, looking up at Abdul, began to emit a low growl. He had taken an immediate disliking to this man.

'You cannot eat my soldier dog!' Haji protested.

'Be quiet, my son!' Haji's father said with exasperation. 'No one will be eating this soldier dog. Is that not so, Commander?'

Baradar nodded. 'This infidel soldier dog is much too valuable to go into a cooking pot.'

The three Taliban men shouldered their rifles, then, with a traditional touch of cheeks, farewelled Haji's father and thanked him for his hospitality. But as Baradar and the third man headed for the gate, Caesar refused to budge when Abdul pulled on the rope, planting his front legs in front of him. In response, Abdul kicked the dog in the ribs. Caesar let out a yelp of pain and, rather than receive another kick, reluctantly allowed the man to haul him out of the kal.

Haji, standing with the other men of the family and

watching the Taliban party depart, said, half to himself, 'Farewell, soldier dog. I will not forget you.'

Standing behind Haji, his brother Nasir was smirking. 'See, little brother, how foolish it was of you to try to keep the soldier dog for yourself. You are only a child, and soldier dogs are the business of men.'

Haji did not reply, but only watched until he saw the last trace of Caesar's drooping tail passing out the gate as he was led away by the Taliban. Haji could not know, nor could any of the members of his family know, what the future held for Caesar. Little could they imagine that Caesar had many adventures ahead of him in Afghanistan. Adventures that would make him famous.

CHAPTER 15

In a busy Sydney cafe, newspaper reporter Amanda Ritchie looked up from the laptop on the table in front of her and saw a uniformed man standing across the room at the entrance. The man wore the khaki slouch hat of an Australian soldier and had two stripes on his sleeve, denoting that he was a corporal. This, Amanda decided, must be the Corporal Ben Fulton who had arranged to meet her here. Smiling, she waved at him, catching his eye. He nodded, then began to make his way toward her. The cafe was close to full, and was noisy with lively chatter and the sounds of coffee-making. It was December. Christmas decorations hung on the walls and there was a sense of seasonal joy in the air.

With a bob of thick blonde hair, Amanda was slim, and dressed in a jacket and jeans. Closing her laptop, she rose to her feet and held out her hand in greeting. 'Corporal Fulton?' she asked.

'Call me Ben,' he replied, shaking her hand. She reminded him a little of his late wife, Marie. Same hair colour, similar age. And she had the same confident air about her that Marie had possessed.

'And I'm Amanda,' she said, sinking back into her chair. 'Please, join me.'

'Thanks.' Ben sat down across the table from her, removing his hat as he did.

Only then did Amanda get a good look at Ben Fulton's face. She gasped as she took in his battered, lumpy cheeks and chin, still red and raw.

'Not a pretty sight, am I?' Ben remarked, with an embarrassed smile. 'Frag wounds,' he explained. 'From a mortar. The docs tell me they can make me look like new with plastic surgery, but I have to wait awhile for the scar tissue to settle before they'll operate. Meanwhile, I have to live with this face. My kids, Josh and Maddie, and my mum got used to it faster than I did. Only took a week after the bandages came off for them not to notice any more.'

'You got that in Afghanistan?' she asked.

'Uh-huh. Confidentially, I was involved in the Special Forces engagement you wrote about a couple of months ago – the one outside FOB Python.'

'Oh, yes. But you're not SAS?' Amanda had been writing about the military long enough to know that SAS soldiers wore a sandy-coloured beret, not a slouch hat like the one Ben had arrived wearing.

'I'm with the IRR, the Incident Response Regiment. I'm Caesar's handler. Or, at least, I was.'

Amanda frowned. 'Caesar? I'm sorry, I don't . . .'

'Caesar, the explosive detection dog. The one that went missing during that mission.'

A look of realisation came over the reporter's face. 'Ah, of course! Caesar was *your* dog? You must have been really upset to lose him over there.'

'Devastated. I still am. That's why I asked you to meet me.'

'You want to talk to me about your dog?' she said, sounding disappointed. 'When you rang the office and asked to meet me, I thought you might want to give me some juicy military secrets to print in my paper.'

'I was hoping you would be the one providing the information, Amanda.' He tried to put on his most appealing smile.

'Such as?'

'Where did you hear that Caesar hadn't returned from that operation?' Ben said, leaning in. 'The Australian Army never officially released the news.'

'I heard it from an American officer in Tarin Kowt. I was over there on assignment at the time and he happened to mention it in passing. Apparently all the troops in Uruzgan knew the story about an Australian war dog missing in action. The American officer joked that maybe Caesar had been deliberately sent on a secret mission behind Taliban lines, but had become a prisoner of war. Cute idea, don't you think?' She grinned.

Ben wasn't smiling. 'Cute? Not really. Caesar has been missing for a couple of months now. Winter has set in over there in Afghanistan. If Caesar's not with people who will look after him, he'll die.'

Amanda's grin quickly faded. She now looked embarrassed. 'Sorry. You and that dog must have been pretty close.'

'Caesar was like my brother, and in other ways like my child. It's hard to explain. Without him, I feel like I'm missing my right arm. And he was as much a soldier as I was. At least I volunteered for what I do – Caesar had no choice. I was responsible for him and I let him down. *I* left him behind.'

Amanda was feeling guilty now. 'It was insensitive of me to joke about your dog like that. Forgive me.'

'Do you have a dog?' Ben asked.

'No, I travel too much for my job to keep a dog. My daughter would love one, but she's at boarding school. If I had a dog, it wouldn't be fair on the animal – locking it up in kennels every few months when I go away on news assignments.'

Ben nodded. 'Most people,' he said, 'especially those who don't have dogs of their own, don't appreciate the bond that exists between an EDD and his handler – and the handler's family. My son, Josh, has been scouring the net every day for any mention of Caesar. So far, your article is the only thing we've found – the only news we've had of him.'

'That must be rough on you and your children.'

'Yes, but in a way, Caesar's loss has brought my family closer together. Before I went to Afghanistan on my last tour of duty, my boy wasn't a big fan of Caesar. But since Caesar has been missing, Josh has dedicated himself to helping me find him.'

'That's good to hear.' Amanda smiled.

'The problem is, both my children have been losing sleep worrying about Caesar. Even if we learn that Caesar is in Taliban hands, at least we'll know he's alive. I was hoping, Amanda, that you might be able to use your contacts to give us some hope to hang on to. It occurred to me that reporters like you hear things – rumours, gossip – that they don't always end up using in their media reports. Even a rumour about Caesar's whereabouts would be a great Christmas present for my family.'

Amanda nodded. 'I'll see what I can do. I'll try the contacts I made with the Australian and US military while I was in Afghanistan. I can't promise anything, Ben, but I'll give it a try. Where are you going to be? Are they sending you back to Afghanistan soon?'

Ben shook his head. 'I'll be at Holsworthy for a while. In their wisdom, my superiors have decided to send me on a promotion course, to get my sergeant stripes. At least I'll have Christmas with my family.'

'Okay, Ben. Let me see what I can find out for you and your kids.' She held out her hand.

As Ben took her hand and firmly shook it, he looked into her eyes. When he departed the cafe, he felt sure, from what he'd seen in those eyes, that Amanda Ritchie was genuine, and that he could count on her to do all she could to help him find Caesar.

Outside the caves, the snow was a metre deep. Deep inside the mountain, a series of caverns had been fashioned into quarters for Taliban fighters, with beds, heating and cooking facilities, ventilation equipment, and lavatories. Many Taliban fighters went home to their families for the winter – back to the kals, villages and towns they came from. Some Taliban fighters were from neighbouring Pakistan, and they crossed back over the mountains to cities and towns there. Other men who fought for the Taliban were from more distant Muslim countries and they, like the better known Taliban leaders, spent the winter in the eastern mountains bordering Afghanistan and Pakistan to await the spring melt and new campaigning season.

In these particular caves, Commander Baradar and the core of his insurgent fighting group lived out these winter days, only occasionally venturing out to obtain information and supplies, and to bury IEDs to be activated in the spring. With the reduced Taliban force this winter was a brown labrador – their prisoner. Caesar's coat had grown thick for the winter, as labrador coats do. While he was being fed daily, the quantity of food was not great and, as a result, he had lost a lot of weight. For many weeks, Caesar was left in a dark corner of a cave and only saw Abdul, his keeper, once a day when he brought Caesar food. Then, one evening, Commander Baradar came with Abdul.

'The animal is looking thinner,' Baradar remarked, surveying the Australian dog as it sat, tied via a three-metre rope to a ringbolt in the stone wall, waiting for his food. 'What are you feeding the infidel soldier dog, Abdul?'

'Scraps,' Abdul grunted.

'Improve the animal's diet,' Baradar commanded. 'Give it more meat.'

'Why would I do that?' said Abdul. 'Our supply of meat is poor. Even we must eat meat sparingly over the winter months here.'

'Because, Abdul Razah,' said Baradar, with rising anger, 'I am the commander here. I do not have to explain myself to you or anyone else.' He paused to calm himself, then went on. 'Because I am a wise man, I shall share my wisdom – even with a fool such as you. There is no point keeping this infidel soldier dog. I have decided to exchange it for my captive father and a great deal of American money. With that money, we shall buy much ammunition and explosives in Pakistan.'

'How would such an exchange be arranged?' Abdul asked, sceptical.

'With the coming of the spring, I shall send a malek to the infidels to propose such an exchange. And when they demand proof that the dog is alive, you shall photograph it on a mobile telephone to show them. But the dog must look well-fed if I am to win my price. Now do you understand why this dog must eat more meat even than yourself, Abdul Razah?

'Yes, Commander, I understand,' Abdul sulkily replied.

CHAPTER 16

Ben walked out of an office at Holsworthy army base. It was March, and Ben had just been informed that he had passed his examination and been promoted to sergeant. He had also received orders to take over the training of a new EDD after its assigned handler had come down with a long-term illness. This news both pleased and saddened Ben. It meant that he could get back to doing what he did best – working with elite explosive detection dogs – but it also meant that now Caesar had been missing for six months, the Australian Army had given up all hope of finding him.

As he was walking, Ben's mobile phone rang. When he answered, a female voice said, 'Hi Ben, this is Amanda Ritchie.'

'Oh, yes, the reporter. Hi, Amanda.' Ben hadn't heard a word from her since their meeting just before Christmas, and he'd recently been thinking of contacting her again to push for information. Now, his heart rate increased in sudden expectation. 'Do you have any news for me?'

'Actually, Ben, I thought you'd like to know, I've heard from one of my American contacts in Uruzgan Province.' She paused. When Ben said nothing, obviously waiting for her to tell him whether the news from her contact was good or bad, she continued. 'The US Army there has been approached by a malek who says he's operating on behalf of the Taliban's Commander Baradar. This guy says that Baradar has your Caesar and is willing to exchange him for his father and $100,000 in cash.'

Ben's mouth dropped in astonishment. 'You're joking! Is it a hoax?'

'No, seems like the approach is for real. This malek even showed the Americans a photo of a brown labrador, on his mobile phone.'

'Amanda, this is amazing!' said Ben, with a rare outburst of excitement. 'How did Caesar look? Was he fit and well?'

'Ben, slow down, slow down! The malek says that it's Caesar in the photo, but there's no way of knowing for sure – the picture could be of any brown labrador.'

'I know, I know,' Ben responded, taking deep breaths to calm himself. 'So, what's the US Army going to do about it?'

'They're asking for proof of life. They want to see this dog in the flesh. But I've got to warn you, Ben, even if this dog *is* Caesar, my contact doesn't think the US would agree to the price. And I know the Australian

Government wouldn't pay $100,000 for him. That's like paying ransom for a terrorist hostage – and they never do that.'

'They'd find a way of paying $100,000 if the Taliban were holding one of their men,' Ben retorted with frustration.

'They might be able to haggle the figure down . . . There is another problem. It's unlikely the Afghan Government will agree to release Baradar's father – not as a trade for your dog, or anything else.' Realising this sounded discouraging, she added, trying to be more upbeat, 'But you never know what might eventuate. I'll keep you posted.'

When Ben ended the call, he had new hope of Caesar's return. But as he drove home that evening, he weighed up in his mind whether he should tell Josh and Maddie the news. Would it raise their hopes of Caesar's return, only for those hopes to be dashed if the brown dog on the malek's phone turned out not to be Caesar?

It eventuated that he didn't have to make that decision anyway – Josh and Maddie already knew. When Ben pulled into the driveway, his two children were waiting for him at the front door with big smiles on their faces. Both ran to him as he climbed from his vehicle.

'Dad, Nan helped me find stuff about Caesar on the net,' said Josh excitedly. 'The Taliban have got him, and they're trying to sell him back to us. Come see!'

'Yes, Daddy, come see,' said Maddie, taking Ben's hand.

They led him inside to the computer, where Josh showed Ben the Facebook page of an American soldier in Afghanistan. It told the same story Amanda Ritchie had passed on to Ben that afternoon – of the malek and the offer from Commander Baradar for the return of Caesar in return for the release of Baradar's father and a large sum of cash. The soldier also said that the malek had told the US military his own son had looked after Caesar following the battle outside FOB Python, and that the Taliban had later come and taken the dog from him. Ben, Josh and Maddie couldn't know that this malek was none other than the father of Haji Haidari, who was keeping his promise to Commander Baradar by acting as an envoy between the Taliban leader and the foreign military.

'We will get Caesar back, won't we, Daddy?' said Maddie, studying her father with wide, trusting eyes.

Looking up, Ben saw his mother standing in the doorway, wiping her hands on her apron. And he saw the look on her face that signalled the need for a cautious approach in case things didn't work out and the children faced a big let-down. But Ben's own determination to be reunited with Caesar, no matter what, shone through. 'We sure will get him back, princess,' he replied, giving Maddie a cuddle. 'I'll do whatever it takes to get Caesar back, don't you worry. And Josh, keep up the good work on the net. You told me about this even before the army did!'

'I'm on it, Dad,' said Josh, smiling proudly.

Later that night, when Josh and Maddie were in bed asleep, the Fultons' house phone rang. When Ben answered, he found, to his surprise, Major General Michael Jones on the line, calling all the way from Tarin Kowt, Afghanistan. Generals usually don't telephone sergeants – and certainly not from halfway across the world.

'Fulton, I promised you six months ago that I would do everything I could to get your EDD back,' General Jones said. 'Well, it looks like Commander Baradar might have him.'

'I know, sir,' Ben replied. 'I'd already heard. Baradar's offering a swap – Caesar for his father, and $100,000.'

'News travels fast.' The general sounded surprised. 'Of course, we're not going to give the Taliban $100,000. They'd only buy more arms and ammunition to use against us. And we would have to convince the Afghan Government to release Baradar's father. But, first things first. We need to establish that this dog really is Caesar. Can you email me a good photograph of him? One we can compare with the photo the malek's provided.'

'Right away, sir,' Ben responded, enthusiastically. 'By the way, my gut feeling is that it *is* Caesar that the Taliban are holding.'

'Mine too,' the general agreed.

That night, Ben didn't email General Jones a photo of Caesar – he sent him a dozen, showing Caesar's head from a variety of angles.

The next day, Amanda Ritchie's newspaper ran her story about the latest turn of events, the headline reading: 'Taliban Demand Ransom for Aussie War Dog'. Ben, while trying to prevent Josh and Maddie from becoming too excited about the possibility of Caesar's return, was determined not to let this opportunity slip. Picking up the telephone, he sought a meeting with his local member of Federal Parliament, Warren Hodges MP, aiming to get him to push the Australian Government for Caesar's return.

It helped that Hodges had once been an officer in the Australian Army. Hodges knew all about EDDs, and since publication of Amanda Ritchie's latest newspaper article about Caesar, which had been followed up by countless other newspapers and radio and TV stations, he had been following Caesar's story with keen interest. He agreed to a meeting at his electorate office.

When they got together that weekend, Ben was able to tell Hodges that General Jones had come back to him the previous night. The general had said that he and his staff in Tarin Kowt had compared the Taliban's photo of the brown labrador with the pictures of Caesar that Ben had sent, and were ninety per cent certain that Caesar was indeed the dog in Taliban hands. The main problem now was meeting Commander Baradar's ransom demands for Caesar.

'It's a tricky situation, Sergeant Fulton,' said Hodges to the uniformed Ben, who now wore the three stripes of a sergeant. 'Officially, the Australian Government will never agree to pay the Taliban a cent. But this Baradar character might settle for a much lesser amount than $100,000. If he did, is there any way you could organise the money?' He looked questioningly at Ben.

Ben hesitated for a moment then said, 'You mean, set up a "Bring Caesar Home Fund" that people could donate to? My kids have suggested we do that.'

Hodges shook his head. 'No, our government would frown on something as public as that. It would signal to the world that Australia was giving in to the insurgents' demands. Personally, I'm all for doing whatever it takes to get your EDD back, but the ransom money would have to be raised secretly. And that wouldn't be easy.'

'If it was a matter of a few thousand, sir, I'd gladly pay it out of my savings to get Caesar back,' Ben quickly volunteered. 'Even if it was $10,000.'

'Okay, good,' said Hodges, nodding. A fit-looking, broad-shouldered man with a very military-style moustache, he decorated his office with photographs from his years in the army. It was as if, in his heart, he had never entirely left the military. Helping Ben, a serving soldier, was something Hodges felt compelled to do, like helping a brother. 'Hopefully, a much smaller figure can be negotiated,' he went on. 'The other problem we have to overcome is getting the Afghan Government to agree to free Baradar's father from prison.'

Ben, recognising that the MP was already talking in terms of 'we', a sign that he was very much on Ben's side, asked, 'Can we put pressure on the Afghan Government to do that, Mr Hodges? To free Baradar's father?'

'I'm not sure.' Putting his hands behind his head, Hodges lay back in his chair. 'We'll have to go to the top,' he said, thinking aloud. 'We might be able to call in a favour from the President of Afghanistan to get his government to order the authorities at Tarin Kowt to release Baradar's father. There are a few things the Australian Government has done for the president behind the scenes over the last few years. He owes us. Let me see what I can do.'

Ben rose from his seat and shook the MP's hand firmly and gratefully. 'Thank you, sir. And my children thank you.'

Coming to his feet to walk Ben to the door, Hodges smiled. 'Sergeant, I too have young children. And you know what they said to me once the story about Caesar and the ransom offer broke in the media? They said "Daddy, we have to get Caesar back!". So, you see, you and your children are not alone in this.'

A couple of weeks later, in late March, Ben told Nan to prepare Josh and Maddie for a special visitor. A human visitor. Then, on a Saturday morning, a taxi equipped to carry passengers in wheelchairs pulled up outside 3 Kokoda Crescent. As Josh and Maddie peeked curiously out the front window's louvre blinds, their father walked to the taxi's rear door. Ben's wounded face had lost its red-raw appearance. His cheeks and jaw were still lumpy, but before many more months had passed he would go into hospital to start having those bumps smoothed out in the first of a series of plastic surgery operations.

With a loud hum, an electric ramp at the rear of the taxi lowered a wheelchair-bound figure to the ground. Taking hold of the wheelchair's handles, Ben began to wheel it up the front path. The figure in the wheelchair was dressed in army uniform, had sergeant stripes on his sleeves, and wore a sandy-coloured beret. A blanket covered the lower part of his body.

'Charlie!' Maddie cried with glee. 'It's our Charlie!'

'I thought he was in hospital!' Josh exclaimed with a mixture of surprise, excitement and delight.

The two Fulton children rushed to the front door, and with Nan following along behind, came running down the path to greet Charlie. Both gave him a hug, making sure to do so with care, knowing that Charlie was still recovering from very serious battle wounds.

'When Dad said we were going to have a very special visitor, I never imagined it would be you, Charlie,' said Josh.

Maddie looked at the blanket covering Charlie's legs. 'Does it hurt, Charlie?' she asked. Her father had told them that both of Charlie's shattered legs had been amputated by the doctors in Germany – one below the knee, the other above the knee.

Charlie smiled. 'No, it doesn't hurt, Maddie. And haven't you both grown since I last saw you.'

'We're a year older now,' said Josh. 'Hey, can we play computer games while you're here?' Then Josh had a disturbing thought, and he wondered if Charlie could still play computer games now that he was in a wheel-chair. 'Or . . .'

Charlie could just about read his mind. Smiling, he said, 'Josh, I might have lost my legs, but I still have my hands – and my wits. I reckon I can still whip you in any video game you care to name.'

He could, too. Josh and Charlie played computer games for an hour before they all sat down to lunch, and Charlie won every time. 'He beat me!' said Josh with amazement, as he took his place at the lunch table. 'Every single game.'

Thrilled to have their father's best friend back with them, the children chattered away over lunch, and after months in sterile hospitals, Charlie enjoyed every minute of the family atmosphere.

'I'm a little bit famous at school,' said Maddie, 'because Caesar is my dog.'

'Me too,' said Josh proudly. 'I've had to give two talks about Caesar – one to my class and one to the whole school. Kids I never even knew before keep coming up to ask me if there's any news about Caesar coming home. Just about every kid in the school wants to meet him.'

Charlie smiled at Ben. 'Looks like the whole family misses Caesar,' he said, with a wink. He could remember back to the last time he was here, when Josh wanted nothing to do with Caesar.

Ben gave him a wink in return. 'They sure do.' Ben was quietly thrilled with the way the entire Fulton family had pulled together during the Caesar crisis. Josh had his old spark back, and Maddie just seemed to meet every crisis with acceptance – and curiosity.

'Charlie,' said Maddie, 'will you always have to live in a wheelchair?'

'Not always, Maddie,' Charlie replied. 'The doctors will give me artificial legs one day, but that won't be for a while yet.'

'So, you'll be able to walk?' Josh asked.

Charlie nodded. 'Roger to that, Josh. Eventually, I will.'

'How will you walk?' Maddie wondered out loud. 'If the doctors took away your real legs, or part of them –'

'Now, don't pry, children,' said Nan.

'But, if one of Charlie's legs is shorter than the other now . . .?' Maddie persisted.

'Maddie, what did I tell you?' Nan scolded her.

'That's all right,' said Charlie. 'Josh and Maddie can ask me whatever they like.' He turned to Maddie with a reassuring smile. 'I'll learn to walk with the artificial legs, Maddie. Prosthetics, they're called. One prosthetic will be longer than the other, so, between the two of them, they'll even me up and I'll be back to my old height.'

'You should get them to make you really long artificial legs,' Josh suggested. 'You know, so that you're three metres tall and tower over everyone. That would be really cool! You could go in the Olympics and run really fast. And the high jump – you'd win the gold medal in that, easy.'

'Steady on, Josh,' Ben spoke up. 'Before Charlie does any running or jumping, he'll have to learn to walk again in the prosthetics.'

'Really?' said Josh with surprise.

'The doctors tell me I'll be a bit like a baby learning to

walk for the first time,' Charlie explained, 'but I'll master it.'

'That's funny,' said Maddie, giggling. 'You being like a baby.'

Josh laughed too, and Charlie smiled a tight smile. But behind the smile, Charlie the war hero was quaking a little at the thought of having to learn to walk all over again. It wasn't the pain he was worried about – Charlie could take all the pain that was dished out to him. And he was totally confident that he would master artificial legs, and be back to walking and running again one day. But for someone who had been so independent and physically active all his life, the thought of having his life on hold for months, maybe years, and having to depend on others to help him in the meantime, was daunting. But for the outside world, and for his 'family' at 3 Kokoda Crescent, he would put on a brave face and pretend that nothing bothered him.

'When will you get your artificial legs, Charlie?' Josh asked enthusiastically.

'Not for a year or two yet, mate. I've got a bit more surgery to go through before I'm at that point. In the meantime, this wheelchair will get me around just fine. Give me a couple more months to build up my arm strength and I'll race you.'

'A race?' said Josh with a perplexed frown. 'How?'

'Me in the wheelchair, and you running.'

'Really?' Josh grinned. 'I'll beat you.'

Charlie laughed. 'We'll see about that, mate.'

The phone began to ring. Excusing himself, Ben left the table and answered it. When he returned a few minutes later, he was beaming.

'Good news?' Charlie asked.

'The best news possible,' said Ben. 'That was Warren Hodges, the MP, on the phone. He rang to tell us that the President of Afghanistan has agreed to release Commander Baradar's father in exchange for Caesar.'

Josh, Maddie and Nan all cheered in unison.

'Apparently,' Ben went on, 'the president couldn't understand why we would go to such lengths to get a dog back.'

'Ah, but the president doesn't realise that Caesar is not just any dog, mate,' said Charlie.

'What happens next, Ben?' Nan asked.

'Now,' said Ben, 'we wait to see if the Taliban will present Caesar in the flesh, to prove that the dog they're holding really *is* Caesar. Once that's been sorted out, and a reasonable sum of ransom money has been agreed to, then an exchange will be set up. Caesar could be returned to us within weeks!'

The week after Charlie's visit, Ben was back at EDD training school. The new dog he had taken over was a sandy-coloured labrador named Soapy – but Ben felt the dog would be better named Dopey. Soapy had passed the obedience phase of his training, but when it came to detecting explosives he could be lazy and unreliable. Some days, Soapy would be on the ball and find every trace of explosives and pass every test. Other days, he would quickly lose interest and want to follow any intriguing scent he came across. It was clear Soapy didn't possess Caesar's intelligence, character or endearing ways. He didn't even have any of Caesar's bad habits, like a compulsion for digging. Compared to Caesar, Soapy was a very ordinary dog. But, Ben told himself, Caesar was an exception, and few other dogs in the world could match up to him.

Although the difference between the two dogs made him think of, and miss, Caesar all the more, Ben persisted with Soapy's training. Tens of thousands of dollars had already been spent getting Soapy to this point – and Ben had gained a reputation as one of the best EDD handlers in the Australian military – so he was not going to give up on the new dog. Soapy would never make it to Special Forces training the way Caesar had, but when Soapy was focused, he *could* detect explosives. That made him worth persevering with.

Besides, Ben's spirits were high. Word had come from Afghanistan that, in exchange for Caesar, Commander Baradar was prepared to accept $10,000 in addition to his father's return. This was way down from the $100,000 originally demanded. When Ben had heard this, he'd immediately gone to his bank and transferred $10,000 of his own money into a separate account. He'd then emailed Major General Jones in Tarin Kowt with details of that account and had told him to use the money to pay Baradar when the time came for Caesar's return.

This was all highly irregular – and unofficial. General Jones was helping Ben behind the scenes because he had given his word to do everything in his power to get Caesar back. If and when the money was handed over, the general could still officially deny that the Australian Government had paid the Taliban a cent, because it would be Ben Fulton's money that was paid as ransom for Caesar. Ben and the general did worry about the Taliban using the money to buy weapons and ammunition, but both consoled themselves with the thought that this was the only way they could save Caesar's life. Both knew that if the Taliban failed to receive the ransom they were demanding, Caesar would be of no use to them and they would most likely shoot him.

One afternoon in early April, just as Ben was locking Soapy away in the Holsworthy kennels for the night, his mobile phone rang. When he answered, he found the caller was General Jones.

'Major General,' said Ben, with sudden expectation. 'Any word of an exchange for Caesar?'

'Fulton,' said the general in a flat voice. 'I regret to say the news is not good. Things have been complicated by a death, I'm afraid.'

'A death?' Ben's heart almost missed a beat. 'Not Caesar, Caesar's not dead?'

'No, no, no. As far as we know, Caesar is still alive and well. It's *Baradar's father*. He's had a heart attack in Tarin Kowt Prison. The man is dead.'

Ben was so shocked he couldn't speak. Without Baradar's father, there was nothing left to swap for Caesar other than money. Ben began to calculate how much more money he still had in the bank.

'Fulton, are you there?' said the general.

'Will Baradar still exchange Caesar, sir?' Ben now asked. 'For more cash?'

'We don't know,' was Jones' sobering answer. 'The whole deal for Caesar's return could fall over now. We can only wait to hear from Baradar's malek again. Keep your fingers crossed that Baradar will still want to do a deal. If not, you may have to prepare yourself and your family for the possibility that we will never see Caesar again.'

Commander Baradar was praying when a messenger arrived at his camp in the hills. With the spring, Baradar and his men had moved down from the mountains to resume their attacks against the troops in the valleys. Already, they had blown up several American military vehicles with IEDs. Agitatedly, the messenger waited for Baradar to complete his prayers.

When, finally, Baradar rose up from his knees and folded away his prayer mat, the messenger approached him. 'Commander, I bring grave news from Tarin Kowt,' he announced.

Baradar scowled. 'What manner of grave news?' he demanded.

'Commander, I regret that your esteemed father has died. In the prison at Tarin Kowt.'

Baradar became suddenly ashen-faced with shock. 'My father . . . dead? How?'

'The provincial governor says that your father died from a heart attack in his prison cell.'

'Heart attack?' Anger began to boil inside the Taliban commander. 'My father's heart was strong!' he declared. 'He could not die from a heart attack. Not my father. Of all men, not my father.' He looked away to the south, in the direction of Tarin Kowt. 'The government has murdered him! That can be the only explanation. And they are trying to cover it up by calling it a heart attack. They must have tortured my poor father, an old man, and he died at the hands of the torturers. I know it!'

Abdul Razah was standing close by when the news was delivered. 'What now of the exchange for the infidel soldier dog, Commander?' he asked.

'The infidel soldier dog?' Now, Baradar's face was red with rage. 'Give me your gun.'

'My gun?' said Abdul. 'Why?'

Reaching out, Baradar ripped away the AK-47 that was draped over Abdul's shoulder. Automatic rifle in hand, Baradar strode to where Caesar was tethered and lying down. Abdul and the messenger hurried along on Baradar's heels. Coming to a halt in front of the dog, who sat up, Baradar pointed the AK-47 at Caesar's head. 'Accursed animal!' he exclaimed, close to tears.

Caesar, sensing peril, lowered his head, but continued to look the threatening Afghan in the eye.

Baradar's finger curled around the rifle's trigger. Then, after a long pause, the commander lowered the weapon. 'No,' he said. 'There is a better way.' He thrust the AK-47 back into Abdul's hands. 'We will honour my father's memory in a more glorious way. We shall send this infidel soldier dog back to its masters.'

'You will give the dog back to them?' Abdul could not understand his commander's sudden change of heart.

'This we shall do,' Baradar affirmed. 'And this soldier dog will take many infidel lives. You, Abdul Razah, will fashion a suicide vest for this animal.'

'You mean to make it into a suicide dog?' said Abdul, with amazement.

Baradar nodded. 'You have made such suicide vests before, for humans. Now you shall make such a vest for this infidel dog. Pack the vest with explosives, Abdul. Then, we shall send the dog back to its masters. The dog will run to them, wagging its tail with joy. And when it is among them, *I* shall have the joy of detonating the explosives in the vest by mobile telephone. Begin work at once, Abdul. With this dog, God willing, much infidel blood will be spilt in revenge for my beloved father.'

With Caesar tethered by rope several metres away, watching him guardedly, Abdul sat on a rock and toiled over the vest that Baradar had ordered him to make. Using canvas, shears and a large needle, he worked away creating a vest that would wrap around Caesar's body, and which would contain pockets for plastic explosives. All the while, he mumbled complaints to himself. 'This is a woman's work!' he moaned. 'Bad enough that a man should have to be keeper of a dog. Now I must make a vest for that dog while my brothers are away dealing death to our enemies.'

Suddenly, Abdul noticed that Caesar had become alert. The dog's ears had risen. Abdul did not know it but Caesar had picked up the high-pitched whine of a helicopter in the distance. As the sound grew nearer, Caesar rose, with twitching ears, to a sitting position. To Caesar, helicopters and Ben went together like tennis balls and fun. The deeper sounds made by the approaching heelo now reached Abdul's ears. 'Infidel helicopter!' Abdul yelled, warning the few insurgents who had remained in camp with him.

Abdul and his comrades threw themselves into hiding and watched as a US Apache gunship passed overhead, several thousand feet up. The insurgents did not fire at it – that would only attract attention to their hidden camp. Meanwhile, Caesar also watched the helicopter pass. Seeing it continue on, he barked at it, repeatedly, as if to say, *Ben, Ben, I'm down here!*

'Stupid infidel dog!' Abdul growled, once the helicopter had gone from sight.

It took Abdul a day and a half to complete the vest. When he was satisfied that it was finished, he made

Caesar stand, then knelt beside him. Wrapping the vest over Caesar's back, he felt beneath his chest and tugged roughly on the canvas ties that would secure the vest in place. In a flash, Caesar turned his head and bit Abdul's hand. Caesar had never bitten a human before in his life, but he had grown to hate this particular human who treated him so badly.

'Yow!' Abdul cried, jumping to his feet and wringing his hand. 'Evil infidel dog!' To punish him, Abdul crashed a booted foot into Caesar's side. Letting out a yelp, Caesar scampered away, as far as his tethered rope would allow. But Abdul was not finished with the brown dog. Looking at his hand, and seeing blood flow from where Caesar's teeth had pierced the skin, Abdul cursed, then bent and picked up his AK-47. He stomped to where Caesar now stood facing him. The dog's teeth were bared, and a savage growl rumbled deep in his throat.

'Evil infidel dog. I will teach you who is master here!' Abdul raised the wooden butt of the AK-47 to crash it down on Caesar's skull. Caesar, seeing the blow coming, ducked out of the way, then leapt to the attack and nipped Abdul on the ankle. Abdul went hopping away, holding his ankle and yelling with pain, 'Devil of a dog! Devil of a dog!'

Furious now, Abdul turned the barrel of his AK-47 toward Caesar. Pulling the trigger, and without taking proper aim, Abdul let off a burst of fire. Bullets kicked the stony ground in front of Caesar, sending him reeling back.

Summoned by the noise of gunshots, sixteen-year-old Omar, a new Taliban recruit, came running, fumbling with an AK-47 he had never fired in anger. 'What is it, Abdul?' he anxiously asked. 'Why did you shoot?'

'This devil dog bit me!' Abdul exclaimed, balancing on one foot to relieve the pressure on his paining ankle, and grimacing at the sight of his bleeding hand. 'Twice!'

'But you cannot kill this dog,' said Omar. 'Commander Baradar has plans for it.'

'I know, I know,' Abdul conceded. 'You try tying that vest around the devil dog.'

Putting aside his rifle, Omar slowly approached Caesar. Omar didn't want to be a Taliban fighter. His father had sent him to fight for Commander Baradar's band. 'Good dog,' he said to Caesar. 'I will not harm you.'

There was a scent of innocence about this youth that Caesar associated with his friend Haji. Feeling little threat from Omar, Caesar allowed him to fasten the vest beneath his chest.

'There,' said Omar to Abdul. 'What was the problem, Abdul Razah?'

Abdul glared at the youth, then at the dog, but did not reply. Both had made him look a fool.

The next day, Commander Baradar and a party of Taliban fighters returned to the camp after staging a raid in which several of their members had been wounded. But Baradar wasn't interested in the wounded – he was most interested in the infidel soldier dog. Going over to where Caesar was tied up and wearing the suicide vest, he stood there looking admiringly at it.

'A worthy effort, Abdul Razah,' Baradar said approvingly, smiling as he surveyed the dog vest. 'It is good. Now show me how it appears with explosives.'

Abdul went away, soon returning with packages of plastic explosives, which he handed to Omar. Abdul had made pockets on the sides of Caesar's vest large enough to snugly hold packets of explosives and a mobile phone that would be used to detonate them from a distance. Once Omar had slid the explosives into the pockets, Abdul stood back with Commander Baradar to study his handiwork. Meanwhile, Caesar was made restless by the scent of explosives right beside him, and he alternated uneasily between sitting and lying down.

'Observe, brothers,' said Baradar proudly, as other fighters crowded around to see. 'Our band will be the first to use this new weapon, the suicide dog. Our children and our children's children will speak of us with awe in times to come.'

'Where shall we use this new weapon, Commander?' asked one of his men.

'At Tarin Kowt,' Baradar revealed. 'This animal came from the infidel base there. And there, too, my poor father was killed in prison by our enemies. At Tarin Kowt we shall return the infidel soldier dog to his masters – and kill them. This act will strike terror into the hearts of soft-headed infidels who hold the life of a dog equal to that of a man. All of you, prepare to break camp at dawn tomorrow. We will move south to Tarin Kowt, staying at friendly kals along the way.'

For several days, Baradar's Taliban band moved south, walking by night, sleeping by day in the kals of farmers who were either sympathetic to the Taliban or were too afraid to turn them away. All the way, Caesar was tugged along at the end of a rope by Abdul, who would kick him if he attempted to pull back.

The insurgent band was fifty kilometres from Tarin Kowt, their destination, when they arrived in the early hours of the morning at their next stop, a kal. It was like many kals that Caesar had been in before, with low buildings and courtyards surrounded by a high mud wall. Abdul locked Caesar in a small shed several metres wide and built against the kal's western outer wall. For travelling, Abdul had removed the suicide vest he had made for Caesar. As he had done whenever they'd halted on the march, Abdul put Caesar in an outbuilding, throwing the suicide vest in with him, complete with explosives in its pockets.

The vest confused and unsettled Caesar. Its scent of explosives was so powerful it almost blocked out every other scent. This was the scent that Ben had trained him to detect. And every time that he had found that scent, Ben had been pleased with him and had rewarded him. Caesar could not rest. Sometimes he lay down. Other times he sat. In between, he paced around the locked shed. A rope was still attached to his collar, although Abdul had not tied the other end to anything. He hadn't thought it necessary as there was a padlock on the door, ensuring that Caesar could not get out. This meant that Caesar could roam around the earth floor of the shed, with the rope trailing across the dirt behind him. He went over to the explosives vest and nosed it time and again, before pacing restlessly around and around the shed once more.

The sun rose and, with several of their men on watch, most of Baradar's Taliban fighters lay down in the kal's buildings to sleep through the day. The residents of the kal went about their usual daily routine, pretending that they did not have guests. The morning passed, and in the storage shed Caesar was still pacing. The presence of the explosives vest was playing on his mind, and he began to obsess about finding a way to escape from this place so he could rejoin Ben.

One of his circuits of the earth floor brought Caesar to the western wall of the shed, which was actually the outer wall of the kal. When he made a closer inspection, Caesar's nose detected that the earth floor at one point smelled different from the surrounding dirt. Caesar could not know it, but the owners of the kal had dug a short tunnel from that very spot inside the shed the previous year. The tunnel had been for Taliban fighters to use as an escape route when they were staying there, if Afghan Army or foreign soldiers paid the kal a visit. But when the US Army and Australian Army had begun to search every kal in the valley for signs of the Taliban later that year, the residents had quickly filled in their tunnel, fearing that the troops would recognise its purpose and arrest them as Taliban sympathisers.

Now, Caesar's acute nose could detect the difference between the disturbed earth of the tunnel and the packed earth around it. Caesar began to dig. As the replaced earth of the tunnel was not as compacted as the soil around it, Caesar's scooping paws swiftly made an impression on it. Soon, he had created a hole a metre deep. Occasionally, he would take a break to lap up dirty water left for him in a bowl by Abdul. His front legs ached, but he would not stop, and he quickly resumed digging. Through the afternoon, Caesar continued to dig down, then, following the course of the old tunnel, he dug parallel to the ground and under the wall.

Twilight was falling over the valley. At a town away in the distance, a Muslim *mullah*, or priest, was singing a wailing song into a microphone, calling local people to evening prayer at the town mosque. At a spot outside the western wall of the kal, the earth began to crumble and fall away. A hole appeared. And then Caesar's snout emerged from the earth.

Carefully, Caesar poked his head out and sniffed the air, studying all the scents on the evening breeze. Hearing the chatter of men and boys coming in from the fields, Caesar ducked back down into the hole and waited for them to pass. The next time he poked his head up, not a soul was to be seen or heard – or smelt. Satisfied that no Afghans were now close by, Caesar wriggled back down into the hole. With difficulty, on all fours, he backed his way through the tunnel, re-emerged inside the shed and went to where the explosives vest lay. Clamping his teeth around a corner of the vest, he carried it to the tunnel. Pushing the vest ahead of him with his nose, he again struggled through the tunnel. Ben, he was certain, would want this vest. At one point, a little earth fell from above and almost covered his head. With a snort and a supreme effort, Caesar pushed on.

By the time it was dark, Caesar was shoving the vest up through the hole under the wall and out into the open. With a flurry of legs and dirt, he dragged himself out of the tunnel. First, he gave himself a vigorous head-to-tail shake to remove the loose dirt clinging to his coat. Then, he listened intently and sniffed the air for sounds and scents of danger. Confident that all was clear, Caesar again picked up the vest, and, with it between his teeth, trotted away from the kal, the rope attached to his collar trailing behind him.

About five hundred metres away from the kal's western outer wall, Caesar stopped to gain his bearings, then turned south. Determined to find Ben, and to please him by bringing him the explosives vest, Caesar resumed the trek to Tarin Kowt that he had begun eight months before.

It was several hours later that Abdul came to the outbuilding to feed Caesar. In one hand, he carried a burning oil lantern. In the other, he carried a little portion of cooked meat on a plate. Ever since the death of Commander Baradar's father, Abdul had deliberately reduced Caesar's meat ration. He himself had eaten most of the meat allocated by Commander Baradar to the dog. Setting down lantern and plate, Abdul took a key from his pocket and unlocked the door. Pushing it open, he entered the shed with lantern and plate.

'Here is your ration, infidel dog,' he growled. 'I hope you choke on it!'

Then Abdul froze. Nowhere could he see the dog. Setting down the plate, and frowning in disbelief, he searched the shed from top to bottom with lantern held high. He could not believe it – the dog had vanished. Once more, Abdul searched high and low. Only on his second search did he notice a dark patch in the floor beside the western outer wall. Walking closer, he dropped to his knees, and discovered the hole that Caesar had dug. Lowering the lantern into the hole, he could see that this was a tunnel that led out under the wall. The blood drained from Abdul's face as he realised what this meant. Getting to his feet, he hurried from the shed and, with a waddling run, went to the room where Commander Baradar was dining with the men of the kal.

Bursting in, Abdul breathlessly exclaimed, 'Commander! Commander! The infidel soldier dog has escaped!'

Baradar turned to him with a furious scowl. 'How can the dog have escaped? How could you permit this, Abdul Razah!'

Abdul, dreading punishment by his intolerant superior for allowing their prisoner to escape, gushed, 'It is not my fault, Commander – there is a tunnel!'

'A tunnel?'

Abdul thought fast. Not in a million years would he have given the dog credit for digging his own way to freedom. 'The infidel devil soldiers must have tunnelled into the kal to rescue their dog.'

'Show me,' Baradar snapped, pulling himself to his feet.

Abdul led his commander to the outbuilding, as the other Taliban fighters came running to find out what the commotion was about. Inside the shed, Abdul showed Baradar the hole in the ground through which Caesar had made his escape.

'See there, Commander. As I said, a tunnel dug by the infidels.'

'Why would the infidels have gone to so much trouble to rescue their animal?' said Baradar, accepting Abdul's assumption that someone had tunnelled into the outbuilding to rescue Caesar. Baradar failed to notice that the earth from the tunnel was spread around the floor of the shed. If someone had dug their way in from outside, as Abdul suggested, earth removed from the tunnel would have to be on the outside. 'Perhaps it was locals who helped the animal escape,' Baradar mused, thinking back to the kal where he had been presented with the dog, and remembering how the headman's youngest son had resisted parting with the animal. 'Perhaps it was the family of Mohammad Haidari.'

Abdul shook his head. 'The devil soldiers came to rescue him. I'm sure of it, Commander.'

'Why would they do that?'

'I have heard that Westerners place microchips beneath the skin of their dogs.'

'Yes, I too have heard this,' Baradar acknowledged. 'What is the relevance to this dog and its escape?'

'Could it be that the Americans have invented a new weapon – one that they bury beneath the skin of dogs?' said Abdul, his imagination running wild.

'Yes, that is the very thing that the evil Americans and their allies would do,' Baradar agreed, stroking his beard as he thought. 'They send unmanned drone aircraft against us. Why, indeed, would they not send unmanned dogs against us? This could be a new turning point of the war.'

'Was the dog meant to explode among us?' said Abdul, thinking aloud. 'Did it have explosives implanted beneath its skin?'

Baradar shook his head. 'I think not. Why then did it not explode while it was among us? No, they have done something more sophisticated with this dog. They must have implanted a listening device and transmitter beneath its skin, allowing them to hear our every word for many months past. That animal was an infidel spy dog!'

'No!' Abdul gasped, horrified. 'They must have heard all our plans for the spring campaign. Now that I think of it, Commander, that infidel dog raised its ears much too often for my liking. I think it must have an antenna implanted in its ears, and every time it raises them, it transmits to the infidels. I saw with my own eyes how it one day summoned an infidel helicopter.'

Baradar was not listening to Abdul's fanciful deduction. Intent on recapturing the four-legged escapee, he stormed out into the night. 'All of you,' he called to his men, 'the infidel dog has escaped!'

'With the help of infidel devil soldiers,' Abdul added, coming behind Baradar.

'It is a spy dog, and must be recaptured!' Baradar told his men. 'If indeed infidel devil soldiers were involved in its escape, we will track them down. If locals helped the dog escape, they will be made to suffer. But while that animal remains on the loose, it poses great danger to us. The dog is all-important. Normal operations are suspended until that brown dog is brought to me. I must discover the secrets that the spy dog carries.'

'And if any of you see it raise its ears, beware,' said Abdul. 'It will probably be transmitting your location to the enemy and calling in a drone or helicopter strike.'

'Go now, all of you!' Baradar commanded. 'You too, Abdul.'

Unshouldering their weapons, Baradar's men hurried out the kal gates. In the darkness, they began to search the surrounding countryside for the escaped dog.

All the talk of Caesar being equipped with a secret microphone and transmitter was fanciful, of course, although Caesar did carry a microchip. After he passed EDD school it had been implanted painlessly beneath the folds of skin at his neck. It contained his army identification details – and that was all. Otherwise, there was nothing special or threatening to the Taliban about EDD 556, apart from the fact that he had pluckily succeeded in escaping from them. And Caesar's escape would go on to disrupt all Taliban offensive operations in Uruzgan Province, as Commander Baradar called in more and more Taliban fighters to join a frantic search for the fugitive labrador.

CHAPTER 18

With no word back from Afghanistan about whether Commander Baradar was willing to exchange Caesar for cash, Ben, Josh, Maddie and Nan Fulton had tried to get on with their lives and think about other things, hoping that good news would soon reach them. Ben's biggest fear was that the Taliban had killed Caesar after learning of the death of Baradar's father. Then, one day in late May, during a lunch break at the EDD school, Ben received a phone call from reporter Amanda Ritchie.

'Ben,' said Amanda, 'I thought you'd like to know that there are two interesting rumours doing the rounds over in Uruzgan Province.'

'Rumours involving Caesar?' Ben asked anxiously.

'One most definitely is. According to what the Americans are hearing on the ground, Caesar has escaped from the Taliban, and is on the run.'

Ben whooped with joy. 'This is fantastic!' he exclaimed. 'Do they know how he escaped?'

'Something about our Special Forces digging a tunnel to reach him. But I've spoken to Major General Jones and he says that no Special Forces mission has been mounted to rescue Caesar. What have you heard?'

'General Jones would've told me if there was a Special Forces mission to get Caesar out,' Ben assured her. 'What was the other rumour?'

'It may not be connected with Caesar,' Amanda replied. 'Then again, it may be. According to the second rumour, the Taliban in Uruzgan Province have suspended their normal spring operations to conduct a manhunt.'

'A manhunt . . . for who?'

'Supposedly for some mysterious spy.'

'A spy?' Ben was intrigued. 'Does this spy have a name?'

'That's the curious thing, Ben. According to the rumour, the Taliban are calling this spy 'brown dog'. The Americans think that 'brown dog' must be a codename for the spy. But could it be that the Taliban are really referring to Caesar?'

Ben smiled to himself. 'Knowing that dog as I do, Amanda, I would have to say that anything is possible. It would be just like Caesar to totally disrupt the Taliban in Uruzgan.'

That night, Ben was able to go home with the good news that Caesar had escaped from Taliban hands. This news meant that the Fulton family could again hope that

Caesar would find his way back to Australian forces, and come home to them.

Ahead, Caesar could see a river slicing across the flat valley plain. It was dawn, and he had been on the run for more than two days since escaping from his Taliban captors. Several times, he had seen and heard Afghan voices and civilian vehicles in the distance, and each time he had avoided them. Coming to the shaly river-bank, he set down the vest containing the explosives. Carrying the vest all this time had made his jaws ache, but Caesar was determined to take it to Ben – it was his driving quest. Giving his jaws a rest, he drank from the fast-flowing river of green water.

Caesar's ears pricked up. Hearing vehicles approach along the dirt road running beside the far riverbank, Caesar grabbed the vest and quickly ducked into the long grass to hide. From here, lying flat, he watched the road beyond the river. Before long, a convoy of heavy trucks and armoured vehicles lumbered into view and began to pass Caesar's position. All the vehicles were sandy-coloured, and the uniforms and equipment of the soldiers riding in them looked familiar to Caesar. They were, in fact, US Marines.

Caesar knew at once that they were friends. Deciding

to try to reach the convoy, Caesar took up the vest and came out of hiding, trotting over the shale to the water's edge. Putting a paw in the water, he felt the water temperature. It was cold, but not too cold. Taking the plunge, and still clutching the vest between his teeth, Caesar launched himself into the river.

A fast current was soon drawing him along, taking Caesar away from the trundling convoy. Meanwhile, the vest in his mouth grew heavy, and it took all his strength to keep his head above water. By the time he had reached the middle of the river, Caesar could no longer maintain his grip on the vest and was forced to release it. Unhappily, he watched the racing waters take the almost-submerged vest further and further away from him. And then he could see it no more. Focusing on the far bank now, he paddled toward it with greater ease.

Emerging from the water, he shook himself, then climbed up onto higher ground beside the river. The convoy had come and gone. A dust cloud hung on the still morning air, marking its passage. Running to the road, Caesar could just make out the last vehicle far, far away. He barked in the convoy's direction, as if to say, *Look, here I am, friends! It's me, Caesar!*

But the convoy was too far away for him to be heard. Then the last vehicle disappeared from view and Caesar was alone once again. Returning to the river, he trotted along the bank for some distance, trying to spot the vest in the water or washed up on the bank. But the vest had sunk. Eventually giving up the search, Caesar turned away from the river, deciding to follow the road south. Increasingly hungry, weary, and dejected at losing the vest that had been so important to him, he recommenced his journey.

Skirting around villages and kals, Caesar kept moving all day until, late in the afternoon, on a fresh breeze, he caught a whiff of meat cooking. Leaving the road, he followed the tantalising smell of food across a field, to a side road. Ahead, on a rise, stood a battered old van. A canvas awning stretched from the side of the van, forming a sort of tent. A fire glowed outside this tent, with a bubbling pot above it. Two young men sat on boxes at the fire, talking animatedly to each other. Remaining downwind of the men so that he could smell them but they couldn't smell him, and sinking onto his chest, Caesar studied the scene and analysed the scents that reached his powerful nose.

The two men that Caesar observed certainly sounded and dressed like Afghans but seemed to him to be different from the Taliban fighters and farmers he had come in contact with. Although both men wore turbans, only one had a beard and it was neatly trimmed. There was no military scent about them or their vehicle. With the Taliban, Caesar had always been able to smell a hint of explosives on them, even the common aroma of the oil they used to clean their AK-47s. There was none of that scent about these men. They smelled more like Haji and the men of his family. And Haji had been his friend. But the most important scent of all to Caesar was the delicious smell of meat cooking. He began to drool at the thought of it. Driven by the demands of his empty stomach, he made the choice to risk approaching these men in the hope they would give him food. Rising up, he slowly padded toward the pair at the fire.

One of the men, the bearded one, stopped talking. He had seen Caesar out of the corner of his eye. 'Brother, do you see what I see?'

Caesar, realising he had been spotted, froze in mid-step.

The second man followed the gaze of the first. 'A dog,' he said, sounding a little afraid. 'Is it a wild dog, brother?'

'No, see, it wears a collar, to which is attached a rope,' the first responded. 'It is only some stray kal dog. A runaway.' Coming to his feet, he folded his arms and glared at Caesar. 'Go away, dog!' he yelled, stamping his feet. 'Go away, I say!'

Caesar did not move a muscle.

The clean-shaven man reached down and picked up a stone from the ground. Then, getting to his feet, he tossed the stone at Caesar. Seeing the stone coming, Caesar nimbly sidestepped it. The man picked up another stone and, taking careful aim at the dog this time, threw it. Again, Caesar avoided the missile. Resuming his original pose, he stared at the men and at the cooking pot on the fire.

'Go away, dog!' the second man yelled impatiently. Grasping an unburnt end of a piece of wood from the fire, he threw it at Caesar.

In the fading light, the burning end of the piece of wood flared red and orange as it tumbled through the air toward Caesar, glowing sparks flying from it. Even though the throw was accurate, Caesar not only didn't let the piece of firewood hit him, he jumped into the air and caught the unburnt end in his mouth!

The bearded man, grinning broadly, was so impressed that he applauded Caesar. 'Did you see that, brother?' he said with delight. 'That is a talented dog.'

Given confidence by this reception, Caesar trotted up to the pair with the burning wood in his mouth. Dropping it at the foot of the man who'd thrown it, he sat and looked up at him expectantly, his tongue hanging out.

'A talented dog indeed, brother,' said the clean-shaven man. 'Perhaps it would like to join our little troupe.'

'That is not such a bad idea, brother. Shall we give this talented and skinny dog some of our meal?'

'Why not?' The clean-shaven man smiled. Like his elder brother, he could see the dog's potential.

So, Caesar was invited to join the two men for dinner, and he gratefully sat and ate the meat they shared with him, then, to the amusement of the pair, he licked their one serving plate clean. When the food had all been consumed, Caesar sat in front of the pair, licking his chops and looking at them, as if to say, *Okay, what's next?*

'You see the dog's collar, brother?' said the bearded man. Both men could speak and read a little English. 'This is the collar of a foreign military dog. American? British? Australian, perhaps? Such dogs are very well trained by the soldiers.'

'Very well trained indeed,' the other agreed with a smile.

'So, talented and very well trained dog,' said the bearded man to Caesar, 'let us introduce ourselves. I am Ibrahim and this is my brother Ahmad. We are travelling acrobats and jugglers. We are like a two-man circus.'

Caesar angled his head to one side and looked at Ibrahim with a puzzled expression.

'Perhaps this dog has never seen a circus, brother,' said Ahmad.

'Then let us show him what we do,' said Ibrahim, getting to his feet.

Ahmad went to the van, quickly returning with three rubber balls. Caesar's eyes flashed with recognition. Rubber balls? He loved nothing better than chasing rubber balls. He fixed his eyes on the balls as Ahmad proceeded to toss them into the air and juggle them. Caesar was mesmerised by the sight of the flying balls. He had never seen anything like it before in his life. Grinning at Caesar's rapt attention, Ahmad added two more balls and juggled all five. When he missed one, the ball dropped to the ground and bounced away. Caesar's eyes followed it, tracking it like radar. His front legs quivered. How he wanted to chase that ball!

'Fetch the ball, intelligent dog,' said Ibrahim, pointing to it.

It was the cue he had been waiting for. In a flash, Caesar was up and giving chase. Moments later, he returned, dropped the ball at Ahmad's feet, then sat, panting excitedly, hoping that Ahmad would throw it again for him to fetch. In his mind, he could picture Ben and Maddie, and long, happy hours in days past spent playing with tennis balls.

'Brother,' said Ibrahim, 'I think this must be our lucky day. This dog has much potential to become a part of our act.'

'And it does not have to be paid,' Ahmad returned with a laugh.

'Let us show the dog the shoulder juggle.'

Ahmad climbed onto Ibrahim's shoulders, and while balancing there on his brother's shoulders, he juggled three balls. Caesar sat looking at this in amazement.

Seeing the balls flying high above him, he stood up on his back legs, and pawed the air, trying to reach them.

'Very good, intelligent dog,' said Ibrahim, grinning. 'Welcome to our troupe. You are now our third brother.'

As the brothers' van drove up to the gates of a remote military base near the border between the provinces of Uruzgan and Kandahar, Caesar was sitting happily on the front seat between Ibrahim and Ahmad. Realising that Caesar's Australian Army collar would identify him to the foreign troops, and cause them to take Caesar from them, the brothers had removed the collar and buried it. In its place, they had simply looped a piece of rope around his neck.

Ibrahim and Ahmad made a living by touring throughout Afghanistan, performing for foreign troops at outlying bases like the one just ahead. They didn't perform for Afghan troops – those men were poorly paid and had no money to spare. Foreign troops were much better paid. Neither did the brothers perform at large bases such as the one at Tarin Kowt, where many Australians were stationed, and where Caesar had lived with Ben. Those larger bases often received visits from overseas entertainers, and small local acts like that of the brothers could not attract an audience. Men at the outlying bases, on the other hand, were starved of enter-tainment, and they welcomed the brothers, often giving them big tips if they enjoyed their act.

Most of the troops at this base were American, and open to watching the brothers perform. But a wary and difficult Afghan Army captain needed convincing that he should give his permission.

'What is this act of yours?' the squat, perspiring officer demanded. 'What is it you do? What is your background? Where did you learn English?' He glared at Caesar. 'And what is the purpose of the dog?'

'When we were boys in Kabul, sir,' Ibrahim explained, 'we trained as gymnasts, using old Russian equipment and inadequate Afghan facilities.'

'All the while, we were dreaming of competing for our country at the Olympic Games,' Ahmad added with a sad shrug. 'But that dream was not to be.'

'It was while we were in Istanbul, Turkey,' Ibrahim went on, 'studying for degrees, learning our English, and learn-ing from Turkish television that Westerners have a curious affection for pet animals, that we heard the Taliban had been driven from power in Afghanistan. We returned home to our country full of high hopes, sir, only to learn that our parents had been killed in the Taliban's last days of power. Our father had been a teacher – a professor.'

'We also learnt, sir,' said Ahmad, 'that our degrees could not feed us here.'

'It was then,' said Ibrahim, continuing on from his brother, 'that we turned our acrobatic skills into an occupation. We did not expect that we would also become animal trainers, but we have.' He looked down at Caesar, who sat at his feet guardedly observing the Afghan officer – the man had the scent of explosives on him, which unsettled Caesar.

'What we do does not make us rich, sir, but it puts food in our mouths,' said Ahmad.

'And food in the mouth of our dog,' Ibrahim added with a grin. 'In fact, this dog eats almost as much as we do!'

Urged by his American colleagues, the Afghan officer permitted the brothers to proceed with their act. In a courtyard, with high walls and machinegun towers surrounding them, the brothers performed for the US soldiers, who stood or sat there watching them while still carrying their weapons. Afghan soldiers at the base, meanwhile, paid them no attention. At the beginning of the performance, Ibrahim introduced their new, enlarged act, as he, Ahmad and Caesar stood before the gathered troops, with all three performers deliberately wearing borrowed US military helmets.

'Gentlemen of America,' Ibrahim began, in English, 'we are the Three Brothers. I am Ibrahim, and these are my brothers Ahmad and Intelligent Dog.'

This introduction brought a resounding laugh from the troops. 'Which one's the dog?' someone joked in the audience, generating more laughter.

The brothers had spent several weeks teaching Caesar circus tricks. His best trick was to jump in the air and catch balls tossed by the brothers. In another part of the act, he jumped over the pair as one knelt on all fours while the other balanced with one hand on his brother's back. Later, Caesar dived between their legs as both lay on their backs with their legs forming a 'V' in the air. With the brothers patting and praising him, and the audience applauding, Caesar's tail wagged more than it had since he'd been separated from Ben. At the end of the show, Ibrahim led Caesar around audience members with a US marine's floppy cap in his mouth, seeking money. As Caesar nosed around the audience members, soldiers patted him, spoke to him and parted with their cash. The hat was filled several times over.

'Intelligent Dog liked the American soldiers,' said Ibrahim as they later counted their takings in their van.

'More importantly, brother, the American soldiers liked him,' said Ahmad.

'This was one of our most profitable performances of all time,' Ibrahim remarked as they rolled up their newly gained American dollars, with Caesar watching on.

'Intelligent Dog is a swift learner. We must teach him many more tricks.'

'And he will earn us many more dollars,' said Ahmad with a grin.

Little did the brothers know why Caesar had so eagerly passed among the American audience members. His nostrils filling with familiar scents of soap, shaving cream, freshly washed uniforms and a Western diet, and hearing English spoken, Caesar had been looking for Ben.

CHAPTER 19

In the Fulton household, the joy of the news of Caesar's escape from the Taliban had faded. It was now July, and a couple of months had passed without any fresh reports from Afghanistan about Caesar. To Ben and his family, it was as if Caesar had vanished from the face of the earth.

Ben was now stationed at Holsworthy with Soapy, helping new dog handlers learn the ropes, and every now and then he brought his best friend Charlie home for the weekend. In hospital, Charlie had nurses to look after him. At the Fulton house, Ben and Nan helped him in and out of bed, and in and out of the bath, on Sunday mornings. Charlie had always been a proud and independent man, and he hated being helped. But when you have no legs, you can't walk on pride, and Charlie reluctantly accepted their help.

This weekend, when Ben brought Charlie home, he also brought exciting news, although it wasn't news directly related to the missing Caesar.

'Charlie is to be awarded the Victoria Cross,' Ben told Josh, Maddie and Nan at dinner on the Saturday night.

'The Victoria Cross!' Josh exclaimed.

'Is that good?' a mystified Maddie asked, looking at the faces around the table.

'Is that good!' said Josh. 'It's only the most toppest medal that an Australian soldier could ever get, Maddie!' Josh looked at Charlie in awe. 'Charlie, that makes you a *hero*!'

Charlie looked embarrassed. 'I was only doing the job I was trained to do, mate,' he responded. 'And your dad is getting a medal, too – the Medal for Gallantry.'

'Our dad is getting the Medal for Gallantry?' Josh couldn't believe it.

'Is that a toppest medal, too?' Maddie asked.

'It's almost as good as a Victoria Cross,' Josh answered. 'Isn't it, Dad?'

It was Ben's turn to be embarrassed. 'Yes, it's a pretty good medal,' he replied.

'Congratulations, the pair of you,' said Nan, beaming. 'I am so proud of you both.'

'What did you do to get the medal?' Maddie asked.

'Both medal recommendations came out of the same battle in Afghanistan,' said Charlie. 'Our last engagement there.'

Charlie's Victoria Cross was being awarded because he had repeatedly exposed himself to enemy fire, while covering his comrades' withdrawal and while carrying Ben and Kareem the interpreter to safety, saving their lives. Ben was receiving his medal for saving Bendigo Baz.

'That was the battle when Caesar was left behind, wasn't it?' said Josh.

'Poor Caesar,' said Maddie, suddenly feeling sad.

'Yes, poor Caesar,' said Ben, nodding. He added, with a sigh, 'I'd give up my medal in a flash if it meant getting Caesar back.'

'Roger to that,' Charlie agreed.

With the addition of Caesar, Ibrahim and Ahmad's act was proving so popular as they moved around the provinces, and so profitable, that in August they were able to buy a second-hand trampoline from Danish soldiers in Helmand Province. As youths, both brothers had mastered the trampoline, with Ahmad excelling at it. Now, they would introduce it into the Three Brothers' act. Only a small trampoline, it conveniently folded in half to fit into the back of the grey van for travelling, but was only large enough for one of them to use at a time. At their next overnight stop, the brothers set it up for a practice session.

Caesar, sitting with his tongue hanging out, watched

in amazement as Ahmad rose and fell like a bounding kangaroo, then progressed to elegant flips and somersaults.

'You have not lost your skill on the trampoline, brother,' said Ibrahim. 'And look, Intelligent Dog approves.'

Ahmad followed his brother's gaze, then laughed, as he saw Caesar's head going up and down as he watched Ahmad's bouncing figure.

The brothers decided that Ahmad would bounce and somersault while Ibrahim juggled balls beside the trampoline. Then, Ibrahim would throw the balls to Ahmad, who would juggle while he bounced. Out of the blue, while they were practising this, Caesar suddenly took a running jump at the trampoline, and, aiming to grab one of the flying balls after Ahmad had fumbled it, passed neatly under the flying Ahmad, landing on the other side of the trampoline with the ball in his mouth. Delivering the ball at Ibrahim's feet, Caesar looked up at him, expecting one of the tiny pieces of cooked meat the brothers had gotten into the habit of giving him as a reward for a good performance.

'Did you see what Intelligent Dog did, brother?' said Ibrahim.

'I did, brother,' Ahmad returned, continuing to bounce.

'Spectacular, yes?'

'Could we train Intelligent Dog to do that on command?'

'Do you know, brother, I think this special dog could be taught to do almost anything.'

'Perhaps we can teach him to drive our van,' Ahmad joked.

'Then we could sleep all the way to our performances,' Ibrahim returned with a laugh. Looking down at Caesar, he said, 'So, Intelligent Dog, show us how very clever you are. Perfect the trampoline trick, and you shall have your reward.'

In September, as the northern summer neared its end, the Three Brothers entered Kandahar Province. Australian soldiers were stationed at Kandahar airfield but, that being a large base, the brothers would not go there. As each day passed, Caesar's chances of being reunited with Ben Fulton and his family became slimmer and slimmer. At the same time, being fed by friendly army-base cooks and receiving tasty rewards from his acrobatic partners, little by little the formerly skinny Caesar became fatter and fatter.

As Ibrahim and Ahmad had thought, Caesar was a fast learner. Not only did he now dive between the brothers' legs when they did handstands, he dived on cue across the trampoline and beneath the bouncing Ahmad, ending up with a ball in his mouth. In another part of the act, Ahmad hung Caesar around his neck as he himself balanced on Ibrahim's shoulders. This was similar to the fireman's lift that Ben had taught Caesar, and the trick reminded him of Ben every time he performed it.

Caesar never stopped looking for Ben. At every military camp the troupe visited, he always sought Ben in the audience. But foreign troops serving in Afghanistan came from more than forty countries – from Bosnia to Britain, New Zealand to Norway – and none of the provinces that Ibrahim and Ahmad now passed through contained Australian soldiers.

The audience reaction to Caesar was always the same. He was a big hit. At a camp in the northern Kunduz Province, a German major said to Ibrahim and Ahmad, in English, 'That is a very fine hound you have there.' And, taking out his wallet, he asked, 'How much do you want for this hound?'

Ibrahim and Ahmad both shook their heads. 'This dog is our brother, sir,' said Ibrahim. 'He is not for sale.'

'We would never sell our brother,' said Ahmad.

In late September, when the autumn arrived, the brothers decided it was time to return to Uruzgan Province.

A year had now passed since Caesar had been separated from Ben Fulton in Uruzgan.

By the first week of October, the brothers' van arrived at a forward operating base in a lonely valley in the northwest of Uruzgan Province. This base was occupied by American troops, including a detachment from the US Rangers, a Special Forces unit. And on the Saturday morning, Caesar and the brothers gave a performance to a small but enthusiastic audience of American soldiers.

One of the Rangers in the audience was Sergeant Tim McHenry. A soldier with twenty years in the US Army, McHenry was a massive man, and as tough as granite. He wore army camouflage, but on his feet were cowboy boots, and a broad black Stetson sat comfortably on his head. The sergeant and his men weren't even supposed to be here. The previous night, they'd been in a Black Hawk helicopter that had crashed while taking them into the hills on what was supposed to be their final secret mission before their tour in Afghanistan ended. The Rangers, having all survived the crash, had hiked to the FOB to await further orders.

This was Caesar's best performance to date. Jumping, catching balls, balancing – he was in his element. The audience applauded, cheered and whistled its approval, and Caesar's tail wagged with pleasure. Following the end of the performance, while Ahmad packed away their trampoline and juggling equipment, Ibrahim led

Caesar around the audience, cap in mouth. The soldiers were generous, and Caesar's cap was close to overflowing with cash when, finally, he came with wagging tail to Sergeant McHenry, who lounged on a pile of ammunition boxes. Urgently, Caesar sniffed the sergeant's camouflage pants, to see if he could find any trace of Ben on him.

McHenry reached into his pocket for money. 'A downright clever animal you got yourself there, my friend,' he said to Ibrahim, speaking in a slow Texan drawl. 'Where'd you find him?'

'We did not find this fine animal, sir,' Ibrahim answered, thinking quickly to concoct a lie that would hide Caesar's true identity and origin. 'My brother and I – we raised Intelligent Dog from birth.'

'Is that right?' said McHenry. Putting a ten-dollar note in the cap in Caesar's mouth, McHenry looked down into the labrador's gleaming brown eyes. And as dog and man gazed at each other, a memory was triggered in the back of the sergeant's mind. A memory of a report of an Australian Special Forces dog that had gone missing in Uruzgan the previous year. McHenry had heard that, ever since, the Australians had been looking for that dog – a brown labrador, just like this clever dog in front of him. And McHenry wondered if this could be that very dog.

Ibrahim, concerned that the American sergeant might

discover the dog's true identity, tugged on Caesar's leash. 'Come, Intelligent Dog.' But Caesar would not budge.

'Hold on there, pardner,' said McHenry. Easing down from the ammunition boxes, the sergeant came to his feet. 'Hey there, dog . . .' He pointed a firm finger at Caesar, who watched his every move. 'Sit!'

Caesar immediately sat, then looked expectantly up at the American, as if awaiting more instructions.

McHenry smiled. 'What do you know about that?' he said to Ibrahim. 'The dog understands English.'

'The dog is very obedient, it is true, sir. My brother and myself – we have made it so. It is our dog.'

'You know what, buddy, I don't believe you,' McHenry came back. 'I've never seen a fine labrador retriever like this in the hands of Afghan men. Never in a month of Sundays. The dogs you people usually have are scrawny underfed mongrels. Personally, I think this dog is a missing military dog – an Australian Special Forces dog. I've worked with Australian Special Forces. I like those guys. I respect them. There is no finer soldier. And they've saved a pile of American lives in this country. Best of all, they are honourable men. It would give me the greatest pleasure to give them back their missing dog.'

Ibrahim looked suddenly anxious. 'No, no, sir. This is an Afghan dog. A performing Afghan dog.'

Ibrahim hauled on Caesar's rope, but still Caesar

would not budge. He sat with his eyes glued on McHenry. Now Ahmad arrived to join Ibrahim, and he bent to grab the rope at Caesar's neck and help Ibrahim drag him away. 'We must go,' said Ahmad. 'Come, Intelligent Dog.'

'Not so fast, the pair of you,' said McHenry. Casually, he slipped a massive Colt Python six-gun from the finely engraved leather holster on his hip. Using the tip of the revolver's barrel, he pushed his hat to the back of his head, cowboy style. 'You're not taking that dog any place.'

Other Rangers crowded around, preventing the brothers from leaving as, making Ibrahim and Ahmad wait, Sergeant McHenry had a message radioed to headquarters at Tarin Kowt. In that message, the sergeant enquired about the missing Australian military dog. Within half an hour, a reply came back: yes, the Australian Army was still looking for EDD 556 Caesar, after the dog had been separated from its handler, Sergeant Ben Fulton, during combat.

'Are you Caesar, boy?' said McHenry, bending closer to the labrador. 'Are you Ben Fulton's dog?'

Here, to Caesar, were the magic words – his own name and Ben's name. He barked once, then wagged his tail so hard that his entire rear end quivered from side to side. Unable to contain himself, he jumped up at McHenry and tried to lick him.

'Okay, okay, boy,' said McHenry, grinning as he gave the brown dog an energetic pat. 'Gentlemen, I think we have the answer to my questions – from the dog itself. This is Caesar, the Australian war dog.'

'We will sell this dog to you,' Ibrahim hastily suggested, deciding to try to cut his losses. 'A thousand dollars, perhaps? This fine and intelligent animal is worth very much more.'

McHenry shook his head. 'I got a better idea. Why don't you two brothers just mosey on out of here and I'll take the dog off your hands.'

Ibrahim and Ahmad looked at each other, as both saw the canine star of their show melting from their grasp and their income vastly reducing overnight. Ibrahim made one last desperate attempt to profit from the impending loss of the clever brown labrador. 'You pay us five hundred dollars?' he said to McHenry. When the sergeant's flat expression didn't change, Ibrahim smiled weakly, then suggested, 'Three hundred dollars?' Still no response. 'One hundred dollars?'

'I guess,' McHenry slowly countered, 'I *could* pay you a couple of hundred bucks for the dog. Or, I could have you guys arrested for stealing – this dog just happens to be valuable military property.'

'No, no, we did not steal this dog!' Ahmad protested, glancing fearfully at his brother. 'It attached itself to us. This I swear, sir!'

'We are innocent of any crime, sir,' said Ibrahim, suddenly picturing himself behind bars. 'Please believe us.'

'Okay. Option three: you both hit the road, without the dog, and I forget I ever saw your sweet, innocent faces. What do you say? Deal?'

Ibrahim and Ahmad needed no more prompting. 'It is, as you say, sir, a deal,' said Ibrahim with a resigned sigh.

Letting go of Caesar's leash, the brothers pocketed the money from the cap, then hurried off. As they reached their van, both turned to cast a sad parting glance Caesar's way. But Caesar, busy lapping up the attention of Sergeant McHenry and his friendly Rangers, failed to notice the brothers' departure.

'We should have sold Intelligent Dog to the German officer in the north, while we had the chance,' said Ibrahim sourly.

'It is true,' Ahmad agreed. 'The German would have paid us thousands.'

And then the brothers climbed into their van and sped away, glad not to be bound for a prison cell for 'stealing' Caesar.

Caesar, meanwhile, was left sitting at the feet of Sergeant McHenry, looking up at him expectantly.

'Now, Caesar, boy,' said McHenry, 'how do we get you back to Sergeant Fulton?'

CHAPTER 20

It was a late night call from Tarin Kowt that brought Ben the news.

'Sergeant Fulton,' came Major General Jones' voice from far away. 'The US Army has your dog. Caesar has been recovered in Uruzgan.'

The next morning, Ben woke Josh and Maddie with the news. He said that General Jones had also told him that the brown labrador that had been retrieved by the Rangers was on his way to US military vets who would check for a microchip inserted beneath the skin, to confirm his identity. Until that had been done, no official statement would be made to announce that the dog was Caesar. But everyone in the Fulton household knew in their hearts that their Caesar had been found. Nan couldn't stop smiling. Maddie ran around the house squealing with joy. Josh went straight onto the internet and soon showed his father several blogs from American soldiers talking about a US Rangers' sergeant who had rescued a missing Australian war dog.

Josh and Maddie were almost too excited to go to school, but nothing would keep them away. Even though Ben asked them not to say anything until it was officially confirmed that the dog in American hands was their Caesar, neither could keep the news to themselves. By lunchtime, between the two of them, they had told their entire school. And, until her teacher heard about it and stopped her, Maddie even sold her classmates tickets for twenty cents each to see Caesar when he came home.

'Maddie Fulton!' said her teacher, Miss Brankovic, 'I'm all in favour of enterprise, young lady, but I'm sure your father did not give his permission for you to sell tickets to your dog's homecoming. Did he?'

Maddie, standing before the teacher, hung her head. 'No, Miss Brankovic.'

'You will give that money back to the other children at once – every last cent!'

Maddie gave the money back.

Later that same day, Ben received a call from Amanda Ritchie, who was waiting on confirmation from the Australian Government that Caesar had been located, before she published a news story about it. Amanda had become so involved in the quest for Caesar's return she was almost as excited by the turn of events as Ben's children. Ben also received a call from his delighted member of parliament, Warren Hodges, who had likewise heard the unofficial news and wanted to congratulate Ben.

The commanding officer of the Incident Response Regiment, the following day, officially informed Ben that the check of the brown labrador's microchip had proven positive. There was now no doubt – the dog retrieved by the US Rangers was definitely Caesar. Ben asked what plans the army had for Caesar now, and was relieved to be told that, even though Ben was now working with Soapy, Caesar would be returned to Ben's care and would remain with Ben until it was decided whether Caesar was physically and mentally able to return to work.

That evening, Amanda rang again. 'Ben, I was wondering,' she began, 'what are your feelings about your dog's future? Do you think you'll eventually be able to take Caesar back on operations?'

'Well, between you and me, Amanda, off the record,' Ben responded, 'my superiors are concerned that after being away from the army for so long, and being in Taliban hands, Caesar might no longer be able to serve as a war dog. If that proves to be the case, Caesar would be sent into honourable retirement.'

'Who will make that decision about Caesar's future?'

'The decision would be jointly mine, after Caesar and I have spent some time together, and the instructors at the EDD school, after they've assessed him. But, to be honest, I'm worried that Caesar has been so badly stressed by his ordeal that he won't even recognise me.'

'Oh, I'm sure Caesar will recognise you, Ben,' Amanda assured him, her voice softening.

'I really hope so, Amanda.' Ben sounded genuinely concerned. 'It's been over a year since he last saw me. Who knows what he's been through in that time?'

The possibility that Caesar would fail to recognise him was a genuine concern of Ben's as he prepared for their reunion in Afghanistan. As it happened, the Prime Minister of Australia was in Afghanistan that week, meeting with the Afghan President and visiting Australian troops. The Department of Defence decided it would be a good idea for Caesar to be returned to Ben in front of the Prime Minister at Tarin Kowt, because it would make a great news story.

So, Ben was put on an Air Force Globemaster and flown to the Middle East, then on to Tarin Kowt.

The handover ceremony was to take place in a large aircraft hangar beside the airstrip at Tarin Kowt. Hundreds of Australian and American troops had assembled for the event. Huge Australian and American flags decorated the hangar wall behind a dais where the Prime Minister, the commanding US general in Afghanistan, and Major General Jones stood. A bevy of reporters and press and TV cameramen was arrayed in front of them.

In dress uniform, Ben marched up to the dais, came to rigid attention and snapped the PM and generals a perfect salute. On his chest, Ben wore the orange ribbon of the Medal for Gallantry, which had been presented to him in Canberra months before. The generals returned the salute. The prime minister then stepped forward and shook Ben's hand. 'A pleasure to meet you, Sergeant. I've read a lot about you and Caesar. You must be looking forward to getting your lost pooch back?'

'You can say that again, Prime Minister,' Ben replied.

A commotion could be heard from the other side of the hangar. Photographers were rushing to snap a brown dog being led in by a sergeant in green US Rangers' dress uniform and beret. That sergeant was Tim McHenry. Ever since he had recovered the dog from Ibrahim and Ahmad, McHenry had been given the job of looking after Caesar until he was officially handed back to the Australian Army.

The cameramen had been told by the army that they could not show the faces of either Ben or McHenry. As Special Forces soldiers who sometimes went on undercover missions, their identities had to be protected – for the enemy often read foreign newspapers and watched Western TV, and they might keep a record of their faces if they were shown, to later identify them when they were on a covert mission. Not even their names were released. Officially, Ben was referred to as Sergeant F, and McHenry as Sergeant M.

In contrast, the media was free to show Caesar's face and broadcast his name. He was the hero of the hour – the Australian military dog who had escaped from Taliban custody and survived in enemy territory for thirteen months. So, cameras flashed and whirred, and within hours his image and the name Caesar would appear on newspaper pages, television and computer screens around the world. This happy ending to the story of the missing war dog had made Caesar an international celebrity.

Ben Fulton's heart raced as he stood waiting, hoping that Caesar would recognise him. A hundred metres away, circled by a crowd, Sergeant McHenry came to attention. Beside him stood the brown labrador, on a metal leash. 'Caesar, sit!' McHenry commanded.

The labrador promptly sat at McHenry's side. The dog's eyes were scanning the cameramen as they pointed their cameras at him, and taking in the look and scent of the Australian and American soldiers who had crowded around to take a look at him. McHenry now bent and unfastened the leash from the new collar that US Army veterinarians had provided the dog with days earlier. McHenry then came to attention once more. An expectant hush fell over the hangar.

'Go ahead, Sergeant F,' said the American general to Ben. 'Call your dog.'

Nervously, Ben cleared his throat, then called loudly, 'Caesar, come! Come to Ben!'

The labrador's ears shot up. Urgently, he scanned the people in front of him. But soldiers and media men and women blocked his view of the owner of that voice.

'Clear a space there!' the American general ordered, and the spectators moved back.

'Caesar, come!' Ben called again.

Now the dog saw Ben. And Ben saw the dog. Ben had been concerned that Caesar would have lost a lot of weight in Taliban hands. But the brown labrador across the hangar was, if anything, overweight. And he was not responding to Ben's call. The dog just sat there, gazing blankly at him, as if dazzled by all the attention. Momentarily, Ben was gripped by a dread that there had been a mistake, and that this was not Caesar after all. Yet it did look like him. It had to be him! Now Ben was revisited by his old fear – that Caesar no longer recognised him.

In as firm a voice as he could muster, Ben repeated, 'Caesar, come!'

Letting out a single bark, Caesar sprang to his feet and

came bounding across the hangar floor. Just metres from Ben, Caesar took a flying leap at him. As Caesar knocked his slouch hat flying, Ben caught him. With his dog's head over his left shoulder, Ben clutched him and staggered back several steps until he regained his balance. 'It's okay, mate,' said Ben, close to tears. 'It's okay.'

The watching crowd cheered with delight. Caesar, turning his head, tried to feverishly lick Ben on the face. When he couldn't achieve that, he let out a frustrated whine, then scrambled to be free again. Ben let go of him, and Caesar slipped back to the ground, then began jumping up, again trying to lick Ben's face. Ben, laughing with joy and relief, squatted down and pulled Caesar into an embrace.

'Calm down, boy, calm down,' he said. 'We're back together again. Good boy. Good Caesar. Well done, mate, you made it back to me.'

With Caesar sitting beside him, Ben Skyped the family from the Tarin Kowt base. 'The military vets have given Caesar a clean bill of health,' Ben told Josh, Maddie and Nan.

'That's good, Ben,' said Nan, eagerly. 'I read somewhere he could have picked up rabies out there in the wilds of Afghanistan.'

Hearing Nan's familiar voice, Caesar gave a single bark of recognition.

'No, he's fine,' said Ben, fondling Caesar's ear.

'Does that mean you can bring Caesar home now, Daddy?' Maddie asked, leaning in to get a better look at Caesar.

Again, Caesar let out a bark, and his tail thumped the floor.

'I won't be able to bring him home just yet, sweetheart,' Ben replied. 'Australian Government quarantine regulations say he'll have to wait six months.'

Both Maddie and Josh groaned on hearing this and looked disappointed.

'But he'll spend those six months in really nice government-approved kennels in Dubai,' Ben assured them. 'The time will fly for all of us. I promise you it will.'

Ben kept Caesar with him at Tarin Kowt for a week while quarantine arrangements were being made. Rather than put him in the base kennels, he let Caesar sleep beside him in his quarters every night that week. Caesar went to sleep with his head resting on Ben's chest. During their first few days back together, Caesar would not leave Ben's side, and Ben worried that Caesar would suffer from separation anxiety during the long quarantine period to come. To his relief, within a few days, Caesar was feeling so reassured at being back with Ben he was chasing tennis balls thrown by anyone, and made a nuisance of himself with the cooks on solitary visits to the kitchens looking for handouts. When Ben put him in a steel travelling cage for the flight to Dubai in the United Arab Emirates, Caesar seemed to know they would be reunited before long and settled down happily with a bone.

As Caesar flew off to Dubai for his six-month 'holiday', Ben flew home to Australia to resume duty with EDD Soapy.

One April Saturday, Ben met Caesar at Sydney Airport after his flight from Dubai. Caesar was overjoyed to see him, and would have licked his bumpy face for hours had Ben let him. Putting him in the back of an army Land Rover, Ben drove him home to Holsworthy.

The Fulton family was waiting excitedly on the front lawn of 3 Kokoda Crescent when Ben pulled up in the Land Rover. Most of the neighbourhood had also turned out to see the return of Caesar the famous war dog – Josh and Maddie had told everyone they knew that he was coming home today. Hundreds of adults and children lined the street, then crowded around as Ben opened the vehicle's rear door. There was a mighty cheer from the crowd when Caesar jumped down at the end of his leash. Ben then knelt beside Caesar and unfastened the leash. 'Go say hello to the family, Caesar,' he said.

With a woof, Caesar bounded over the grass. First, he went to Josh, giving him a lick on the face as he bent to pat him. Then he went to Maddie, almost bowling her over in his enthusiasm. Finally, he went to Nan, who gave him a long cuddle.

'That was amazing, Dad,' Josh said proudly to Ben later.

'What was, mate?' Ben asked.

'Caesar came to me first again. Do you think Caesar knows I helped you track him down?'

'I wouldn't be surprised, Josh. Anything's possible with Caesar,' Ben said, smiling to himself.

Ben let Josh and Maddie take Caesar to say hello to the many waiting children, who all wanted to pat him, give him sweets and have their photos taken with the four-legged hero. Patiently enduring all the attention, Caesar accepted the strokes and cuddles with a wagging tail, and sat with his tongue hanging out as children draped themselves over him and their parents' cameras clicked. After his days as a circus performer in front of applauding audiences in Afghanistan, Caesar had become used to being a star.

Ben had put off the first of the planned plastic surgery operations on his damaged face until he had Caesar back home. Now, Ben made the necessary arrangements. He knew that Josh and Maddie worried about him going into hospital for these procedures. Both had become accustomed to his scarred face. And neither could work out how doctors could 'sculpt skin', as one plastic surgery leaflet their dad brought home described it. So, to keep their minds off him while he spent a week in hospital for the first round of surgery, Ben arranged for Caesar to stay at home with them all that week. Meanwhile, Charlie had recently returned from an exhausting round of public appearances where he'd spoken about receiving the Victoria Cross, and he offered to come and stay for ten days to also keep the Fulton children company.

Charlie was still in a wheelchair, but had built up his arm strength to such an extent that he could now get himself in and out of bed, shower, you name it. And, as he had threatened before, when he gave Josh a race at the local cricket oval, Charlie beat Josh over 400 metres. So, knowing how fond Josh and Maddie were of Charlie, and how proud they were of him now that he was the famous Sergeant Grover VC, Ben accepted Charlie's offer and went off to hospital, leaving the children in Nan, Caesar and Charlie's care.

Charlie sat in his wheelchair in the Fulton living room watching a golf tournament on TV. He had been a good golfer before being wounded in Afghanistan. Now that he was unable to walk, his golf clubs were gathering dust back at his quarters at the SAS home base in Perth, Western Australia.

It was a quiet weekday morning. Ben was in hospital, Josh and Maddie were at school, and Nan Fulton was out shopping. But Charlie had Caesar for company. Lying with his eyes closed, the labrador was contentedly curled up on the mat in front of Charlie's wheelchair. After a while, Charlie lost interest in the golf tournament – watching other people play golf only reminded him of the long list of things he was restricted from doing. Deciding to change the channel, he reached for the TV remote control lying in his lap. But in his haste, he knocked the remote flying, and with a *clunk* it landed on the wooden floor to one side of his chair.

'Clumsy nitwit!' Charlie growled to himself. With a grunt, he tried to reach down to pick it up, but it was just out of his reach. Cursing to himself, he strained to try again, only to fail a second time. Hearing Charlie struggle, Caesar opened his eyes. Suddenly, he rose up and went to where the TV remote lay. Carefully, Caesar picked up the remote between his teeth, then gently dropped it on Charlie's lap.

'Caesar, what a clever dog!' said Charlie with a laugh in his voice, giving Caesar a vigorous pat. 'Good boy! Good boy!'

Caesar stood there in front of Charlie, eyes glinting, tongue hanging out and tail wagging from side to side, seeming to say, *Come on, then, let's play. Give me something else to fetch, Charlie.*

'Okay,' said Charlie, getting the message. 'Let's see how smart you really are, mate.' Looking around the room, he saw his mobile phone lying on the dining table where he'd left it. 'My mobile phone, Caesar. Get my mobile phone.' As Caesar put his head questioningly to one side, puzzling about what Charlie meant, Charlie thought quickly. 'What is it that Ben says to you? Oh, yeah. Seek on!' Putting one clenched hand to his ear, as if holding a telephone, he said, 'Mobile phone, Caesar. Mobile phone. Seek on! Bring me my mobile phone, Caesar. Seek on!'

In an instant, Caesar was on the move. Charlie watched with fascination as, with his head raising and lowering, Caesar trotted around the room, looking on the floor, looking on chairs and sofas, looking on shelves, until he came to the dining table. Then Caesar stopped, and put his front paws up on the table so he could survey its surface. Spotting the phone lying there, he took it in his teeth, dropped back to the floor, and delivered the phone into Charlie's lap beside the remote control.

'Caesar, you are brilliant!' Charlie exclaimed, pulling him into a cuddle.

Caesar licked Charlie on the cheek. Then he pulled away and barked, just once, as if to say, *This is fun! More, Charlie! More!*

Charlie grinned, 'Okay, Caesar, my friend. Let's see what you can really do. What can we try next?' Scanning the room, Charlie sought more difficult challenges for Caesar.

Ben was in for a surprise when he returned home after seven days in hospital, his face covered with light bandages.

'You'll never guess what Caesar has done while you were away, Dad,' said Josh.

'Yeah! Caesar's the cleverest dog that ever lived!' Maddie declared.

'I think you're being a bit biased there, Maddie,' Ben responded, with a chuckle.

'No, I have to agree with the kids, Ben,' said Charlie. 'Caesar is phenomenal!'

Caesar, meanwhile, sat looking at Ben with his head cocked to one side, as if to say, *What's that stuff covering your face, boss? Where am I supposed to lick you a hello?*

Ben, amused by Caesar's mystification, knelt and gave him a hug.

Caesar managed to lick him on the neck, then, as Ben straightened, he ran to the back door and barked, as if to say, *Come on, there are tennis balls outside that I want you to throw.*

'I'm serious about Caesar, Ben,' said Charlie. 'Watch this.' Clicking his fingers, he called, 'Caesar! Attention!'

Caesar's head snapped around to Charlie.

Charlie now pointed to his own head. 'Caesar, seek on,' he said.

Caesar bounded from the room.

Ben shook his head. 'What's going on?'

'Just watch, Dad,' said Josh proudly. 'It's amazing.'

'Amazing!' Maddie repeated, jumping up and down with excitement.

Moments later, Caesar returned with Charlie's beret in his mouth. Carefully, he lay the beret on Charlie's lap, then sat beside Charlie's wheelchair, and received praise and a rewarding pat. Charlie then proceeded to give Caesar a series of hand signals – two open hands together, a square drawn with two fingers, a fist to the ear – and for every signal Caesar would hurry away and return with a specified item: the newspaper, the TV remote, and Charlie's mobile phone.

'Fantastic!' Ben exclaimed. 'You mean to tell me you've taught Caesar all this while I've been in hospital?'

'That's not all,' said Charlie. 'Watch this.' He gave Caesar a signal of tumbling hands, and away Caesar went. 'Come on,' said Charlie to Ben. 'To the laundry.'

With Charlie wheeling himself, they all followed Caesar to the laundry. Nan joined them from the kitchen, and with a wide smile, stood back as Caesar went to work – Nan knew what was coming, as she'd seen the trick before. First, Caesar used his teeth on the handle of the front-loading washing machine, opening the door. Then he went to the clothes basket, took every item of dirty clothing from the basket one by one and stuffed them into the washing machine. When the basket had been emptied, Caesar closed the washing machine door with his nose.

'Incredible!' Ben exclaimed. 'You taught him to do that . . . in a week?'

'He's a fast learner, mate,' Charlie replied. 'You, of all people, should know what he's capable of.'

'What's more,' said Nan, 'Caesar can unload the machine again, after the washing is done. Every house-wife needs a Caesar!'

'You know,' said Charlie, 'the army has offered to get me a trained care dog.'

'That's a great idea, Charlie,' said Ben.

'Well, if I do get a dog to help me,' Charlie mused, patting Caesar, 'I want a dog just like this bloke.'

With Charlie due to leave the Fulton house the next day, Ben took Josh and Maddie aside just before it was time for bed.

'Guys,' he began, 'there's something I wanted to discuss with you in private.'

'You're not going away from us again, Daddy?' said Maddie, with sudden alarm.

'No, no, nothing like that,' Ben replied, stroking her hair. 'You remember, the other day, when Charlie was saying that he would love to have a care dog just like Caesar? What if we gave Caesar to him?'

Josh and Maddie both looked at their father with surprise. 'What do you mean?' Maddie asked.

'We would let Charlie have Caesar – to be his care dog,' Ben explained.

'Why would we do that?' Josh asked. 'Caesar's our dog.'

'Well,' said Ben, 'you saw how quickly Charlie was able to train Caesar to help him.'

'Yes, but . . .' Josh protested, then faltered.

'That would save Charlie a heap of time.' Ben had a very serious look on his face. 'It takes months for a care dog to get used to its new owner. Charlie and Caesar are old friends. And no ordinary care dog could do what Caesar can do.'

'Could we still see Caesar?' Maddie asked.

'Of course we could.'

Josh was shaking his head. 'I don't want to give Caesar away. He's ours, Dad!' Tears began to form in his eyes. 'He's part of our family. And we only just got him back.'

Ben pulled Josh close, then gently wiped away his tears. 'I know, son. But I owe Charlie. He saved my life over in Afghanistan. Giving him Caesar is the least I can do to repay him.'

'But we love Caesar, Dad,' said Josh. Time, first-hand involvement in the search for Caesar, and Caesar's unconditional affection for him had combined to change Josh's attitude to the brown labrador. '*I* love him!'

'We all love him, son,' Ben responded. 'We will always love him, and he will always love us. That's not the point. Do you remember when Charlie came to visit a couple of years ago, there was something very important he said to you?'

Josh shook his head. 'I can't remember.'

'Charlie said, "Sometimes, we have to put others before ourselves and make sacrifices for the sake of others. To do that is the mark of a man of courage and compassion".'

Josh nodded. 'Now I remember.'

'That's why Charlie won the Victoria Cross,' Ben went on. 'I wouldn't be here today if Charlie hadn't put others before himself. And now we have to do the same. What do you say? Can we be brave and compassionate like Charlie, make the sacrifice and give Caesar to him?' He paused and then added, 'It has to be a family decision.'

'What does Nan say?' Josh asked.

'Nan says "yes",' Ben replied.

'I think we should say "yes" too, Josh,' said Maddie. 'I can be brave.'

Josh was silent now, so Ben said, 'We'll always be able to see Caesar at weekends, you know, Josh. And whenever Charlie comes to visit, he'll bring Caesar with him. It's not as if Caesar will be disappearing from our lives.'

'Really?' said Josh, perking up a little at the thought.

'And he won't stop loving us just because he's living with Charlie. One day, when you and Maddie are older, you'll move out of this place and live in homes of your own. That doesn't mean we'll love each other any less. The same goes for Caesar.'

'I'll never do that, Daddy,' said Maddie, earnestly.

'What's that, sweetheart?' Ben asked. 'What wouldn't you do?'

'Move out of here,' Maddie replied.

Ben smiled. 'Don't you want to have a home of your own one day, with a husband and children? You once told me you wanted seven children when you grow up.'

'Oh, yes, I still want that,' said Maddie, 'but they can all come and live here with us.'

Ben's smile broadened. 'Well, we'll see if you still feel that way in twenty years' time.'

All the while his father had been in conversation with Maddie, Josh had been deep in thought. Now he said, 'So, Caesar going to live with Charlie would be like Maddie going to live with Charlie? Maddie would still be my sister. And Caesar would still be my dog . . . well, *our* dog.'

'Exactly,' said Ben. 'Very well thought out, Josh. I couldn't have put it better myself. In principle, nothing much will change – only Caesar's living arrangements.'

'So, Josh,' said Maddie, 'have you decided?'

'Yes,' said Josh, 'I've decided. I can do it for Charlie. After all, Caesar will still be our dog, in principle.'

'That's really noble, and mature, of you, Josh,' Ben responded, giving him a hug. 'I'm very proud of you, mate. Very proud of both you and Maddie.'

Josh beamed, and Maddie beamed.

'And we're proud of you, Daddy,' said Maddie. 'You're the most bravest one of all.'

The next morning, Ben told Charlie what he and the children had decided. Charlie was immediately conflicted. On the one hand, the idea of having Caesar as his companion and helper delighted him. But, on the other hand, Caesar was Ben's dog. 'Mate, I can't do that to you and the kids! I can't take Caesar away from you.'

'Too late,' said Ben, with a shrug. 'The family has voted on it. They know we'll all get to see Caesar regularly if he's with you.'

'Yeah, but –'

'Besides, it's getting more and more dangerous for war dogs in Afghanistan. Five of our dogs have been killed over there now. Spider, a dog that Caesar and I worked with, was blown up by an IED in Uruzgan just two weeks ago. Do you really want Caesar to go back over there – to that?'

'Ah,' said Charlie. 'Now you put it like that . . . But when I said the other day that I'd like a dog like Caesar, I wasn't angling for you to give him to me.'

'I know that. You're the most unselfish person I've ever known. But how about you and I are both a bit selfish, just this once, by keeping the Caesar we love safe, the way he kept us safe in Uruzgan? He deserves it.'

'Roger to that,' Charlie finally agreed.

CHAPTER 21

Hundreds of excited schoolchildren lined a Canberra courtyard as a military band played and a troop of soldiers marched out bearing the Australian flag and the unit banner of the Special Operations Engineer Regiment (SOER), as the Incident Response Regiment had recently been renamed to better reflect its core Special Forces role. Following the soldiers came Charlie, propelling himself along in his wheelchair and dressed in SAS dress uniform adorned with his Victoria Cross and other medals. Caesar trotted along beside him on a leash.

Scores of guests occupied plastic chairs in the centre of the courtyard. In one of the middle rows sat Ben, wearing a civilian suit and sunglasses. His plastic surgery was complete, and as if by magic, his face was now as smooth as silk. Beside him sat Josh, Maddie and Nan Fulton. All four, bursting with pride, focused on Caesar as he passed. Officially, Caesar was a serving member of the SOER. Army records showed him as now on special assignment to Sergeant Charles Grover VC, as his 'personal assistant'.

Caesar wore a special emerald-green dog jacket. Trimmed with white and emblazoned with the SOER's emblem, the jacket had two Australian Army medals pinned to it.

'Dad!' Josh whispered urgently to Ben. 'Are those Caesar's new military medals on his jacket?'

'Yes,' Ben replied in a hushed voice.

'The War Dog Operational Medal, and the Canine Service Medal?' Josh knowledgeably asked. In his excitement, he spoke at full volume this time.

'That's right, son,' Ben returned, signalling with a finger to his lips for Josh to keep quiet.

An elderly retired general sitting in front turned and glared at them. Ignorant of the family's connection with the two heroes out front, he too put a finger to his lips, then went, 'Ssshhh!'

Maddie giggled at this. 'That man doesn't know that we're related to Caesar, does he, Daddy?' she whispered.

'That's right, sweetheart,' Ben whispered back. 'It's our secret.' Then he caught sight of Amanda and Warren in the audience. Both gave him discreet waves.

Right at the back, wearing civilian clothes, baseball caps and sunglasses to disguise their identities, sat Bendigo Baz and Lucky Mertz. Both had fully recovered from their battle wounds and returned to SAS service. Neither would have missed this day for the world, for Charlie and Caesar were their comrades in arms.

On a dais stood a beaming Major General Jones, alongside Lieutenant General Martin McBride, chief of the Australian Army, and Catherina Roma, head of the Royal Society for the Prevention of Cruelty to Animals, the RSPCA.

As Charlie and Caesar sat facing him, Lieutenant General McBride commenced his speech. 'Ladies and gentlemen, we are here to present another medal to a special member of the Australian Armed Forces. If there were a Victoria Cross for dogs, EDD 556 Caesar would have received it. Not only did Caesar risk his life time and again to discover explosives and other enemy material, on one occasion he helped pull an Australian soldier into cover during an engagement. And, most plucky of all, Caesar, while missing in action, succeeded in escaping while a prisoner of the Taliban. He then disrupted Taliban operations in Uruzgan Province for weeks as he evaded recapture. While I know that Caesar's former handler, Sergeant F, must sorely miss him, it is fitting that Caesar is today partnered with Sergeant Grover VC, one of Australia's most decorated soldiers. For, today, in receiving the RSPCA's rarely awarded Purple Cross, Caesar becomes the most decorated dog in Australian history.'

Anonymous in the audience, Ben and his family watched with heart-thumping pride as Catherina Roma now came down from the dais to Caesar, and, bending low, draped the Purple Cross around his neck on a purple ribbon. In return, Caesar licked her on both cheeks, which generated squeals of joy from the watching children. Then, as Charlie had recently taught him, Caesar held out his right front paw for a handshake. Laughing, Catherina shook his paw as cameras clicked away, capturing the moment for posterity.

'Three cheers for Caesar!' called Lieutenant General McBride. 'Hip-hip . . .' And the courtyard resounded to hundreds of voices giving three loud cheers.

Following the medal ceremony, there was a garden party on the lawn. As guests drank tea and nibbled sandwiches, Charlie brought Caesar over to the Fulton clan. With a wildly wagging tail, Caesar dispensed licks to them all.

Josh pulled a tennis ball from his pocket, and Caesar's eyes immediately latched onto it. 'Charlie,' Josh said, 'do you think Caesar could . . .?'

'Roger to that, mate,' said Charlie, unfastening Caesar's leash at the collar. 'Caesar, seek on!'

Caesar went loping away with Josh and Maddie to play ball on the grass. As Ben, Nan and Charlie were watching, Major General Jones and Lieutenant General McBride came up to them. 'So, Fulton, Grover,' said Jones, after returning their salutes, 'you should be very proud.'

'Enormously proud, General,' said Ben. 'Of Caesar,

and of Josh and Maddie – they've been very grown-up about allowing Caesar to work with Charlie.'

'Roger to that,' Charlie agreed.

'I suppose,' said General McBride, 'we can now close the book on EDD 556 Caesar. He'll go down in history as an exceptional animal.'

'Oh, Caesar's still got plenty to offer his country, General,' said Charlie, as he watched the brown labrador romp with Josh and Maddie. 'Don't go writing either him or me off just yet. What do you reckon, Ben?'

A grin stretched across Ben's face. 'Roger to that, mate.'

As they spoke, Caesar bounded over to drop the tennis ball in front of them, then barked, once, as if to say, *Come on, guys, you're in this game, too!*

Caesar would sleep well that night, and would dream with twitching snout and quivering paw of playing with the people he loved and who loved him.

Charlie and Ben were right, of course. Far from being over, Caesar's amazing career had only just begun.

LIST OF MILITARY TERMS

AK-47	Russian-made assault rifle
ammo	ammunition
ANA	Afghan National Army
Anzacs	originally, soldiers of the Australian and New Zealand Army Corps, but also used as a term to describe all Australian and New Zealand troops during the First World War
Apache, AH-64	twin-engine helicopter gunship
ASLAV	Australian light armoured vehicle. It is amphibious, has eight wheels and can carry six troops plus a crew of three.
asset	a general military term that is sometimes used to describe war dogs, but can also mean a human spy behind enemy lines
bears	military intelligence personnel
Black Hawk, S-70A	military helicopter used as a gunship as well as a cargo and troop carrier
Bushmaster	Australian-made troop-carrying vehicle, four-wheel drive and can carry eight troops plus a crew of two

carbine	rifle with a shorter barrel than an assault rifle
Chinook, CH-47	twin-rotor medium-lift military helicopter that carries cargo, vehicles and troops
clicks	kilometres
Colt Python	large-calibre Magnum revolver
convoy	a group of vehicles of any type travelling together on land, or a fleet of cargo ships that sails together for protection
Diggers	nickname for Australian soldiers
doggles	protective goggles for war dogs
drone	unmanned military aircraft used for reconnaissance and bombing raids
EDD	explosive detection dog
extraction	pickup of troops from hostile territory by air, land or sea
FOB	forward operating base
frag	shell fragments from an exploding artillery shell, grenade, bomb, or missile
F-16	American jet fighter-bomber aircraft

Globemaster III, C-17	four-engine jet heavy transport aircraft used to rapidly deploy troops, combat vehicles including tanks, heavy equipment and helicopters over long distances
Green Berets	unofficial name of the US Army Special Forces, because they all wear a green beret
heelo	helicopter, also written 'helo'
Hercules, C-130	four-engine, propeller-driven military transport aircraft similar to but smaller than the Globemaster, pronounced 'Her-kew-leez'
hostiles	enemy fighters
Humvee	American military vehicle, four-wheel drive
IED	improvised explosive device or homemade bomb
insertion	secret landing of troops behind enemy lines
insurgent	guerrilla fighter who does not use a regular military uniform or tactics, and blends in with the local population
intel	intelligence information

IRR	Incident Response Regiment, Australian Army Special Operations Command unit deployed against terrorist and insurgent threats. In February 2012, the unit was renamed the Special Operations Engineer Regiment to better reflect its core Special Forces role
ISAF	International Security Assistance Force
jumpmaster	aircraft crew member who supervises parachutists
kal	an Afghan farm compound, pronounced 'karl' and also sometimes spelt 'qal'
loadmaster	crew member in charge of cargo and passengers in military cargo aircraft and helicopters
LZ	landing zone
malek	a neutral Afghan envoy trusted by both sides
MRE	Meal, Ready-to-Eat, sealed military ration pack of pre-cooked food
operator	Australian SAS soldier
ops	operations or military missions
ordnance	ammunition

PE	plastic explosive
puppy Peltors	protective earmuffs for war dogs
Ranger	a member of the US Army Rangers
roger	'yes' or 'I acknowledge'
round	bullet
RP	rendezvous point or meeting place
RPG	rocket-propelled grenade
SAS	Special Air Service, elite Special Forces unit in the armies of Australia, New Zealand and the United Kingdom
seek on	a handler's instruction to an EDD to find explosives
SOER	Special Operations Engineer Regiment, *see IRR*
special ops	special operations or secret missions
trooper	lowest rank in the SAS, the equivalent of a private in other army units
VC	Victoria Cross for Australia, the highest-ranking Australian military medal for gallantry

FACT FILE

Notes from the Author

There were two real war dogs by the name of Caesar that served with Australian and New Zealand soldiers in the past. One was a New Zealand bulldog, whose job was to search for wounded Anzacs and carry water to them during the First World War (1914–18). The other was an Australian Army tracker dog that went to the Vietnam War in 1967. A black labrador–kelpie cross, that dog was left in Vietnam when Australian troops withdrew from that country several years later. The fictional Caesar in this book is based on several real dogs of modern times – Sarbi, Endal and Cairo – and their exploits.

I was prompted to write this book when I read how Australian Army explosive detection dog Sarbi, a female labrador, went missing in war-torn Afghanistan for thirteen months. To this day, no one knows precisely what happened to Sarbi during that time. If only she could talk! However, several reports from various sources about this period of Sarbi's life do exist. One account claimed that Afghan guards shot at Sarbi when she found her way back to the forward operating base (FOB) where she had been located with her handler prior to the battle in which they were separated. Another report alleged that, shortly after the battle, Sarbi was taken in and cared for by an Afghan boy. All accounts agree that sometime later she came into the hands of the Taliban, who sought to exchange or ransom her. And finally there was a report that Sarbi was spotted in Afghan hands by a US Special Forces soldier, who was responsible for the dog's return.

Those titbits of information inspired the creation of several characters in this book: the Afghan boy Hajera Haidari and his family, the Taliban's Commander Baradar and Abdul Razah, Ibrahim and Ahmad the acrobats, and the US Rangers' Sergeant Tim McHenry. Using these characters as a starting point, I was able to imagine what the lost Australian dog might have experienced during those thirteen months.

Similarly, all the other characters in this book are of my creation, and while they were often inspired by real people, every one of them is fictional and not intended to represent any particular real person. Ben Fulton, our Caesar's handler, is quite different from Sarbi's handler, Sergeant D, whose full name has not been released by the Australian Government for security reasons. For example, Sergeant D didn't have two children.

The character of Sergeant Charlie Grover VC was also inspired by real people – SAS soldiers Trooper Mark Donaldson VC and Corporal Ben Roberts-Smith VC. Although Charlie's appearance and background are very different, his courage and valour mirror theirs. In the same way that Charlie won his Victoria Cross for his actions during the Taliban ambush in which Caesar was separated from Ben, Trooper Donaldson won his Victoria Cross for his actions during the Taliban ambush in which Sarbi was separated from her handler. He was the first Australian soldier since the Vietnam War to receive the rarely awarded Victoria Cross.

Here are a few more facts about the real dogs, people and military units that inspired this book.

EXPLOSIVE DETECTION DOGS (EDDs)

The Australian Imperial Force used dogs during the First World War, primarily to carry messages. Sarbi was preceded by a long line of sniffer dogs used by the Australian Army to track the enemy during the Korean War (1950–53) and, later, in the Vietnam War. In 1981, the current explosive detection dog program was introduced by the army's Royal Australian Engineer Corps, whose base is adjacent to Holsworthy Army

Barracks in New South Wales. In 2005, Australian EDDs were sent to Afghanistan for the first time to join Australian Army operations there as part of the International Security Assistance Force (ISAF). A number of Australian EDDs have served in Afghanistan since then. Several have been killed or wounded while carrying out their dangerous but life-saving duties.

SARBI

Sarbi, whose service number is EDD 436, is a black female labrador serving with the Australian Army. She began the EDD training program in June 2005 and graduated from the 19-week training course with Corporal D, joining the Australian Army's top-secret Incident Response Regiment (IRR) – now the Special Operations Engineer Regiment (SOER) – whose main job was to counter terrorist threats. In 2006, Sarbi and Corporal D were part of the security team at the Commonwealth Games in Melbourne, and in April 2007, the pair was sent to Afghanistan for a seven-month deployment. They primarily worked with Australian engineers who were part of the ISAF reconstruction team in Uruzgan Province, locating IEDs and saving many lives. In June 2008, Sarbi and Corporal D returned to Afghanistan for their second tour of duty there. This time they went to work with Australian SAS and commando units that were part of Special Operations Task Group 7.

On 2 September that year, Sarbi and Corporal D were members of a joint Australian–American Special Forces operation launched from a remote forward operating base 100 kilometres northeast of Tarin Kowt. The operation went terribly wrong when five Humvees carrying Australian, American and Afghan troops were ambushed by a much larger Taliban force. In the ensuing long battle, Corporal D was seriously wounded and became separated from Sarbi, who was also injured. While the ambushed men managed to fight their way back to the FOB, nine of the twelve Australians involved were wounded, as was their Afghan interpreter. Several of the American soldiers were also wounded in the battle. The handler of the American EDD on the mission died as a result of his wounds, although his dog was unharmed. It was during the last stages of this battle that Sarbi went missing on the battlefield. And so began the saga of Sarbi's months – lost in Taliban territory.

After being 'missing in action' for thirteen months, Sarbi was wrangled back into friendly hands by a US Special Forces soldier. A month later, Sarbi and Corporal D were reunited at Tarin Kowt in front of the Australian Prime Minister and the commanding US general in Afghanistan. At the time of writing, Sarbi is still serving in the Australian Army. She is the most decorated dog in the history of the Australian military, having been awarded all the medals that Caesar receives in this book.

ENDAL

I was motivated to have the Fulton family give Caesar to Sergeant Charlie Grover VC to serve as his care dog after hearing the astonishing true story of Endal, the British service dog. Endal was a sandy-coloured male labrador who was trained by the UK charity Canine Partners. Initially thought to be of no use because of his poor health, Endal went on to qualify as a service dog and, in the late 1990s, was partnered with Allen Parton, a former Chief Petty Officer with Britain's Royal Navy.

Parton had sustained serious injuries during the Gulf War, and was thereafter confined to a wheelchair. Initially, he couldn't speak, so he taught Endal more than 100 commands using hand signals – just like the commands that Charlie teaches Caesar in this book. Endal could even put Parton's cash card in ATMs and take out the money. Endal was so clever he could pull the plug out of the bath if Parton was to become unconscious, so that his master didn't slip down and accidentally drown, before going to find help.

In 2009, Endal suffered a stroke – just as Ben Fulton's

former dog, Dodger, did – and had to be put down. During his lifetime, Endal became famous in Britain, receiving much media coverage and many awards for his dedicated and loyal service to his master. A young labrador named EJ (Endal Junior) took Endal's place as Allen Parton's care dog.

CAIRO

Cairo is a long-nosed Belgian Malinois shepherd that was trained as an EDD for service with the United States Navy SEALs (Sea, Air and Land teams), a unit within the US Special Operations Command. In 2011, Cairo was part of SEAL Team 6, which landed by helicopter in a compound in Pakistan to deal with Osama bin Laden, the leader of the terrorist organisation Al Qaeda. Cairo's job was to go in first to locate explosives in the compound. Cairo and all members of his team returned safely from the successful mission.

Because he and his unit are top secret, little more is known about Cairo. It is known that he was trained for insertion by helicopter and by parachute, strapped to his handler, just as Caesar is in this book. And it is also known that Cairo later met US President Barack Obama, when the SEALs were presented with the Presidential Unit Citation for the bin Laden operation.

AUSTRALIAN MILITARY INVOLVEMENT IN AFGHANISTAN

In 2001, the Australian Government sent SAS troops to participate in operations with US, British and other coalition forces in Afghanistan, following Al Qaeda attacks in America. Although those Australian troops were withdrawn in 2002, Australia resumed its military involvement in Afghanistan as part of ISAF in 2005. By 2012, Australia had 1500 troops in Afghanistan, the largest military presence of any foreign nation other than members of the North Atlantic Treaty Organisation (NATO). Most of these Australian troops have either been involved in reconstruction programs, rebuilding destroyed or run-down infrastructure in Afghanistan, or the training of the Afghan National Army. Three hundred members of the Australian contingent have been SAS operators and commandos from the Royal Australian Regiment, involved in special operations against the Taliban and other anti-government militias.

SAS

The original Special Air Service was created by the British Army during the Second World War for special operations behind enemy lines, with the motto 'Who

Dares Wins'. In 1957, the Australian Army created its own Special Air Service Regiment (SASR), commonly referred to as the Australian SAS, two years after the New Zealand Army founded its Special Air Service.

Australia's SAS is considered by many to be the finest Special Forces unit in the world, and its members help train the Special Forces of other countries, including those of the United States of America. Operating all over the world, the unit has received numerous awards, including the prized US Presidential Unit Citation for exceptional service. The Australian SAS Regiment's extremely tough selection course is only open to serving members of the Australian military, with very few soldiers who begin the course completing it.

The Australian SAS is based at Swanbourne Barracks in Perth, Western Australia. A top-secret unit, its men are often involved in covert anti-terrorist work, so their names and faces cannot be revealed. The only exceptions to this rule are SAS members who receive the Victoria Cross. The unit is divided into three squadrons, with one squadron always on anti-terrorist duty and the others deployed on specific missions, such as those undertaken by the SAS in Iraq and Afghanistan in the 21st century.

The primary role of the SAS in wars such as that in Afghanistan is to provide information about enemy movements and operations. They generally do this by mounting secret patrols in enemy territory for a week or more at a time, being inserted by helicopter, parachute, submarine, small boat or special long-range patrol vehicle, depending on the location. Usually, but not always, working in teams of six 'operators' including a signaller, they will observe and report, or will seek to capture enemy leaders. Sometimes, they will call in air attacks on enemy targets they locate, or in support of other units under enemy attack.

During the war in Afghanistan, Australian EDDs and their handlers have increasingly worked with Australian SAS and commando units on special operations.

THE TALIBAN

The Taliban is an armed political movement that originated in southeast Afghanistan and is confined to Afghan tribes that speak the Pashto language. By 1996, the Taliban had gained control of much of Afghanistan by force, after which they permitted terrorist groups such as Al Qaeda to set up training camps in Afghanistan. In late 2001, foreign coalition troops joined Afghan Northern Alliance forces in driving Taliban and Al Qaeda fighters out of Afghanistan, after which an elected Afghan Government was established in the country's capital, Kabul.

ISAF militias and extremist Muslim fighters from many countries, and operating from mountainous regions of eastern Afghanistan and western Pakistan, have waged a fierce insurgent war against the Afghan Government and ISAF forces. In 2011, secret talks were initiated between Taliban leaders, the Afghan Government and the US Government to seek a peaceful solution to the war. ISAF troops, including those from Australia, are currently scheduled to pull out of Afghanistan by late 2014, after which the Afghan Government will be solely responsible for security in Afghanistan.

If you love this book, please recommend it to a friend, and help send Caesar around the world. Thank you.

STEPHEN DANDO-COLLINS
April, 2012
www.stephendandocollins.com

Read more of Caesar's adventures in
Caesar the War Dog: Operation Blue Dragon

Available now